Goes Without

Saying

Goes Without Saying

Saying

Luisa A. Jones

GOES WITHOUT SAYING

For Martin

"A man travels the world over in search of what he needs and returns home to find it."

— GEORGE AUGUSTUS MOORE

Chapter One

Diamond Jubilee Bank Holiday:
Tuesday 5th June 2012
Saunton, North Devon

Four hours. Four interminable, aching hours wedged into a bucket seat with a baby trampolining on her bladder and ankles swollen up like water bombs about to burst. Four hours alternately gnawing at her nails, clutching her bag, checking her phone and twisting the thin fabric of her skirt into a crumpled rag.

A bump in the road sent a spasm across her lower back, making Megan wince and arch her spine.

"Sorry," Matt said again from the driver's seat. He'd been apologising on and off all morning; anyone would think this hopeless escapade was his fault. Perhaps he felt a need to apologise on Tom's behalf, or on behalf of all useless husbands who put their wives through hell. Poor Matt: he'd been a star, giving up a precious bank holiday to act as chauffeur on a wild goose chase.

She would have to find a way to repay his kindness one day, when she had stopped simmering with fury. Although, now she came to think of it, the rage she felt towards her husband had never merely simmered. It started at a full-on rolling boil last Friday, condensing into a bitter stew of indignant wrath, and there were no signs of it abating yet. Making things up to her sister and brother-in-law could wait until she had worked out whether she still had a marriage. When she had decided whether her daughters' father was worthy of the title.

How, she wondered, do you trust someone enough to stay with them once you know they might vanish without warning whenever the mood took them? Surely you'd end up with butterflies in your stomach every time they failed to answer a text, or whenever you arrived home to find their vehicle wasn't on the driveway? Bloody Tom. The stupid, useless, irresponsible, feckless bloody idiot didn't deserve a wife and children after this.

Her blood pressure must be off the scale; the midwife would probably have her hospitalised if she could see her now. Well, if she ended up having a stroke or something, everyone would know who to blame. A grown man behaving like a runaway teenager; he should be ashamed of himself.

And another thing: just how long had he spent planning this little jaunt of his? Assuming it was just a jaunt, and not a full-on moonlight flit. No... that thought was too frightening to confront just yet. Best to save that one until she had found him and could demand a proper explanation.

Forty-eight hours after he left, still with no news to enlighten her as to his whereabouts, she had abandoned all respect for Tom's privacy and mined his laptop for his internet browsing history. It could hardly count as snooping, in the circumstances. She had discovered a trail of searches into beaches and places to stay. Most recently, these had focused on North Devon. She couldn't be certain that this was where he had gone, but it was the only clue she had as to his possible destination. Hence the road trip, to either drag him back to face reality or tell him she'd be changing the locks and contacting a solicitor. Right now, the latter seemed the more appealing proposition.

Matt and Megan's first abortive stop in their hunt for her errant husband had been Woolacombe, followed by a somewhat nervous trip along winding narrow lanes to conduct similarly unrewarding searches of the next couple of coastal villages. Greta, Tom's ancient orange camper van, should be easy enough to spot, or so they hoped; so far there had been no sign of it.

As Matt's sleek black Audi hit another painful pothole, Megan bit her lip. How long could she reasonably expect him to continue combing the car parks of Devon before they would have to give up, head back to Wales and break the news to her daughters that their daddy was nowhere to be found?

They rounded a headland and Matt whistled between his teeth, disturbing her reverie. "Look at that for a view."

Ahead of them, a beach arched for what must surely be miles, a long band of pale caramel like a pastry crust edging the shore. In the distance, a dark band of cliffs huddled on the horizon where Devon reached out towards Cornwall. Lord only knew how many beaches might be found along there, and how many hours or even days it might take to search them all. Megan's knuckles whitened as she gripped the crumpled edges of the road atlas resting on her bump.

Don't panic. Keep it together, at least until you find the heartless shit. Then you can scream and cry all you want. Wherever Greta is, that's where he'll be; they're bound to be around here somewhere.

"There! That's the turning for Saunton. It's the next beach along the coast."

She scanned the area for any sign of Tom's camper van while Matt negotiated the tight bend towards the car park.

"Bugger," he muttered. "There are loads of the bloody things!"

"Is that her? There aren't any other orange ones as far as I can see." She pointed to an orange van in a corner; but her spark of hope was stifled by Matt's response.

"No. It's the wrong registration number, look - that one's a P reg. Greta is a T."

She barely noticed as Matt paused to fumble in his back pocket for cash, handing it to the attendant in exchange for a ticket.

It was obvious that Saunton must be a popular spot, despite lacking the facilities offered by a larger coastal town like Woolacombe. Families, couples and solo travellers, many with dogs or surfboards, strolled to and from the beach laden with assorted bags and mats to make the most of the sunshine. Little did they realise how lucky they were to be out enjoying themselves, instead of spending their day trapped in a car on a wild goose chase.

The car park stretched away from the sands for some distance, with numerous rows of vehicles to search through.

"Let's start at the furthest point from the beach and drive around the whole car park so that we don't miss him if he's here," Matt suggested, offering what he presumably hoped was a reassuring smile. "Don't worry. We've got all day if need be. I'd put money on him being somewhere in this area, even if he's not at this particular beach. We won't give up until we find him."

"Thanks." She turned back to the window to hide the hopelessness in her eyes. This was such a dumb idea. Tom must have wanted to disappear. If he'd intended for her to know where he was, he would have told her in his note.

She swept her hand across her face and focussed on the rows of vehicles. She had never seen so many Volkswagens flocking together in one place before: or, indeed, such a variety of new and old vans. Didn't surfers use anything else for transport?

She started when, without warning, Matt grabbed her wrist.

"Look! There she is! He must have got here early to be able to park so close to the beach. He's here, Meg. He's definitely here. That's Greta, for sure."

The driver of the car behind tooted her horn, making them jump. Clearly they couldn't sit here staring at Tom's van all day. Megan tossed the atlas behind her seat and opened the door.

"I'll get out here; you drive round again and find a space."

She ignored his apologetic smile into the rear view mirror as she eased herself out of the passenger seat. The impatient woman in the car behind, drumming her fingertips on her steering wheel, had plainly never been pregnant. If she had, she must have forgotten what it was like to be unable to move at anything faster than an undignified waddle. Well, she'd just have to wait. Trying to move a body like this out of a sporty little hatchback was like trying to lift a boulder out of quicksand without a winch.

She uncoiled, rubbing her back and watching the car ease away in search of a parking space. Matt would be relieved to get away from her miserable face for five minutes, no doubt. Still, fair play to him: he'd got her here. Greater love hath no man than to waste a day of his holiday sorting out his wife's sister's marital woes.

And here was Greta, Tom's beloved little ray of sunshine, her cheery orange paint mocking Megan as she shuffled over to peer in through the windows. She shielded her eyes from the glare of the sun against the glass.

There was nothing out of place in the van, nothing left lying around, nothing to tell her any damned thing. Only his guitar rested in its case on one of the seats. She frowned. Why on earth did he take that with him? He hadn't picked the thing up in two years, maybe even longer.

She tutted, groping through the muddle in her handbag until at last her fingers bumped against the cold metal of the spare keys. With moist palms she fumbled with the lock and slid the side door open until it clicked into place at the end of its runner. A smell of warm vinyl and Tom's familiar deodorant spray poured over her. The air inside the van was thick, as if it had been waiting in the sunshine for hours.

It was an effort to climb in, heaving herself up with a grunt, gripping the side of the van. With the roof clipped down she had to stoop, adjusting her balance to take account of her bump. Her back twinged again in protest.

With no clues to indicate what her husband might be doing, she sank down onto one of the brown and cream checked seats to wait for Matt. They might have found Greta, but she was still no closer to understanding Tom's state of mind. Her initial relief ebbed away. The stale air felt oppressive: it was as if the van itself was telling her she was unwelcome, whispering into her thoughts.

Why would he want you, with your dreary nagging and sniping? When was the last time you had fun together, the way he does with me? Does he smile when he sees you? His face lights up whenever he looks at me.

Hanging from a hook, a dream-catcher turned, its glass beads glittering as the air in the van stirred. Such a frivolous object, every bit as pointless as the garland of silk flowers trailing along the bottom of the windscreen. The back of the tax-disc holder caught her eye: a yellow smiley face, such as she had drawn on the covers of her exercise books at school. Its cheerfulness jarred with her mood.

You know he's a dreamer. You've always known. I allow him to dream. He can be himself with me. When was the last time you allowed him to chase his dreams?

"Oh, sod off," she muttered back.

Her thoughts turned to last Friday, when she found Tom's note. He had left it, scrawled onto the back of a used brown envelope, propped against the kettle where she would be sure to find it. She'd spotted it there when she first arrived home, but assumed it was about something unimportant: he had gone to the gym, perhaps, or her mother had phoned and left a message.

But oh, that moment when she first had a moment to read it. She had already been flustered, after struggling to keep three year-old Nia occupied during five year-old Alys' half-hour swimming lesson. She had resorted to the usual tactic of bribing her with crisps and the promise of something delicious from the vending machine if she would just be a good girl until it was time to go home. Getting Alys dry and dressed had been another battle, the child protesting against the comb while Meg kept a watchful eye on Nia to ensure she didn't run off towards the pool.

Full of excitement at the prospect of the half-term week off school, Alys had chattered all the way home from the leisure centre about her ideas for places to go and friends to see. Arriving home with two hungry, fractious girls, Megan barely noticed that Greta, Tom's camper van, was not in her usual spot on the driveway. She had hastened to empty the wet costume and towel from Alys' swimming bag, then hunted through the freezer for something quick for dinner before the thought of filling the kettle to make a cup of tea even crossed her mind.

The note, seemingly so innocent, so bland and unthreatening while it still leaned unread against the kettle, had made her aching legs tremble so violently she had to stumble across the kitchen to collapse into a chair.

Going away with Greta for half term to get my head together.
Tom.

Its bluntness stunned her like a physical blow. What did it mean? Where was he going? Was he going away for the whole week of the half term holiday? Without her! Without their daughters. Didn't he realise how completely and utterly knackered she was in the eighth month of her pregnancy? How much she could do with a holiday herself? He hadn't even had the decency to offer an apology for leaving her in the lurch. Couldn't even be bothered to put a kiss for the girls after his name. Selfish, arrogant, inconsiderate bastard – what the hell did he think he was playing at?

Anger gave her the impetus she needed to pull herself shakily to her feet and continue preparing the girls' meal. Its heat had sustained her for the past four nights as she lay alone in their bed, the cool sheets vacant beside her, only the shallow sound of her own breathing to be heard in the ominous silence of the room. Where was he? Was he, like her, sleeping alone? Or was he spending his nights with someone else? Had he been lying, as well as keeping things from her? Had he made a fool of her when he convinced her all those years ago that he would never leave her?

Nothing was certain any more. Marriage had been a safe haven up to now; but in the early hours before dawn, without her husband's solid presence beside her, Megan's faith in her future lay in ruins. She pressed her hands against the rhythmic kicking of the baby in her belly and told herself that she could cope alone.

An incident came to mind: it had happened a few weeks ago, but she could still picture it vividly. She had been in the kitchen with Tom, preparing packed lunches for the next day, trying to remember which of the girls liked raspberry yogurt and which preferred peach;

who would only eat ham and who would leave her sandwiches untouched unless they were filled with cheese spread. In the midst of this logistical trial Megan, still fuming because he had bought his stupid orange camper van instead of the gorgeous new oak kitchen she wanted, had finally snapped – and really, who could blame her? The kitchen cabinets were falling to bits; anyone with any sense would invest in home improvements rather than blowing thousands of pounds on an old hippie van.

"Look at this cupboard," she said. "The bloody knob's fallen off again!"

Tom turned the full force of his icy blue eyes upon her and snarled. "Well! Lucky fucking cupboard."

Such a stupid remark. Even weeks later it made her grind her teeth.

"What the hell is that supposed to mean?"

"I'll tell you what it means, Megan: I envy this kitchen. You care more about it than you do about me. The cupboard should consider itself fortunate to get so much of your attention."

She flinched at the violence with which he slammed the jar he'd been holding back into the fridge, half expecting to hear a shower of breaking glass.

"If my knob fell off I don't think you'd even notice." He flashed a piercing, contemptuous look in her direction and stalked out to grab his car keys and gym bag.

"Oh, grow up!" she yelled as the front door crashed shut behind him. Honestly - he was getting more and more like a moody teenager.

When he returned home she was already in bed, her back turned to him, pretending to be asleep. It was so typical of him to avoid conflict by walking out, and she had no intention of rewarding such behaviour by giving him attention when he finally deigned to come home. If he thought she was going to make the first move and apologise after the childish way he had spoken to her, he was very much mistaken.

He had been morose recently, closemouthed and sullen. Sulking over her reaction to Greta's arrival, no doubt. With Alys and Nia, the warmth would return to his eyes and his smile was as broad as ever. But when he noticed her watching he'd turn away, concentrating his attention on their daughters instead. He was a physical man whose strong arms gave the most sublime hugs. It was galling to admit it, but she missed them. It wasn't fair for Alys and Nia to be the sole recipients of such comfort. How much rejection is a wife supposed to take?

Now he had left her alone when she was pregnant and feeling at her most vulnerable. He had ignored her wishes when deciding to spend his money on this clapped-out old van instead of a beautiful new kitchen; he saved his smiles and hearty enthusiasm for their daughters instead of his wife; he neglected to discuss his life or his feelings with her; and finally, of course, there came the ultimate rejection: he went away without consulting her, leaving only the briefest information to ensure she couldn't find him.

He had reckoned without her determination.

"Judging by the number of camper vans in the car park, they are pretty popular," Matt said when he returned. "I just popped to the shop to grab a sandwich, and half of the souvenirs in there are camper-related. They've got key rings, mugs, t-shirts, everything. Maybe Tom's onto something?"

His attempt at humour fell flat as she sniffed and turned away. The muscles across the back of her neck felt as if someone was gripping them in a vice – she raised them higher, rolled them and allowed them to drop. It didn't help.

"Anyway," Matt went on. "I expect you need the loo yet again, and I want to get home to help Bethan with those two girls of yours. Why don't you nip off to the shop and grab something for lunch while I wait here? That way, if Tom comes back we won't miss him."

It wasn't a bad idea. Food was the last thing on her mind, but she would be glad of the chance to stretch her legs and look around. She trudged towards the shop, making every effort not to lapse into a waddle as she crossed the tarmac. Still no sign of Tom.

She crossed her arms as she entered the shop, on edge in the bustle of holidaymakers whose sharp elbows threatened to knock against her swollen stomach. The shop was well stocked with wetsuits, surfboards and the usual array of buckets, spades, balls, kites, hats and souvenirs. Matt was right: there was a plethora of camper-related items. Horrid, tacky things. Meg averted her gaze, her heart as cold and heavy as a stone in the face of their popular appeal. A camper van had lured her husband away. She could hardly be expected to feel any affection for them, however supposedly iconic they might be.

She bought a couple of bottles of chilled mineral water at the takeaway outlet and, despite the knots in her stomach, forced herself to pick out a sandwich. Stowing her purchases in a carrier bag, she threaded her way along the tarmac path towards the beach.

Now, perhaps, she might catch a glimpse of Tom. The thought gave her a strange sensation in her stomach, like the heartburn that had been troubling her for the past few months of pregnancy. Soon she would learn why he had deserted her, and whether he really did plan to come back.

Emerging at the end of the pathway through the dunes, she stood transfixed by the view. A shame she had forgotten to bring her sunglasses: she had to squint against the glare of the sun reflecting off the endless sash of sand edging the shore. To her right, where the coast road continued back towards the village of Croyde, a row of white buildings clung to the cliff like molars in a jawbone.

So this was the place that had lured Tom away from his family. She supposed she could see its appeal, in a way. There was no tacky commercialism of the sort that so often blighted British beaches. No fairground, no donkey rides or stalls, apart from one discreet shed offering the temptation of deckchairs and beach huts for hire. The girls would love it here, having all that space to play. For a long moment she forgot the purpose of her visit and was still, inhaling the crisp, salty air like a drug as warm sand crept in at the edges of her flip-flops. Her sundress flapped around her puffy ankles, and the sun warmed her arms and shoulders.

Blinking, she took in the distance to the water's edge. The tide must be out. Could Tom be among the distant huddle of people with their surfboards and body boards? Was he one of the swimmers, or one of those paddling at the edge of the waves? Her shoulders drooped as she let out her breath, forcing out some of her tension. It was hopeless trying to identify him, and she didn't have the energy to trek all that way across the sand for a closer view.

At last, roused by the tell-tale prickle of the sun's rays threatening her fair skin, she headed back up the slope to join Matt. It was time to send him back home to Bethan. Tom had to be here somewhere, whether in the waves or walking along the wide sweep of sand. He would be sure to return to Greta eventually. As long as she stayed with the van she couldn't fail to find him.

She found her brother-in-law waiting in the van, tapping out an impatient rhythm with his feet. His hasty smile suggested he was making an effort to be upbeat and he sprang up, remembering too late how low the ceiling was in the compact living space. She grimaced as he rubbed his bruised head, but he brushed off her concern, keen to share his latest discovery.

"There you are. You were gone for ages. Before you ask, no, he hasn't been back. I poked around in the cupboards while you were gone and found a leaflet and receipt from a company called 'Wipe-Out! Mobile Surf School'. There's a van over there with their logo on the side, look."

He pointed through the window towards a long, modern VW van. *Wipe-Out!* was emblazoned across its side in bold letters.

"I seem to remember their logo... Their web page must be one of the ones he looked at when he did his research into surfing beaches. So you think he must be with them, then?"

"According to the receipt he's booked a week's course of surfing tuition. The leaflet says they meet you at the beach with the wetsuits and boards and provide lessons for a couple of hours each morning and afternoon. They let you keep the gear until five o'clock, if you've still got the energy to use it. Personally I would find an hour more than enough, but Tom's obviously fitter than I am."

Megan's gaze dropped to his waistline, then slid away. He was undoubtedly right; but in fairness, Tom was fitter than most people.

"Did you find anything else?"

"Not really. There's an open packet of bacon, some milk, eggs and beer in the fridge so I guess we can deduce he's had at least one cooked breakfast, and sat out under the stars with a couple of tinnies to strum away on his guitar in the evenings."

"Hmmm." His forced brightness grated on her. She bit her lip and tried to remember how it felt to see the funny side of a situation.

"I don't know why he brought his guitar. I can't remember the last time he picked it up."

"Maybe that's the point?"

"What do you mean?"

"He doesn't get a lot of time for self-indulgence, any more than you do. This whole thing shouts 'Mid-Life Crisis' to me. Think about it: he hits forty and before you know it he's blown his inheritance on a camper van and driven off into the sunset to surf all day, then drink beer all night. Maybe he's turned into a hippie? He'll be growing a beard and getting his kids' names tattooed over his heart next."

"If you're right and it is a mid-life crisis, I suppose you think I should be grateful he hasn't bought a sports car and run off with a younger woman."

Matt was fidgeting with the keys in his pocket, making them jingle. "I don't suppose he'd dare, Meg. And I don't suppose he'd want to – no need to look like that."

There was an uncomfortable silence.

"Look, I really need to be thinking about heading home. My phone isn't picking up any signal, so I haven't been able to give Bethan an update. She'll be worried about you. Maybe the lack of signal around here is the reason Tom hasn't been in touch? It's not that he isn't speaking to you, just that he can't. His mobile is dead, anyway – I found it in the glove compartment and the battery's completely drained; it won't even turn on. There's no sign of a charger anywhere, so - fair play to him - I guess he had no way of getting hold of you. The Muppet should have thought to pack a charger along with his trunks."

"I imagine there's a payphone in the shop, so if he'd actually wanted to let his wife and children know that he's still alive it wouldn't have been that difficult."

"Maybe there isn't one where he's camping? Anyway, I'm not here to make excuses for him. Perhaps he's just turning into a bit of a prat in his old age."

He leaned his arm across her shoulders in a fraternal hug, and the concern in his brown eyes made her soften a little.

"I hope you can sort things out. You two were always good together. I'm sure you can find a way to make it work again. If you need me, give me a call – even if it's from a payphone in the shop." He smiled tentatively, as if trying to assess her mental state from her expression. "Am I okay to go now? Have you got everything you need? You might have to wait with the van for a good while if he's hired the surfing gear until five o'clock. I don't like to leave a damsel in distress, especially when she's about to drop her sprog, but I don't want to get stuck in the bank holiday traffic on the M5. Northbound will be a nightmare later, if I stay too long."

She couldn't blame him for wanting to get home. He had already been so kind, even if he had been more or less forced into helping. She had been so desperate to confront Tom, her sister Bethan would have given him hell if he hadn't brought her down here. But being an object of pity leaves a bitter taste in the mouth.

"I'm absolutely fine," she insisted. "There's no need for you to worry. The little one won't put in an appearance for at least another month. You get back and let them all know we found Greta. Give Nia and Alys a big kiss from me, and tell them I'll try to call later and let them know when I've found their dad."

Poor little girls, waiting for news. Although confused, they had accepted their father's vanishing act with greater equanimity than she had been able to herself. Unlike her, they were naïve enough to trust him to come home.

Now, as she heaved herself back into the camper van to wait for Tom to appear, rancour stirred again. She propped her aching back against one of the cushions and gazed out towards the beach path, trying to make sense of it all.

Maybe Matt's comment about Tom undergoing a mid-life crisis might have some truth in it. He had never done anything like this before. Disappearing off in a camper van to find himself while his heavily pregnant wife struggled to cope with two demanding young children was outrageous, but it was also uncharacteristic. He must have known she would be furious. Presumably he didn't care.

It had been obvious for some time that he was unhappy. She had put it down to the usual male disgruntlement when sex wasn't forthcoming. It was months since they had been intimate, and he had left her in no doubt of his bitter resentment. He should have understood, should have anticipated that she would be more tired during this third pregnancy: she had so much more to contend with this time around. If she had put lovemaking on the back burner for a while, why should that have surprised him? Who would feel sexy juggling a part-time job, running a household and being a mother to two small children? Alternately feeling sick and swigging down gallons of Gaviscon and Lactulose weren't particularly conducive to a strong libido.

There was so little to like about him lately, a part of her wondered if this disappearance might be the final straw. Did she want to stay with a man who could behave so selfishly? Closing her eyes, she allowed herself a brief vision of all of Tom's possessions dumped in bin bags on the driveway. No more shirts to iron. No more sweaty gym kit. The toilet seat would never be left up; no one would moan that her long red hair looked like a drowned squirrel when it built up and blocked the plug hole in the shower.

No one would say anything much to her at all by way of adult conversation. Or help when she couldn't reach something from a high shelf (which happened a lot). No one to mow the lawn or put the bins out, remind her when the car needed servicing, or climb the ladder when she wanted something brought down from the attic. No one to check the doors were locked before bed. No warm back to snuggle up to when settling to sleep.

She sighed and opened her eyes again. Time to face facts. She had too much invested in their relationship to give up on it without a struggle. Now that she had reduced her working hours he contributed a lot more to their household income than she did. He wasn't one of those useless men who wouldn't lift a finger around the house: he didn't expect a medal for nipping round with the hoover or getting on with dinner if he arrived home before she did. More importantly, her daughters shouldn't have to grow up without a father, as she had.

To think it had come to this, contemplating the possibility of ending their marriage. Only a year ago she would have said they were happy together. There had been a time when she and Tom seemed to have it all.

How had it all gone so wrong? Was he planning to come home, as his note seemed to suggest? Or had he decided, whilst strumming his guitar or surfing the waves and "getting his head together", that he had had enough of responsibilities and domesticity? Was he planning to make a fresh start without her?

Now here she was, stuck in an unfamiliar place, with only Greta for company, the van that symbolised Tom's treachery. Wondering whether he would have an adequate explanation for his actions. Waiting to find out whether they had reached the end of the road.

It had all seemed so different in the beginning.

Chapter Two

Seven years earlier: Saturday, 18th December 2004
Cardiff

Nothing says Christmas party like a sticky dance floor in a shabby hotel festooned with fairy lights, tinsel and balloons, Megan thought. Garish foil decorations twirled from the ceiling with the heat and cigarette smoke of the couple of hundred party-goers who had congregated in the function room, where a moth-eaten Christmas tree failed to compete with the flashing lights of the disco. Megan's footsteps tottered, due in part to too much Bacardi, and partly because the balls of her feet stung from dancing in vertiginous heels. With ears ringing from the too-loud second-rate music of her parents' generation blaring from the enormous speakers, and an extravagant dose of roast turkey dinner and plum pudding lying like a stone in her stomach, she was loving every second.

Better start pacing myself, she decided, striking out in a meandering course towards the bar: after only one term working as an English teacher at St Dyfrig's High School, it wouldn't do to show herself up by getting too embarrassingly inebriated at the staff party. But before she could order a soft drink, her colleagues Rachel and Claire appeared at her elbows.

"We're off to the ladies. You coming?"

"What a night!" Megan said as they joined the inevitable queue. "I'm seeing a whole new side to everyone. Is Sue always like that after a few drinks?"

Rachel nodded. "Always. Mind you, she probably hasn't had a night out since September. You can always tell the ones who don't get out much, can't you?"

"Mmmm. Poor old Sue – she does work so hard. I bet she loves having a chance to finally let her hair down now and then, even if it isn't exactly a glamorous occasion. Can you believe the DJ tonight? I mean, does he know any recent music at all? I can't remember the last time I danced to Y.M.C.A; I'm surprised I remembered the actions after all these years."

"Hmm…You gave quite an impressive performance. It's a shame I can't join you in a Bacardi or two – it might loosen me up a bit, help me look more like a dancer and less like a hippo," Claire said, eyeing her pregnant stomach glumly in the mirror.

Megan patted her on the shoulder. It must be tedious being the only sober member of the party. "Aww. Your self-sacrifice is very noble. You look radiant, not like a hippo at all."

Rachel groaned, stooping to examine a ladder in her tights. "Damn it, look at these – brand new and I've gone and snagged them already…" She straightened up and puffed out her cheeks. "God, I'm as full as an egg. I should have declined the coffee and mince pie. I haven't been this stuffed since the cruise I went on last summer…"

Megan nodded agreement, pausing in the task of touching up her make-up. If she concentrated very hard she could just about manage to apply the lipstick in a straight line. Good job it was pale coral, a wobbly edge wouldn't be too obvious.

She caught Rachel grinning at her in the mirror. "It isn't only the crap music and dancing round our handbags that reminds me of school discos. I'm not sure if you've spotted them, but I've noticed that you have some secret admirers, my girl."

"You're joking! Who? I haven't seen anybody looking."

"The P.E. guys. They've been watching you from the bar."

"I didn't notice. Must have been too busy enjoying myself. I'll take a peek when we get back to the dance floor." She slipped her lipstick back into her bag, began to zip it back up and paused as a new thought struck her. Rachel had finally gone into a cubicle, so Megan called through the door.

"Rach, please tell me you didn't mean Duncan. He's sweet, but I honestly think I'd die if he tried to chat me up."

"No need to sound so worried," Rachel called back. Emerging from the cubicle, she headed to the washbasins barelegged. "All yours. I hope you've got a tissue in your bag – there's no paper left. No, Duncan wouldn't be brave enough to chat anybody up, even if he wanted to. I meant Tom Field and Garin Pugh."

Meg had encountered Garin at work, but Tom's name was less familiar. She smoothed her skirt with a quick backward glance to reassure herself that she hadn't accidentally caught the hem in her knickers. "Garin is the really tall, lanky one, isn't he? The one who looks at every woman as if he's picturing her naked."

"Yep, that would be him."

As they washed their hands, Claire primped her updo in the mirror, teasing the tendrils that framed her cheeks. "Garin must be around six foot two, maybe even taller. I rather like him, actually. If I wasn't already taken - and up the duff, obviously – I'd consider making a pass at him myself. I've always had a soft spot for bad boys."

Rachel stuck out her tongue. "Ugh, no – Garin isn't so much a bad boy as a boorish oaf. The sort who'd imagine he could charm a woman by serenading her with a stirring rendition of *Get Your Tits Out For the Boys*."

"Get away, he's a laugh. Even if he is the sort of bloke your mother warns you about." Claire grinned, but Rachel shook her head.

"He's too gangly for my taste. I like a man with a bit of muscle on him. And he's a cocky bastard. If I had to choose one of the two, I'd go for Tom. He may be a bit shorter, but he's better looking, if you ask me. Quieter, not so full of himself. And always terribly polite. If you went out with Garin, you wouldn't get a word in edgewise. Not even our Little Miss Chatterbox here." She patted the top of Megan's head playfully.

"Wouldn't you find him a bit posh, though? Whenever he speaks I'm always half expecting him to offer to drive me round his country estate in a beaten-up old Land Rover, looking for some peasants to shoot. You'd have to buy a tweed suit and a headscarf for the first date. Whereas Garin's salt of the earth, a regular Cardiff caveman."

"Stop exaggerating," Rachel said. "He only seems posh compared with the Valleys blokes you're used to. What do you think, Meggie? Which one will you go for?"

Megan held up her hands. "To be honest, neither of them sounds like my type. I'll be quite content to just enjoy the dancing and then go back to my grotty flat in Splott for a nice cup of cocoa on my own."

"Nonsense. It is a truth universally acknowledged that a single English teacher in possession of a grotty flat in Splott must be in want of a shag."

She couldn't help but laugh. It may have been a few months, but she wasn't yet desperate enough to settle for a Neanderthal or an upper class twit.

They headed back to the function room, weaving around the women dancing at the edge of the floor to squeeze into the only space available at the bar.

Meg nudged Rachel.   "Alright. Which one is Posh Tom, then?"

"At the other end of the bar, look. Dark shirt, fair-ish hair. He's got his back to us at the moment… Careful, now: Garin's seen us looking. You should be playing it cool, not gawping over there. Have you never heard of 'treat 'em mean to keep 'em keen'?"

Ducking her head unfortunately meant that catching a glimpse of Tom Field was impossible.

"Here, have another Bacardi, and then let's wow your admirers by showing off our moves on the dance floor," Rachel said, passing the glass.

It would be rude to refuse, of course. But this drink would definitely have to be her last.

∞ ∞ ∞

Tom thanked the barman for their drinks and nudged Garin's pint of beer along the bar towards him. His colleague's ability to drink like the proverbial fish was legendary. Despite many drunken rugby tours over the years, Tom knew he would struggle to consume the amount of ale the Welshman was able to pour down his throat, and certainly not after a heavy Christmas dinner.

As Christmas parties went, he didn't think he'd ever been to a worse one. Certainly the DJ was the worst he'd ever had the misfortune to listen to, with an apparent predilection for the Bay City Rollers and Brotherhood of Man. He'd been tempted to fetch his coat when Russ Abbott's *Atmosphere* started blaring through the speakers, but things had improved marginally with *Delilah* and *Green Green Grass of Home*. His Welsh colleagues at least seemed to find these rousing, joining in and waving their drinks around in patriotic abandon.

If the DJ would only play something decent - from within the past decade, for instance - and if he'd been able to join Garin in a few pints, he could have probably enjoyed himself. But with eighty miles to drive the next morning the last thing he needed was a hangover.

Garin gulped down a generous swig of beer and licked the foamy moustache from his top lip.

"You're a positive saint, you are, Tommo. I don't know how you can resist such temptation. Listening to shit like this should be enough to drive anyone to drown their sorrows."

Tom leaned his elbow on the bar and sipped his lime and soda. "You know me, Garin," he said. "My body is a temple."

"Oh, so is mine. Most definitely a temple. That explains why I'm always besieged by worshippers."

"Hmmm. The trouble is, yours is the Temple of Doom, and pretty soon it'll be in ruins."

"Oh yeah - very good. You're reasonably witty for an Englishman, you know? No, my body needs to be topped up with alcohol to stop me getting frostbite on the way home. I should be having whisky or brandy really, served up by a Saint Bernard with a little barrel round its neck, or better still a Nordic blonde with a fur coat and no knickers. It'd freeze the bollocks off a brass monkey outside. I wouldn't be surprised if it's cold enough for snow – what do you reckon?"

"You could be right. It'd be just my luck to wake up to a few inches in the morning."

"A few inches? You speak for yourself. Mine's eight or nine, at least."

Alcohol made him so predictable. Tom quickly manoeuvred his glass of soda away from his shirt as Garin jostled his arm and leaned to growl in his ear:

"Hey, look over there! Talent alert. That new girl from the English department is back on the floor. Cor, I tell you what, she could have it."

Tom reached for a beer mat, his glass dripping. So Garin had spotted the petite redhead dancing with Sue and Rachel. Hardly surprising, since she was arguably the most attractive woman on the dancefloor. Tom had noticed her at work several times since September, but their paths hadn't crossed and he didn't know her name. She wasn't the athletic type he usually went for. Not a bit like Erica... A vivid memory of short, dark hair and slender limbs flitted through his mind. He pushed away the thought and focused his attention on the redhead in her striking emerald dress.

She was tiny, half a head shorter than Rachel even in those spiky heels. Remarkable that she could walk in them, never mind dance. Her smile flashed often, giving her an air of mischievous confidence: laughter frequently rippled through the group at things she said. He liked a woman with wit as well as looks. Not that he was on the lookout for anyone, of course. He was still off women.

She reminded him of someone... He frowned, dredging up the memory. Yes, that was it – his adolescent fantasy: Susan Sarandon in *Bull Durham,* shagging Kevin Costner on the kitchen table. God, to think of the hours he'd spent reimagining that scene of milk cartons and breakfast dishes tossed aside in the heat of passion. Then he'd grown up and realised there wasn't a woman in the world who'd be willing to sacrifice her crockery for sex. Least of all Erica. Damn her – she'd invaded his thoughts again. He'd been doing quite well recently, too.

"What d'you reckon, Tommo? Lush, eh? She'll never be a runner with a rack like that, though, will she? Even a gentle jog would give her facial bruising. I tell you, I wouldn't mind waking up to those puppies on Christmas morning. What do you say? I wouldn't mind her giving my Christmas cracker a pull, to see what comes bursting out."

Tom set his glass down on the bar and arranged his face into what he hoped was a discouraging expression. His colleague's characteristic irreverence tended to descend into outright offensiveness when he'd had a few drinks. He was like a can of cola that had been shaken: effervescent fun until he turned and vented on some unsuspecting soul.

"Do you think she's a natural redhead?" The leer on Garin's face told Tom all he needed to know about his line of thinking.

"I've no idea. Why don't you ask her?" Tom felt a moment's satisfaction at his own cunning: a question like that would be sure to put her off Garin, leaving the way clear for a more gentlemanly approach to achieve success. Not that he was planning to make any kind of move, but still…

"That's a cracking idea, fair play. I'll go over there now and say to her, my mate Tom wants to know if your collar and cuffs match."

While Garin laughed hard enough to slop ale down the front of his shirt, Tom looked him coldly in the eye.

"Did I ever tell you about the time I won a kick-boxing competition?"

The gale of laughter stopped abruptly. "Er – no, I don't think you ever have."

Tom let his blatant lie sink in before changing the subject. "Moving on... Have you noticed Sue? She must have had a fair bit to drink: you have to admit, that Tina Turner impression she's doing is pretty good."

Garin snorted. "Yeah, right. If Tina Turner was white and weighed sixteen stone the resemblance would be positively uncanny."

There was a movement at Tom's elbow: their colleague Duncan had rejoined them at the bar, seemingly unaware of the toilet paper stuck to his sole like a streamer. Tom opened his mouth to tell him, but Garin got in there first.

"Well, look who it is: Duncan Doughnut himself. Come to spot some talent with the big boys, have you Dunc? You're not likely to snare any with bog roll on your hoof, though."

Duncan stooped to detach the toilet paper. He stared at it, apparently unsure what to do with it, then folded it up and tucked it into his breast pocket.

"Talent watching, are you? So that's why you've been looking at Megan Parry. The one with red hair. She's a lovely girl, that one. Very friendly."

"Oho, I like 'em friendly. Friendly girls are just my cup of tea. Cor, I tell you what - I'm having a spiritual experience here, looking at those breasts."

Tom raised a sceptical eyebrow. "Are you sure it's a spiritual experience, not a physical one?"

Garin's smile was wolfish. "Oh yes, definitely spiritual. Because those tits are a miracle and a wonder." He rolled his eyes heavenwards. "'Rock of Ages, cleft for me. Let me hide myself in thee.' I could hide myself very happily in that cleft, let me tell you."

Duncan's cheeks reddened. "Garin, you are a disgrace to whoever taught you in Sunday School," he said.

"I know. If old Auntie Dilys could see me now, she'd be on her knees, praying for my soul. Actually, now I come to mention it, I wouldn't mind having that little redhead on her knees. But then, when I start thinking about that, I think about my cock, and I have another spiritual experience."

"Tsk! How can you describe thinking about that as a spiritual experience?"

Tom winced. Whatever punchline was coming, it was sure to be in the poorest possible taste.

"Because when I think about my cock I say to myself: my God - how great thou art." Garin grasped his crotch, hazel eyes gleaming.

It was time to intervene before poor Duncan had a coronary.

"That redhead is very nice, but she's far too short for you, Gaz. Look at her compared with Sue: she'd make Kylie Minogue look tall. If you're hoping to get off with her you'd better get her a stepladder and pray she's not scared of heights."

"Ah, well – it all evens out when you're horizontal, doesn't it? And, looking on the bright side, she'd be able to give me a blow job without even needing to stoop."

Tom was obliged to give Duncan a few firm smacks between the shoulder blades as he choked on his drink. Outrage furrowed the other man's brow, but Tom knew he was too intimidated by Garin to censure him. He gave Garin a nudge with his elbow, trying a different tactic.

"You'd be better off with that girl on the other side of the dance floor: the one who's been eyeing you up for the past half hour…"

Hawk-like, Garin scanned the room.

"No, no - she's not with our lot. I think she's with that group from the insurance company. Over there, look - the tall brunette. Microscopic skirt; endless legs. No ladder necessary to get off with that one."

"Oh aye, I see the one you're on about. Hmmm, not bad at all. Alright, here we go: start the ball rolling with a bit of eye contact…. Yeah, baby." Garin's gaze latched onto the woman like a crosshair locked onto a target. As he turned his best smouldering expression towards the brunette she giggled and whispered to her friends.

Duncan seemed to be on the verge of choking again. "Unbelievable," he spluttered. "She actually seems to be interested. See her now, she's batting her lashes at him from across the room and they've never even met. And her friend has her eye on you, Tom. I don't know how you do it. It's almost as if you're both irresistible to the opposite sex! Come on now, tell me: what's the secret?"

Garin took a swig of beer, leaned back on the bar and delivered his advice in the manner of a guru dispensing pearls of wisdom, although the slurring of his words tended to mar the effect somewhat.

"I'll tell you the secret, Dunky. It's all in the eyes. Tom and I, we've both got these gorgeous eyes, see. And we know how to use those gorgeous eyes, don't we Tommo? Seduction is all about eye contact, my friend." He pointed to his eyes and Tom's, nodding sagely, presumably believing this would add gravitas to his advice.

Tom obliged by batting his eyelashes, playfully coy. He wasn't above making deliberate eye contact with attractive females, or hadn't been in his younger days anyway. Garin, on the other hand, was downright predatory. Hopefully he'd never have to stoop to that level – he'd want someone to shoot him first.

Duncan waited in vain for some more useful tips.

"So - is that it? Is that honestly the secret? Well I never. You mean, if I stare at them long enough, I'll have a magnetic attraction for the opposite sex? If only I'd known that thirty years ago."

"I hate to break it to you Dunky but you could stare and bat your eyelashes till Doomsday and you still wouldn't pull a bird, not even if she sat on your face. You haven't got the X factor. That's what it is, see. I've got it, yes, and Tom to a lesser extent, not as much as me, obviously. It's known as Animal Magnetism. What you might call an electric personality. Watch this now."

Git. There was no need to be cruel to someone as harmless as Duncan. Tom sent Garin a reproving glare, but he ignored it, raising his glass towards the brunette in a toast.

"Bingo! There you go," he said as she simpered and sent him a flirtatious wave. "Tidy! See you later, losers."

Duncan's lips pursed as Garin strutted across the room and joined the woman, beer in hand, to murmur in her ear. "I don't know what they see in him. The way he talks about them… And the way he treats them! You couldn't meet a greater misogynist in all your life. The way he was talking about Megan was disgraceful."

"Megan being the one with the Rita Hayworth hair?"

"Yes, that's her! She's lovely; far too good for Garin. I'd hate to see him get his hooks into her." Duncan brightened as if an idea had struck him, and he leaned closer. "Why don't you go over there and get talking to her first? Honestly, she's really nice. And you need to put yourself back out there again, don't you? It's about time, after all. You don't want to end up a lonely old bachelor like me."

Tom grimaced. Just what he needed – a bloody matchmaker. He eyed Duncan, whose smile had frayed a bit at the edges with those final words. No, he didn't want to end up like that. Well… she was pretty enough, and it couldn't hurt to say hello.

He drained the last of his soda and lime. Pity it wasn't a Scotch. It was a long time since he'd chatted anyone up; a bit of Dutch courage wouldn't go amiss.

"Go on, then," he said with a sigh. "Introduce us."

∞ ∞ ∞

Megan sat alone at the end of a table. She had removed her high heels and was rubbing her feet, laughing in the face of her friends' taunts from the dance floor.

"Party pooper!" called Sue, gyrating her ample hips with a confidence that suggested she, too, had had more than a few too many drinks. "It's only just after eleven o'clock! You wouldn't have got me off the dance floor all night at your age!"

"I know - I'm a pathetic little wimp with no stamina. But I'd defy anyone to dance all night wearing shoes like these." Under her breath she added, "or after drinking this much." It really was time to start pacing herself with a couple of soft drinks, or she'd end up with a killer hangover in the morning. She slipped her feet back into her shoes with a groan.

"Megan!" Duncan called her name from behind a knot of dancers, waving eagerly to catch her attention.

Oh, dear. Duncan was sweet, but not adept at respecting personal space. She shrank back a fraction as he leaned over to bellow into her ear above the volume of the disco.

"I want to introduce you to Tom Field. He's our rugby specialist."

She nodded. This was an interesting development. It seemed she would get to meet her alleged secret admirer after all. She brightened and sat up a little straighter in her seat, until Duncan patted her bare shoulder with a sweaty hand and made her cringe.

He swayed, blocking her view. "You'll really like him, I'm sure. Thanks to him, our team is at the top of the Welsh league. And yet the thing is – now this is quite ironic, as I'm sure you'll agree, Megan, when I tell you – would you believe, he's an Englishman! There isn't a drop of Welsh blood in his body, yet here he is teaching our Welsh kids to play their national game. What do you think of that, then?"

Until he removed his hand she was too uncomfortable to think anything, really. But it was true that there was an element of irony in the idea. She was about to voice courteous agreement when he moved aside and she glimpsed his companion for the first time.

So this was Tom Field. He did look vaguely familiar: she must have seen him at work occasionally, presumably only at a distance because if she'd had a good look she would most definitely have remembered. Of course, he would wear sweatpants or tracksuits to teach sport. That would be why she hadn't paid attention to him before. Nothing made a man look more unkempt than a tracksuit and trainers.

What an improvement tonight, though. The dark, narrow-fitting shirt and smart trousers transformed him, hinting at a well-formed body underneath: broad shouldered and narrow hipped. Short haired and clean shaven, he had a lean, good looking face. As far as she could tell from her seat, he was fairly tall, but not intimidatingly so like Garin, who would tower over her by more than a foot.

"Miss Parry. Duncan was surprised to hear we hadn't met, so he offered to introduce us. I'm Tom Field."

He was well-spoken, without a trace of a regional accent, but not as plummy as she had been led to expect. As he held out one hand to shake hers the tone of his voice was as warm and appreciative as his eyes.

"Hello there. It's nice to meet the Rugby Field Duncan was just telling me about... But I suppose you've probably heard that line before."

"Hmmm. Maybe once or twice." But he smiled tolerantly enough at her clumsy attempt at wit.

"I think I've seen you around before at school, but you were always scruffing about in your tracksuit. You've scrubbed up quite nicely tonight, though."

That was definitely a gleam of amusement in his eyes. Dammit. Little Miss Chatterbox indeed. Had the Bacardi had loosened her tongue too far, made her look desperate?

"I've seen you around, too. But you usually wear your hair up. The pre-Raphaelite look suits you."

He'd noticed. She tucked a stray tendril behind her ear, pleased.

"Thanks. I thought I'd let it do its own thing for a change. At school I'm always too scared to leave it down in case I get nits."

"We certainly wouldn't want that, would we? May I?" He indicated the empty seat next to her, undaunted by her apparent inability to appear chic and sophisticated. She nodded hastily, wishing she hadn't mentioned nits. She'd start itching in a minute just thinking about them.

She couldn't have been more aware of the close proximity of those broad shoulders and muscular legs if they emitted an electric charge. Better steer the conversation back to safe ground before she made an even greater fool of herself. But what? Rugby – yes, that would do. Nothing safer than getting a man to talk about sport.

"So, Tom Field, rugby specialist… What's your position of choice, then?" She knew she'd slipped again as soon as the words were out.

"Now that's a leading question. Most women wait until at least the first date before asking me that."

"Mine was always Wing Attack. In netball, not rugby, obviously." Best to put him straight, not let him imagine she was thinking about anything more than sport.

"Ah. 'Though she be but little, she is fierce'."

"You know Shakespeare?"

He hesitated. "Not really. Tempting though it is to let you believe that I'm a cultured and literary man, I'm afraid I probably just read it on a t-shirt somewhere."

Disappointing, but at least he was honest.

"Can I get you a drink?"

"Thanks, but I really don't think I should have any more. I've embarrassed myself quite enough this evening already."

Duncan fussed at her elbow; she forced herself to turn towards him, instead of basking in the glow of Tom's gaze.

"No, no - let me buy you both a drink – I won't hear of you getting this round, Tom. You know, it was his birthday two days ago, Megan, and he hasn't let me get him a celebratory drink yet."

"I think he might be your biggest fan," Tom said as Duncan bustled away to the bar, seemingly astonished that they both wanted soft drinks.

"Is he? Bless him – he does seem very sweet. Not as cocky as most of the P.E. teachers I've met."

He seemed unperturbed by the challenge. "I agree: Duncan's a thoroughly good egg. He was a champion swimmer in his youth, did you know? And he ran cross-country for Wales. He still runs, but for charity now. Ultra-marathons and so on. I'm afraid some people see him as a bit of a bumbling idiot, but actually he's rather shy. The kids at school love him because he's a terrific coach, never sarcastic or harsh. He has a way of seeing the best in people and then finding ways to bring that out."

His attention had been caught by something behind her, and she turned to see a huddle of people deserting the dance floor for the bar. The music had been pretty poor all evening, but now the DJ had clearly abandoned the idea of playing anything even approaching contemporary music. A rock and roll track blared through the speakers, eliciting good-natured smiles from those old enough to remember it but sneers from many of the youngest dancers. The sudden warmth of his hand on hers startled her.

"Come on," he said, and pulled her up to her feet.

Before she had time to say a word, they were on the dance floor and she was caught up in a whirling, breath-taking jive that made several of the other dancers whistle their appreciation.

"What are you doing? I don't know any of the steps!"

He grinned. "Don't worry. I do."

And he did. She burst into giggles as he twirled her around, forgetting the stinging of her feet in the effort of keeping her balance. His confidence and obvious enjoyment made her feel that her ineptitude didn't matter, only the pleasure of their hands joining and parting, the swift rhythm of the music and the purposeful, laughing way he directed her movements.   As the song ended she swayed, giddy and grateful for his steadying hand against the small of her back. His eyes were alight, suggesting that he was no more immune to the headiness of touching than she, and he bowed good-naturedly to the ripple of applause from the other dancers.

"You're full of surprises!" she exclaimed on their way back to their seats, conscious of her flaming cheeks and trying not to show that she was so much more out of breath than he. "Wherever did you learn to dance like that?"

"At university. I realised in Freshers' Week that I would meet a lot more girls in the ballroom dancing society than the rugby club."

"Ah, so you're a strategist. Did your tactic pay off?"

"Initially yes, but I'd dated all the good-looking ones by the end of the first year so after that I gave up. I'd been hoping to learn the tango but I'm afraid I was too shallow to want to dance with any of the ugly girls, and the pretty ones had all seen through me and moved on to other partners."

"Well, I'm impressed that you got me dancing like that – twirling around, and everything. The most sophisticated dance I've ever managed before is the *Macarena*."

"Not the *Time Warp*? Or *Agadoo*?"

She liked his deadpan way of teasing her. Nothing sparked her interest like a man who could keep her on her toes, and this one had almost literally swept her off her feet within a few minutes.

A deep Welsh voice boomed out from behind them.

"Well, hello there, Miss Parry. How delightful to meet you at last. I see my old friend Twinkletoes here has muscled in first and got you all pink and panting, just the way I like my women."

Garin Pugh, every bit as vulgar as her colleagues had suggested. She ignored his outstretched hand.

"Pink and panting? Really? If that's a typical example of your conversational skill, I can't imagine any woman allowing you to get close enough to have the same effect."

He raised his eyebrows and looked at Tom. "My, she's got a very sharp tongue, that one has. Very sharp indeed. You want to be careful which body parts you let her use that sharp tongue on, Tommo, in case she cuts you with it."

Not only vulgar but insufferable. "There really is no beginning to your wit, is there, Mr Pugh?" Megan retorted before Tom had time to respond.

Thankfully, Garin took the hint and sloped off, narrowly avoiding bumping into Duncan, who was crossing the dance floor with a glass in each hand.

She scowled after Garin's retreating figure. "Is he always like that?"

"No," Tom said, with the faintest hint of a smirk. "As a rule I'm afraid he's much worse."

"I was warned about him. Turns out the warnings were true. I wasn't given quite the right impression of you, though."

"Should I be worried or flattered that you've been hearing things about me?"

"Neither. I was told you were polite, which seems to be true so far. And that you're posh, which had me thinking you were some sort of stuffy, overgrown public schoolboy."

"Private school, actually. But I thought it best to leave my cravat and top hat at home this evening. They'd be wasted on riff-raff like Garin."

He looked up and smiled at Duncan, who had set their drinks down on the table beside them.

"I'm going to have to love you and leave you, I'm afraid," Duncan said. "You won't mind keeping each other company, will you? I've just bumped into someone I haven't seen for years - she's here with one of the other groups. She's invited me to join her at her table for a drink."

"Go ahead and don't mind us. We don't seem to be doing too badly so far, despite our cultural differences," said Tom.

Duncan beamed delightedly and scurried away as if he couldn't wait to get back to his companion.

"Duncan's evening seems to be looking up," Megan remarked, picking up her glass.

"Mmm. It seems he's pulled, after all. I do love to see Garin proved wrong."

Whatever the reason for his smug expression, there wasn't time to ask. Sue approached, cleaving a path between the remaining dancers like a galleon in full sail.

"I must say it was like watching Strictly Come Dancing, seeing you two doing that jive earlier - even if you did look like you might trip over your own toes and fall over in a fit of the giggles, Megan. I thought I'd better come over and find you because Claire's gone home exhausted and Rachel has offered to take me clubbing for the first time in – oh, probably ten years! You're more than welcome to join us if you'd like to?"

Megan considered her options. A club could be fun with just Rachel, but not so much with their boss, and she'd probably end up succumbing to more alcohol, resulting in a crashing hangover that would spoil the weekend and her Christmas shopping plans. No, given the way her head was spinning after that dance with Tom, it was probably safer to go home.

"Thanks for the offer, Sue, but I think I've had enough for one night. I'll get a taxi home and ease these aching feet. I'm in grave danger of turning into a pumpkin at midnight."

Tom leaned back in his chair and stretched out his long legs. His eyes met hers, holding a hint of a promise. "No need to go to the expense of a taxi," he said. "I've got my car. I'll take you home, if you like."

Chapter Three

Megan let out a sigh of relief when at last the din of the disco was muffled by the fire doors and threadbare, dated carpet in the hotel corridor. Her ears still rang from the intensity of the noise, and her throat was dry from the fug of cigarette smoke in the function room. Her hair and her dress would stink like a stale ashtray in the morning, after the night of partying. Part of her regretted that they hadn't stayed long enough for the slow dances, as she was pretty sure that dancing close to Tom would be even more pleasurable than having him twirl her around the floor; but something told her the DJ's choice of romantic tunes would be corny rather than seductive.

They collected their coats and to her surprise Tom held hers while she shrugged it on. Most of the men she knew wouldn't have thought to do so. While she did up the buttons, he made for the stairs; but she called him back.

"I'm not taking the stairs in these shoes. My feet have had quite enough for one night."

She headed towards the lift, wincing with each step as the balls of her feet burned in her high heels. Glancing back as she stepped in, it occurred to her that he looked none too pleased to be following. What had made his face fall so abruptly? Was he regretting his offer to take her home? Surely he wasn't such a fitness freak that he disapproved of taking the lift instead of the stairs?

He joined her and pressed the button for the ground floor.

Was she imagining a distinct air of tension? No, there was a muscle twitching in his cheek and he was definitely avoiding eye contact, which was a shame because now that they had left the multi-coloured disco lights behind, she had noticed that his eyes were a rather beguiling and intense shade of Aegean blue. A snippet of a song trickled through her mind: *your eyes were bluer than robin's eggs...* It could have been written for him.

"What's up?" she asked as the doors slid closed.

There was a pause, making her wonder if he hadn't heard; but then he muttered: "Nothing. I just don't like lifts... Especially when they're as ancient as this one."

He certainly did appear jumpy, shooting out one hand to steady himself against the wall as the lift juddered into its creaky downward progress.

"It's lucky there's no basement and it's only a short ride, then. If the cable breaks we won't have far to fall.... That was a joke, by the way," she felt obliged to add as he directed the full force of those blue eyes upon her in a distinctly unamused gaze. Really - there was no need for him to be so touchy about a little light-hearted remark.

The lift came to a halt with a shudder and she turned, anticipating the opening of the doors.

Nothing happened.

Tom reached past her to press the button, then pushed it again a few seconds later.

The doors remained stubbornly closed.

This was silly. Elbowing him aside, Megan tried the button a few times herself, ignoring the voice in her head which protested that her attempts would surely be no less futile than his.

"I don't believe this." The colour had drained from his face. He pushed his finger firmly onto the alarm button for several seconds and awaited a response.

Nothing.

She jumped as he hammered his fist against the doors and yelled for someone to let them out.

"Okay, let's just keep calm, shall we?" Meg adopted her most authoritative voice, hoping it concealed her own nervousness. Being stuck in a confined space with a larger, stronger person on the brink of a panic attack wasn't the way she would have chosen to sober up. "Someone is bound to be along in a minute. There are still loads of people in the hotel, and it won't be long before someone realizes the lift isn't working. It's only the doors that are stuck: we definitely arrived on the ground floor."

Tom hammered fruitlessly again, then kicked the doors with a muttered expletive.

Moments passed, increasing Megan's tension. Tom's head was bowed, his ear pressed to the door.

At last they heard a faint voice outside. "Are you alright in there?"

Hastily, she explained their situation.

"I'll fetch the duty manager, if you can wait there for a few minutes," the voice said.

"Alright – we're not going anywhere," she called back, glancing at Tom to see if this attempt at cheeriness had met with another cold glare. He had retreated the couple of steps to one corner and was staring up at the ceiling.

Megan felt better now that she knew help was on its way.

"Why don't we make conversation while we wait for the manager? It might be a welcome distraction," she suggested.

He fiddled with his cuffs, then rubbed his hands against his trouser legs as if to relieve sweaty palms. Clearly he wasn't about to begin making small talk. She sighed.

"Right, I'll kick off then. So… Why were you on soft drinks tonight?"

He cleared his throat and finally met her gaze. "I'm driving to my dad's in Ludlow tomorrow to stay with him for Christmas. My brother and sister-in-law and my Auntie Jean will be there. Knowing Jean, she'll have started boiling the sprouts for Christmas dinner already."

Hopefully his lame attempt at humour was a sign that he wasn't about to start hyperventilating or throwing himself around. Curious that he hadn't mentioned a mother in this cosy family gathering, but now might not be the most tactful time to ask why. Perhaps his parents were as dysfunctional as hers.

"Ludlow? So you're a Shropshire lad. Well, apart from the sprouts, that sounds like a nice way to spend Christmas. I'm going to my mum's in Carmarthenshire. My sister Bethan and brother-in-law Matt are going, too."

She paused, but he didn't offer any response. Maybe she was boring him. There was still no sign of imminent rescue, and the azure gaze was directed towards the doors again. He had the most ridiculously long, thick, sandy-coloured eyelashes. Lucky swine. With a bit of mascara they'd be a knockout.

"Are you married? Or with anyone?" Alright, so it wasn't exactly subtle, but he had danced with her, and had looked at her with undisguised interest, so it was hardly wrong of her to check.

"No. I'm free as a bird. You?" It was impossible to tell whether there was any significance to the grim set to his lips and the gruffness of his voice, beyond his annoyance at the lift doors' refusal to open.

"Likewise. So… Erm… What's your favourite film?" she asked.

"Blade Runner. The Director's Cut, obviously."

"Obviously." That was a bit of a non-starter, given her dislike of science fiction. "Your favourite book?" she continued.

His reply seemed wrung from him for the sake of politeness. "I haven't really got one particular favourite. I quite liked *The Da Vinci Code*."

Not another Dan Brown fan... She grimaced and tried to think of something else to keep the conversation going.

"What's your favourite colour?" This was lame, admittedly, but her mind had gone frustratingly blank. If only the manager would hurry up.

He looked pointedly at the hem of her dress where it hung below her coat.

"Green."

That was more promising.

"Er - favourite food?"

"God, this must be what those dating agency questionnaires are like. I'm surprised you haven't asked me my star sign."

"You don't believe in all that mumbo jumbo, do you?"

"No, of course not!"

"Anyway, I know you're a Sagittarius because Duncan said it was your birthday a couple of days ago." She couldn't help but giggle as his eyebrows flew up.

"So he did."

"Come on, you still haven't told me your favourite food."

"Again, no particular favourite. If I'm cooking, I'll often make pasta or a stir-fry because they're quick. But those aren't necessarily my favourites. I'd just as happily eat roast beef or a nice, hearty pie."

He glanced back at the stubbornly closed doors, shifting his feet as his adam's apple bobbed nervously. His forehead had creased with anxiety again.

Meg redoubled her efforts to distract him, leaning against the carpeted wall of the lift to stop herself swaying with the effects of alcohol and fatigue. Despite their circumstances, she was beginning to enjoy herself now that she'd got him talking. She mustn't spoil it by letting the conversation lull.

"What if you were ordering an Indian takeaway? What would you get?"

"It varies. Probably a Lamb Saag Balti or a Jalfrezi."

"Ah, that's interesting. Honestly, it is - you don't need to look so dubious. It tells me a lot about you."

"Such as?"

"Well, if you'd said Chicken Korma I'd have thought you were a bit of a wimp, to tell the truth. Tikka Masala would have suggested that you're an unadventurous conformist. Whereas if you'd said Vindaloo I'd have to assume you're one of those blokes who thinks he can prove he's hard by eating the hottest thing on the menu, even if he has to wipe the sweat out of his eyes to see what's on his plate."

Tom's eyes flickered back to the doors, but only briefly. "Alright, Sherlock: what does Lamb Saag tell you?"

Megan tilted her head, lips pursed, to give her verdict proper consideration.

"Firstly, and most obviously, it tells me you're not a vegetarian. But it also says you're more interested in flavour than your image. You have a more sophisticated palette than the average British bloke. And you don't feel a need to follow the crowd."

He grunted. "Who would have thought that a man's choice of curry would be so revealing? Tell me, are all women so quick to make assumptions based on food, or are you unusual in that respect?"

"I've no idea. Don't you ever make assumptions based on what people choose?"

"I hope not."

She wasn't having that. "What about if you were out for a meal in a fabulous restaurant with a woman and she didn't order dessert? You'd make assumptions then."

"If a woman doesn't want dessert I'd assume she's already had enough to eat."

"Or?"

He frowned. "Perhaps she doesn't have a sweet tooth, or she's on a diet, or maybe she's diabetic. So yes, it might tell me something; but it wouldn't reveal anything about her character."

His eyes were on the doors again. She racked her brains for a fresh topic of conversation, but they seemed too befuddled by Bacardi to be of much use. He looked as tense as ever. She had to find a way to lighten the atmosphere.

"I'll tell you what," she said. "Let's play Shag, Marry or Cruise."

That got his attention: the quizzical blue eyes were on her again, not the doors. "What's that?"

"I'll give you three names, and you have to say which one you would shag, which one you would marry, and which you would just take on a cruise."

At last! She'd succeeded in making him smile. She pressed on, hammering home her advantage.

"So: you've got a choice of Madonna, Catherine Zeta Jones and – er –- Britney Spears," she finally decided, shifting her weight from foot to foot in an attempt to relieve her sore feet.

"That's easy. I'd shag Britney Spears, marry Madonna and cruise with Catherine Zeta Jones."

"You're not serious?" This was even more disappointing evidence of poor taste than the sci-fi or the Dan Brown novels. "Why would you want to marry Madonna? Catherine Zeta Jones is definitely the most attractive of the three. And she's Welsh. She'd be the best one to marry, surely?"

He sighed. "Well, if I'm honest, none of them are really my type. Britney got the shag because I'd find her too boring to spend time cruising with… I don't particularly fancy her, so at least with just a shag it could be over and done with fairly quickly."

She raised a sardonic eyebrow and he immediately backtracked.

"Not *very* quickly, I should say. In fact, I can make a shag go on for quite some time if required."

"Oh, really?"

"Hours and hours and hours given the chance."

He had the most wickedly provocative grin. Heat rose to her throat, making her feel like a teenager with a crush. She hoped he hadn't noticed, although his knowing gaze suggested that he had.

"Point taken. There's no need to get defensive about your manly prowess."

He leaned against the wall opposite and continued his explanation. It seemed he had forgotten about the doors, temporarily at least.

"I'd cruise with Catherine Zeta Jones because I could probably spend a week in her company without finding it too tedious. Also, she's married to an elderly chap so she's probably used to cruising. She could pass on some helpful hints. How much to tip the room steward; what to wear if we're invited to dine at the Captain's table..."

She snorted at this.

"...And I'd marry Madonna for two reasons."

"Go on."

"Firstly, she's loaded, so I'd make a fortune in the inevitable divorce settlement. And secondly, I've a feeling there's absolutely nothing that she wouldn't be prepared to try; so a quick Wham, Bam and Thank you Ma'am wouldn't be enough to satisfy my curiosity."

"I see!"

"Well, you did ask."

He was watching the doors again.

"Huh! What is it about Madonna that makes every bloke seem to want to get into her groove?"

"Why wouldn't they?"

"I bet she's rubbish in bed: those pointy bras and the crucifixes and all that *strike a pose* business would get in the way of a good time. And anyone who wants to feel like a virgin again must be twp."

"Twp?"

"Sorry – I forgot you're English. It means mad, daft, soft in the head. But really - I mean, would *you* want to feel like a virgin?"

"No, I'll admit you have a point there: I can't say I would. I like to flatter myself that my performance has improved considerably since the first time."

It was fortunate that he couldn't read her mind. Her first time, with a fumbling and equally inexperienced school friend in his single bed while his mother clattered about with pots and pans downstairs, had been an act of teenaged rebellion that was over almost as soon as it began. The friendship didn't last much longer, either, once she found out he had boasted to all his mates about how easy she was. She'd had plenty of better experiences since, of course. What would it be like with Tom? Would he fret about his *performance*, as he put it? Would he be selfish? Or would he make love as playfully and confidently as he danced?

"Well, personally, I don't know what men see in her," she said, forcing herself to focus on the topic of conversation.

He sighed. "Don't ask me to Justify My Love. I just wish someone would Rescue Me."

It took a second for his joke to register.

"Oh yes, I get what you did there. Very witty."

Just as she had seemed to be winning the battle to keep his attention, it fixed once again on the firmly closed doors.

"Your turn now," she said. "You have to think of three celebrities I could shag, marry or cruise with."

He frowned, as if trying to think of some names. At last he gave up and shook his head.

"It's no good, I can't think of anybody…. David Beckham? Um… Look – I'm sorry Megan, but honestly it's hopeless. All I can think about is getting out into the fresh air. As much as I couldn't be trapped with a more delightful person, I'm still not at all comfortable with being trapped."

Bless him – there was something endearing about this broad-shouldered rugby player getting himself into a tizzy over something as mundane as half an hour or so stuck in a lift. He seemed to be counting each breath in and out to help him keep his nerve, and was unable now to meet her gaze. He shuffled from one foot to the other and rubbed the back of his head, obviously embarrassed about being seen in such an anxious state.

She couldn't help herself. There was an obvious solution, one hundred per cent guaranteed to divert his thoughts. And hopefully it would be pretty enjoyable for her, too.

∞ ∞ ∞

Tom's heart was pounding, his fists clenching with the effort of not bellowing and charging at the doors. He'd been mad to follow Megan into the lift, should have known something like this would happen. It was obviously too much to expect the facilities to work in this godawful hotel where the urinals overflowed, the walls were yellow with the build-up of years of nicotine, and the disco would disgrace a senior citizens' party in a working-men's club.

The sudden directness of her move to kiss him took him aback, his first instinct making him tug away from her grasp; but agitation quickly gave way to pleasure. Her lips were soft and tasted not unpleasantly of alcohol. He bent lower, stooping to overcome the disparity in their height, and stole his arms around her, drawing her closer. When her fingers slipped into his hair above his collar, he mirrored the gesture: her hair trailed glorious over his hand, smooth as ribbons as he caressed the nape of her neck.

She broke away briefly, lips millimetres from his, eyes dark and intent as if she wasn't sure he wanted her to continue. He did. He had forgotten how good it was to sink into a woman's eyes and feel that surge of excitement in his belly. Their next kiss grew more ardent, a slow build that made him hungry to feel her skin under his fingers instead of the scratchy wool of her coat. He was unused to passion, he realised, couldn't remember the last time he was the one being seduced, not the seducer.

He was so absorbed in discovering the feel and taste and fragrance of her, he didn't notice the lift doors sliding open. The waiting hotel manager's deliberate cough intruded roughly, making them flinch apart. Tom blinked rapidly, getting a hold on reality again, as self-conscious as a teenager caught in flagrante by a strict headmaster.

Tom cleared his throat. "Ah. Marvellous. Rescue at last." Trying without success to appear unruffled despite the heat in his cheeks, he fumbled to zip up his jacket and stepped out into the hotel lobby.

"Thank you very much." He nodded to the knot of smirking hotel staff and partygoers who had congregated outside the lift, seized Megan's hand and strode towards the exit.

"Hold on! My feet are killing me, remember."

He forced himself to adjust his pace as she stumbled behind him in her pretty, foolish shoes.

Stepping outside, the blast of wet December air hit him hard enough to make him gasp with the shock of it. He turned back to look at Megan. She was huddling into her coat, face alight. Tendrils of hair whipped into her eyes, and she lifted a hand to untangle them.

"Did you know, your ears go pink when you're embarrassed," she said.

As if he needed her to point it out. He kissed her again, hard, and felt the same leap of desire he had felt earlier when she kissed him back equally passionately.

He could hardly believe his luck. It had been in the back of his mind to risk chancing a kiss at the end of the evening, depending on the mood when he dropped her home. He certainly hadn't expected her to take the initiative as she had. If she had coshed him over the head and handcuffed him, he could not have been more her captive than he was now.

Finally they drew apart. She shivered.

"You're getting cold! You'd better wait inside the main doors. I'll fetch the car to save those tiny feet from any further suffering."

He headed off to his car, concerned to get them both out of the chilly wind. She emerged from her shelter in the hotel doorway as he pulled up, sending him an appreciative glance as he jumped out to open the passenger door. He waited until she had tucked her skirt safely around her before closing it.

"You'll need to tell me where we're going," he prompted at last, ready to set off.

"Ah yes, that would help."

He was acutely aware of her eyes upon him as he negotiated his way across the city. The silky chiffon of her skirt spilled over the edge of the passenger seat, brushing against his hand as he changed gear. It took a supreme effort to concentrate upon his driving as the evening's unexpected events scrolled through his mind.

Out of the blue, a thought occurred to him, making him laugh.

"I should have suggested Peter Crouch, not David Beckham, when it was your turn to play Shag, Marry or Cruise," he said.

"Who?"

A shame - she obviously wasn't interested in football.

"Peter Crouch. He's a footballer. He plays for Liverpool."

"I don't get it - what's so funny?"

"The combination of you and him. He's six foot seven."

She rolled her eyes.

"Sorry," he said, hoping he hadn't spoiled his chances by teasing her. Maybe she was sensitive about her height.

"Hmmm. I suppose it could be seen as fair revenge for calling you the Rugby Field." Good - her wry smile suggested she didn't really mind.

"How tall are you, anyway?"

She pursed her lips before replying. "Five feet and half an inch."

"Ah. It wouldn't do to forget that half an inch."

"You're a man: you should know that size matters. I've heard tell that even half an inch can make a big difference."

He nodded acknowledgment, amused.

"How tall are you, then?" she asked.

"Five foot ten… And a half."

"QED, Mr Field. Every half inch counts."

Her snort of laughter was gratifying. Every man likes a woman who could appreciate his attempts at wit.

The disappointingly short drive to Megan's address afforded little time to get to know her better. Regretfully, he manoeuvred the car into a parking space in the terraced street and left the engine idling. He didn't really expect to be invited in, given that she hardly knew him. If she did ask, though, it would take a momentous effort to maintain a cool demeanour rather than betray his eagerness.

"Thank you for a most enjoyable evening. I didn't expect to end it with a ravishing redhead: I must be on Santa's Good List this year."

"Thank you for the lift… The lift home, obviously, not the one we were stuck in."

"It was my pleasure – both lifts, I mean. I'll be visiting my folks until after Christmas, but if you'd like to, perhaps we could go out somewhere after I get back?"

He waited, holding his breath until her reply allowed him to release it again.

"Why not? And next time, Tom Field, I promise to take the stairs."

Chapter Four

"So – bear with me while I make sure I've got this right," said Bethan, tucking her feet up under her on the sofa and leaning against her husband Matt. "You got pissed at the office party; accepted a lift from a man you had never met before; divulged your address to a complete stranger; and pounced on him and snogged his face off when he had a panic attack in the lift."

Megan's cheeks flushed. "It wasn't quite like that. He wasn't actually having a panic attack. Not as such. And he wasn't a total stranger – he's a colleague who was introduced to me for the first time, but I've probably seen him around before. And he's a teacher, which means he's police checked."

Matt chuckled. "You're a fast mover, Meg. Sounds like I married the wrong sister."

Bethan gave him a mock-furious dig in the ribs and glared at him, making him laugh even more. Meg waited, anticipating further questions. Bethan wouldn't have finished her interrogation yet.

Sure enough, Bethan had turned her gimlet eye on her again. "So what's he like, then? You said he's a P.E. teacher so I assume he's fairly fit, but what does he look like? How old is he?"

Sipping her mug of tea, Meg tried to estimate Tom's age. He hadn't been old, by any means, but his face hadn't had that smooth, blank boyishness that a very young man might have. He had an air of confidence that suggested a level of experience. And his car hadn't been ostentatious, just a VW Golf – although for all she knew it could have been some sort of sporty model, a GTI or whatever. He hadn't driven stupidly, though - not like some of the boy racer types she had dated in the past, who believed the best way to charm a woman was to fling her about by tackling roundabouts on two wheels and turning corners using the handbrake.

"I don't know exactly how old he is. I'm guessing early thirties."

"Early thirties and single? Sounds dodgy to me. If he's that great, why isn't he with anyone?"

"I've no idea. I expect I'll find out more when we're back at work. That's if he ever speaks to me again. I was a bit the worse for wear; maybe he was just being polite when he asked for my number. He might have thought better of it today."

"Why, how drunk were you? Don't tell me you did anything else to embarrass yourself?"

"No... Unless you count asking him to play Shag, Marry or Cruise."

Matt hooted with laughter. "How very seductive!"

"Yes, I know. He'll probably never want to see me again."

"Never mind, Sis. I expect you had your beer goggles on anyway. Last time you snogged someone after a few too many, you were mortified the next morning. You did say you'd never noticed this guy at work, so you might get a nasty shock if you see him when you're sober. He's probably got a face like a pig's arse."

"Beth, I wasn't as drunk as all that. He wasn't necessarily an Adonis, but he had gorgeous eyes. A nice, peachy little bum. He didn't have smelly breath or bad teeth. He was lovely: a perfect gentleman, in fact. He opened the car door for me and everything."

"Are you sure he's not gay?" Bethan asked. "I've never known a straight guy to be that polite."

Matt's eyebrows had risen speculatively. "When you say he's a gentleman, does that mean he refused your invitation to come in for a nightcap? If he did, Bethan's right: definitely gay."

"No! I didn't dare invite him in. My flat was in a hell of a mess – make-up in the washbasin, crumbs all over the kitchen, bed unmade, clothes everywhere. You know what's it like when you're getting ready to go out…"

"I know what it's like when *you're* getting ready, yes. Some of us manage to tidy up as we go along."

"… And I was a bit nervous, being so sloshed, that if we had any more to drink I might throw up over his shoes or something. I didn't want to ruin the positive impression. Believe me, there were signs that I made a *very* positive impression when I kissed him – signs which have reassured me that he most definitely isn't gay."

"Okay. So you managed to hide what a slob you are. Now tell me more about this straight man with the supposedly gorgeous eyes and the impeccable manners."

Meg poked her tongue out. "I don't know why you're saying 'supposedly', as if I might have got it wrong. If you're that keen to know what he looks like, there's probably a picture of him on the school website."

Matt grabbed his laptop. "Good idea. We can all check whether you should avoid the ugly bastard next term."

Meg whacked him with a cushion as she moved to join him and Bethan on the other sofa. It took only a few moments for him to find the St. Dyfrig's High School website.

"Aha! Look, there's the English department. Have they got your photo on here?" Before Megan could protest, Matt had opened up the link. "Yes, that's you – it's always easy to spot the little one in the front row."

Megan groaned as she saw the photo.

"I've got to say, Meg, it's not the most flattering photo of you," said Bethan, brutally honest as only a sister can be. "You look a couple of stone heavier there… 'Megan Parry here, my tits enter the room a couple of minutes before the rest of me'."

"Why, thank you. You're too kind."

"More than a handful's a waste, if you ask me."

"That sounds suspiciously like sour grapes, Beth."

Matt screwed up his face. "Would you mind not discussing your sister's breasts in front of me? You'll only slap me if I look."

"Yes, why don't we change the subject and look at the P.E. department's photo, as you were meant to do in the first place?"

Matt clicked away to find the correct page. All three scrutinised the picture eagerly. Duncan, Tom and Garin stood alongside three female teachers on the athletics track outside the school. All wore sports kit and appeared relaxed despite their formal pose, lined up with their hands behind their backs.

Bethan squinted to get a better look. "Are you sure he's not the short, balding, middle-aged one?"

"No, silly, that's Duncan. He's the one I told you about, who's pathetically grateful for any morsel of attention. That's Tom, on the left."

Megan awaited their verdict.

"Hmmm… Not bad," Bethan pronounced at last. "He does look pretty fit in that t-shirt. I can't make out the colour of his eyes but he seems to have quite a nice smile."

"Matt?"

He held up his hands. "Hey, there's no point asking me whether another guy is good looking or not. He just looks… well, normal, really."

Meg huffed, exasperated. "He isn't just normal, he's lush! Look at his chest and those shoulders, he's a dish." She paused, head on one side, and added: "I do hate the sweatpants, though: they're revolting."

"I'd say he looks confident," Bethan said cautiously. "Something has made them all laugh for that photo; he seems quite at ease. Which is more than can be said for your picture - you looked like you couldn't wait to get it over with."

Meg scowled as she headed back to her seat. What did it matter if they didn't rave about him based on a little photo? For her, seeing his picture in the cold light of day was a happy confirmation that she hadn't been imagining how handsome he was last night.

"At least he isn't butt-ugly," Matt said. "I'm not sure what he'll make of you and your aversion to exercise though, if he's a P.E. teacher."

"He's into rugby, I know that much."

"Ah! Crouch, touch, engage! Watch it, he'll just be out for a maul and a good ruck - in any one of fifteen different positions."

Bethan cackled. "Ooh yes - Strong Deliverer, Strong Deliverer! You can sing Hymns and Arias when the conversation runs dry."

"Actually, he's English, not Welsh." Her words fell into the conversation like a stone. She picked at her cuticles, anticipating their response.

With a mischievous glance at his wife, Matt shook his head like a mechanic passing judgment on a worn-out engine.

"Dear, oh dear," he said.

"Oh, behave. Anyone would think I'd told you he was a Nazi or something."

"That might be preferable," Matt said, trying to hide a grin behind his hand.

Bethan patted his knee. "Now, be nice – it's quite romantic really. Love across the cultural divide and all that. He can't help being English, poor sod. It's like a birth defect, isn't it? We'll try to make allowances if we ever meet him."

"What a pair of wind-up merchants you two are! I thought you'd be pleased that I'd found myself a hot date after four months on the shelf."

Bethan relented. "Alright, stand down – no need to be so touchy. Of course we're pleased for you. Can't have my little sis ending up a dried-up old maid, can we?"

The conversation moved on to their plans for Christmas. Bethan and Matt had been married for five years and were putting a brave face on another Christmas without the child they so desperately longed for. Meg knew better than to offer platitudes or to suggest trite solutions: they had considered every option in the past few years, but decided to leave the matter to Fate.

What they all dreaded most was the prospect of a day with Meg and Beth's mother, who was a stickler for her own routine and found it difficult to adjust to other people staying in her tiny house, even her own family.

At around ten o'clock, just as Meg was picking up her coat and bag to go home, her mobile phone tinkled to signal the arrival of a text message. Picking the handset up and flipping it open, she squealed. "It's him! Oh, my goodness!"

In her delight she dropped her phone and a minute or two elapsed while she fumbled to replace the battery and reassemble the cover.

"Come on, come on! Boot up, will you? I want to know what he says."

Finally, the message came back and Meg clutched the phone to her breast.

"I don't know whether I want to read it now. What if he isn't interested after all?"

"I hardly think he'd be texting you tonight if he wasn't interested."

Matt agreed, pausing on his way to the kitchen with an empty mug in each hand. "He'd have managed to conveniently lose your number if that was the case. Come on, we're dying to know what he says."

Megan beamed with pleasure as she read the message. "Get this: not only is it a really lovely text, it's grammatically correct, not 'text speak'!"

Maybe they thought it was ridiculous to be excited about such a triviality, but these things mattered, didn't they? Men who sent texts along the lines of "C U L8R" deserved to get blown out of the water str8 away.

"There we are then, if he's texting in Standard English, he must be a good catch. Come on then, spill the beans. What does he say?"

"He says: 'I went in a lift today and smiled all the way down from fourth floor to ground, thinking of you.'"

"Yay!" Beth draped her arm around Megan's shoulders. "I'm pleased for you. It sounds like you made a great impression. Now, while Matt drops you home, you can start thinking up a suitably seductive response."

Alone in her flat later, Megan put the kettle on, spooned hot chocolate powder into a mug and settled down on the sofa to compose a reply to Tom.

I'm glad the therapy session helped to cure you of your fear of lifts. There is a danger that you could regress without further sessions, however.

Should she put a kiss at the end? Hmm, probably better not to. She hardly knew him, after all. It wouldn't do to appear over-eager. There was no immediate response after she pressed the Send button, so after

By Luisa A. Jones

finishing her cup of hot chocolate she did a bit of half-hearted tidying up, too edgy to settle for bed.

"Now who needs distracting?" she said aloud at her own foolishness.

She had just finished sorting a load of laundry when her phone beeped again. She nearly fell over the laundry basket in her hurry to get back to it.

I think regular sessions could be most helpful. Shall we start on the 28th? I will be back in Cardiff by then.

Triumphant, Meg noted the date in her diary, even though she knew there was absolutely no danger of forgetting it. To ask so soon for a date, he must be keen. This time she allowed herself to add a kiss to her reply. Alright, so she wasn't exactly playing hard to get, but what the heck: she didn't want to let this one slip through her fingers.

Sounds perfect. See you then. X

∞ ∞ ∞

In Ludlow, Tom endured the inevitable round of questions from Auntie Jean, who hadn't seen him for months. Why wasn't he a head teacher yet, or at least a head of department? A higher salary would come in handy, would help him buy a proper house instead of that little flat. He couldn't expect to start a family living on the fourth floor, carting prams and pushchairs up all those steps, seeing as he wouldn't use the lift. No matter that he would need a partner to start a family – apparently that was a minor consideration. She prattled on and on, while he maintained a forced smile and reminded himself that he, too, might be old one day and need some patience from the younger generation. He steeled himself as she continued, raking over the coals of his failed love life. Had he seen Erica recently? She'd hoped he'd settled down at last, after living with her for so long. She couldn't understand why they had split up so suddenly, when Erica was such a nice girl. In fact, Jean had been hoping Tom might make Hugh a grandfather. It was about time Tom thought about children, at his age. Although he'd have to move into more suitable accommodation first, as he couldn't expect a wife to cart prams and pushchairs up all those steps...

Tom had no intention of satisfying Jean's curiosity. Finally he was provoked enough to say firmly, planting a kiss on the top of her head to soften the blow: "There were very good reasons why we split up, Auntie, which I really don't want to go into now. I'd rather focus on enjoying Christmas with you."

Thank goodness his dad would be much less voluble on the subject. Hugh Field was a man of few words. A retired GP, he was a scientist who preferred to deal with facts and statistics, rather than emotions. From what Tom had heard over the years, this had not always been an advantage when dealing with patients, who sometimes took offence at his blunt and seemingly unsympathetic attitude towards their minor complaints. Hugh had often grumbled that he wished he could make flashcards saying "It's a virus, there's nothing I can do for you", or "No, I won't give you antibiotics", to save him from repeating himself.

Having his sister Jean move in with him had been a matter of financial sense rather than sentiment. Hugh's house was too big for one old man to rattle around in, and having someone to care for helped to keep Jean occupied. It was Jean who had invited Tom, his elder brother Rob and Rob's wife Linda to stay for Christmas, relishing the chance to have younger people to fuss over. Hugh, on the other hand, while always pleased to see his sons, seemed to prefer the relative peace and quiet of his daily routine. Tom suspected he would have been quite content with a day-long visit.

It was a relief when Rob and Linda arrived to stay for a couple of days, as the spotlight of Jean's attention swung onto them. Linda was expecting their first child, and Auntie Jean bustled about to make her comfortable, refusing her any access to the kitchen, which was a shame as Linda was a much more competent cook. They made the best of the dry turkey, mushy vegetables and lumpy gravy at Christmas dinner, then as they settled in the living room Jean insisted everyone toast Her Majesty's annual speech with a schooner of sherry.

With Hugh, Jean and Linda all on the verge of dozing off in front of the television, Tom met Rob's gaze. His brother needed no more encouragement than a quick wink towards the door to suggest they make the most of the remaining daylight to take Dandy, their father's Springer Spaniel, for a walk.

It felt good to be in rural surroundings again. Tom was a city dweller for the sake of convenience, not by temperament. There was nothing he enjoyed more than to get out into the outdoors, whatever the weather, and get his limbs moving.

Once past the familiar walls of Ludlow's magnificent castle, the brothers soon crossed the river into the countryside, letting the dog off the lead when they reached open fields. They paused at a gate, watching Dandy sniff along the hedgerows.

Rob took Tom by surprise by blurting out the unmentionable.

"I hate Christmas without Mum. It just isn't the same any more. And I can't bear Jean's fussing. How in God's name will you manage to stand it for a whole week?"

Tom shrugged. "I'm getting out as much as I can. I've been running, and I brought my bike so I can disappear for a few hours. Jean means well, but it is pretty hard going."

"I couldn't do it," Rob confessed. "We're doing the duty call to Linda's parents tomorrow. Come what may, next year Linda and I will be staying at home. We've already discussed it. If people want to see the baby, they'll have to come to us."

"I don't blame you in the slightest, but that will bring its own problems: you'll end up with Dad and Jean staying with you. It's a good job Linda's parents live near you, or else you'd need a mansion to have room for everyone."

"Christmas is a bloody nightmare, isn't it? I hate it. You're far better at the whole Dutiful Son thing than I am."

Tom was taken aback. "You're kidding? You're the one who's a chip off the old block. Compared with you I'm an epic failure."

"Whatever makes you say that?"

He paused and both men gazed back across the fields towards the old town. It seemed like a lifetime since he'd lived here, not just fifteen years.

"I was never all that good at school, Rob, whereas you seemed to get top grades in everything. It wasn't just because you were cleverer, although of course you were – are. You had the motivation to put the work in. I really wasn't the academic type. I did the bare minimum and was happy to scrape through. I spent most of my time on the rugby pitch and the athletics track, if you remember. And when I wasn't chasing personal bests, I was chasing girls."

Rob frowned and tossed the tennis ball he had been carrying. Dandy's tongue lolled as he ran off to retrieve it.

"You did alright, though. You went to university, just as I did. Although admittedly I got most of the brains while you got the lion's share of the looks."

It was a long-standing joke between them, making both men smile now. Where Tom's light brown hair verged on blond, Rob was mousy; Tom's eyes were a brilliant shade of blue, while Rob's were merely grey; and while Tom was lean from regular exercise, Rob's desk job and high-powered business lunches had made him heavier-set. Any youthful rivalry was long dead: Rob had proved himself highly successful in his career, and Tom didn't begrudge him a penny.

Tom sensed his brother watching him, waiting for him to expound further. His mouth twisted a little, and not just because of the disgusting sogginess of the ball when Dandy returned it.

"If I'm honest, I only went to university to please Mum and Dad. I would probably have been quite happy as a fitness instructor or something, doing a bit of coaching and refereeing in my spare time. I didn't really want to carry on studying, but they insisted I had to go on to higher education and get a 'proper' job. Don't get me wrong –

I'm not ungrateful: on the whole I enjoy what I do, and I definitely earn more than I would have done without a degree."

It was Tom's turn to bowl the ball for the dog, and he made a precisely calculated throw, perfectly executed, that far outstripped Rob's feeble attempt. Dandy scurried off to the far side of the field in pursuit, and they set off behind him.

"I don't remember any of that," Rob said, chin down as he strode purposefully into the chilly winter wind to retrieve the ball. Dandy had managed to lose sight of it, and was sniffing along a line of hedgerow now, distracted. No doubt he had caught the scent of a rabbit.

"No, I don't suppose you do. You were already at university when I did my A levels, so you probably didn't hear any of the arguments. Not that a great deal was said. The expectation was there and I didn't want to upset Mum by going against them."

"She'd been ill for a while by then, hadn't she?"

Tom nodded. "Yes. What kind of lousy shit would I have been to have denied a dying woman one of her last wishes? I'm not really the dutiful son you think I am, Rob. I'm basically just a coward."

Rob was silent. How strange, Tom thought, to be discussing this after so many years had passed. But hey, that's what Christmas does to you – it encourages reminiscences.

"Do you know what I think, Tom?"

"What's that?"

"I think Mum would be delighted if she could see you now. You've achieved what you set out to achieve; you live a useful life…"

Tom snorted at this, stooping to scoop up the ball.

"But you do, and you know it – teaching is far more worthwhile in human terms than making money for shareholders and finding ways to thwart the taxman, like I do. You've said yourself how much job satisfaction you get from helping youngsters succeed."

That was true. Tom did enjoy working with teenagers, especially those who perhaps weren't academically successful but could achieve in a more physical arena. Still, he felt his lack of ambition put him at a disadvantage compared with his brother. A more ambitious man would have moved on by now and begun climbing the career ladder, but Tom had worked at the same school since qualifying as a teacher, after making a good impression there on his student placement. Promotion would mean less time for teaching and more time spent on tedious desk work which didn't appeal to him in the slightest.

"And you're much more unselfish than I," Rob continued. "You let go of your own ideas to please Mum and make her proud. You're even willing to give up a week of your holidays to stay here and endure Dad grumbling about Jean, and Jean wittering on interminably about how wonderful Erica is. It must be a bloody nightmare."

"Rob, I'm afraid you overestimate my altruism. My willingness to be here has nothing to do with making anyone proud. In fact, my motivation is pretty selfish: I don't want to spend Christmas on my own in a lonely flat. Nor do I want the flak that would come my way if I upset Jean by not coming. As I said, I'm a coward." He held up a gloved hand to cut off his brother's protests. "Fortunately, next year is going to be much better because by then I'll be an uncle and we'll have your baby's first Christmas to celebrate."

It worked: Rob nodded and patted him on the shoulder, signalling that enough had been said. It was comforting to know that his brother understood.

Daylight was fading depressingly early. Tom whistled for the dog and the two men turned for home, trudging along in a companionable silence, readier now to face not only Auntie Jean's attempts to force them to eat yet more stodgy food, but also Linda's insistence upon watching the Christmas episode of her favourite soap opera. No doubt one of the characters would die, or get divorced, or have a hideous accident. Tom didn't mind, though; he would read the book of sporting trivia he'd had for Christmas, sip some of his dad's single malt, and make the most of the familiar company.

Later that evening when he retired to bed, mellow from the whisky and the fireside, he found a text message from Megan, wishing him a very happy Christmas. He smiled, taking his time to compose his response. 2004 had been one of the worst years of his life, but perhaps now, as it drew to a close, things were finally on the up.

Chapter Five

January 2005
Cardiff

As often seemed to happen to her well-laid plans, Megan's anticipated date with Tom didn't take place. Seasonal 'flu hit without warning the night after Boxing Day, making her ache all over. When her teeth began to chatter from an acute bout of shivering, she gave up and retreated to bed, huddling under every blanket and coat she possessed. By morning she had a high fever and she knew there was no way she could leave her flat. She sent Tom a text message, her eyeballs aching from the effort of looking at her mobile phone's tiny screen. Sweet as it was of him to message back offering to bring chicken soup and sympathy, she turned him down flat. It would be out of the question to allow him to see her sweaty and miserable in her oldest nightshirt, coughing into her pillow and croaking as if her throat contained shards of glass.

When she returned to work in January, she still felt fatigued. The last lesson of her first morning was a sixth form group, a class she always looked forward to as they invariably engaged in heated debate. Today they were reading from *Tess of the D'Urbervilles,* arguing about the principal character.

Megan presided over the group from her usual perch on the edge of her desk, book in hand, a bottle of water and a box of tissues at her side to ward off coughing fits. This was what she loved about her job: throwing in provocative questions to stretch the students' reasoning, drawing out the quieter members of the group, and pushing them all to justify their points of view. It made it worth dragging herself off out of bed that morning and pushing herself to perform.

Ten minutes before the end of the lesson there came a knock on the classroom door, and she looked up to see it open just as one of the more vociferous girls in the class voiced her judgment:

"Honestly, Miss, she gets right on my tits!"

Tom stood in the doorway wearing a startled expression that caused a titter of laughter around the room. Lucy, the pupil who had made the comment, had the grace to blush.

Thank goodness it hadn't been the headmaster barging in. She'd have had to pretend to be thoroughly offended by the girl's remark. And what did Tom mean by interrupting her lesson? He leaned his arm against the door jamb in a manner that showed off his chest and bicep to perfection. A brief glance at several rapt teenaged faces suggested she wasn't the only one who had noticed how his t-shirt clung.

"Good morning, Mr Field," Megan said. "You came in at a bit of an inopportune moment, I'm afraid. Lucy was just sharing her opinion of *Tess of the D'Urbervilles* with the group. In a moment she'll work out a more appropriate way to express her disapproval – won't you, Lucy?"

Lucy blushed again. "Sorry, Miss. We were talking about whether Tess is a pure woman, sir, like Hardy said she was… or whether she's basically just an idiot who needs to get a grip."

"It sounds fascinating. Though in my experience, purity is an overrated virtue in a woman."

She had forgotten his tendency to make teasing remarks while remaining poker-faced.

"My apologies for interrupting your lesson, Miss Parry," he continued. "I just wanted to remind Kayleigh, Dafydd and Will that they've got a P.E. assessment on Wednesday. They need to make sure they've prepared thoroughly – I thought it might have slipped their minds during the holidays."

It seemed an unlikely reason for him to cross the campus and burst in unannounced to stand in her doorway brimming with male confidence. She'd go along with it, but she wasn't going to make it easy for him.

"Ah, a P.E. assessment! Well, naturally I can hardly begin to imagine the difficulty involved in passing a test in P.E… Tell me, Dafydd: what do you have to do to get a high grade? Run all the way around the field? Touch your toes? Do ten star jumps, maybe?"

Dafydd folded his arms, pretending to be insulted. "You're not going to let her get away with that, are you, sir?"

Unabashed, she continued. "I bet the written paper is really hard. Are there any essays, or is it multiple choice? I can just picture the type of questions: 'Which of the following sports does not require a ball? A: Football; B: Basketball; or C: Swimming.' It must be ever so tricky."

The class awaited Tom's rejoinder, enjoying the respite from serious work.

"Sarcasm is the lowest form of wit, Miss Parry. But who am I to try to convince you that English Literature isn't superior to sport? After all, what could be more rewarding than engaging in endless, futile discussions about characters who never existed and their imaginary deeds? Perhaps, in an English Literature exam, one might be required to write a pointless essay entitled: 'Explain in not less than five thousand words why *Tess of the D'Urbervilles* gets on your tits.'"

"I could probably write ten thousand words on that, sir," Lucy volunteered. Megan hid her smile as Tom continued.

"I admire your passion for your subject, Lucy. Personally I'd argue that there's room for both English and P.E. 'Mens sana in corpore sano', after all."

Hmmm. He might have devoted himself to developing brawn, but it seemed it hadn't prevented him from also using his brain.

"For those of you who don't have Mr Field's knowledge of Latin, 'mens sana in corpore sano' means 'a healthy mind in a healthy body'. It means that it's important to exercise the body *and* the brain."

"Indeed: we complement each other perfectly, wouldn't you agree Miss Parry?"

As Tom spoke, the bell rang for the end of the lesson and the students hurriedly moved to pack up their books and pens.

Complement each other? She had a feeling he was no longer referring to their subjects. She busied herself tidying up her desk while the class filed out.

He sauntered into the room once the pupils were gone, his hands in his pockets.

"How are you?" he asked.

"Much better now, thanks. I felt dreadful during the holidays."

"You do look pale. And you must be the only member of staff who actually managed to lose weight at Christmas."

"Every cloud has a silver lining, then. I was more interested in sleeping than eating during the second week."

He was as attractive as she remembered, despite those ghastly tracksuit bottoms. The air of confidence had dropped, though, now that they were alone. He sent her a sheepish smile.

"Actually, the P.E. assessment was just a pretext to catch you before you disappear off for lunch."

"You don't say?"

"The thing is, when you texted me to cancel our date, I wasn't sure whether you were really ill or whether you'd just decided to give me the brush-off. I thought maybe you'd found someone else. Someone who doesn't make an idiot of himself in lifts, perhaps. But now, seeing that you obviously were genuinely unwell… I was hoping you might consider rearranging our evening out?"

A prickle in her chest heralded the onset of another coughing fit, so he had to wait until she had finished and could catch her breath again. His expression of concern was endearing, as was the way he jumped to grab a tissue and pass it to her. She had wondered, in her more miserable moments in her sickbed, if he would tire of waiting and take up with someone else during the holidays; but here he was, making an effort to seek her out. Yes, of course she wanted to go out with him. Silly question.

"Where were you thinking of going?" she asked.

He stroked his chin meditatively.

"Well… what would you say to sausage in batter, chips and curry sauce from Caroline Street?"

Seriously? Cardiff's fast food district, a notorious hot-spot for drunken and loutish behaviour, for a first date? An invitation to McDonald's would have more class.

"What would I say? Well now, that would depend."

"On what?"

"On whether that was a serious question."

She saw his laughter threatening to burst.

"You swine," she said. "You had me going, there."

"Sorry. I couldn't resist seeing that stern teacher face of yours again. So, we'll do Chippy Lane another time, perhaps? How about dinner in the Bay instead? Or, if you prefer somewhere more traditional, we could go to a country pub and have a quiet drink in front of a log fire."

She couldn't conceal her relief. "They both sound very appealing. But, as it's freezing outside, I think the log fire wins."

"Friday?" he proposed. "I could pick you up at seven."

She moved to collect her handbag from the cupboard next to him. She was so close, she could smell the subtle woody notes of his aftershave. Close enough to touch. But a classroom with windows on two sides was about the most indiscreet place in the world to betray attraction.

"Friday at seven it is."

She felt much brighter as she entered the staffroom to join her colleagues for lunch.

Nick, one of the other English teachers, was already there, munching on a sandwich and sipping an enormous mug of coffee while perusing his regular broadsheet. A creature of habit, no doubt within about five minutes he would be quietly engrossed in the cryptic crossword. After wishing him a happy new year and hearing of his relief when his grandchildren's annual visit had finally ended, Megan rummaged in the fridge for her carton of soup. She set it in the microwave to heat up, and refilled the kettle ready for a much-needed cup of tea.

When Claire, Rachel and Sue trooped in, she had just settled down with her soup and was checking her planner to prepare for the afternoon's lessons. She made room for Claire to flop into the seat next to her.

"How are you doing?" she asked. She refrained from patting Claire's stomach, knowing how much Claire hated people doing that. "You're blooming. I'm sure your bump has grown during the past fortnight."

"I'm fine, thanks; just counting down to maternity leave now. I had a lovely rest over Christmas, it was bliss."

"That's good. I went down with 'flu and felt bloody awful. By the time I felt human again it was time to go back to work."

"Oh no, that was bad luck."

Rachel tutted sympathetically, sitting down next to them with a low-fat yogurt and a tangerine. "Here I go, back on the bloody diet food again. I put nine pounds on over Christmas. Can you believe it, nine pounds! And I was only off the wagon for a week."

"That's the best thing about being pregnant," said Claire. "No one expects you to have a waist."

"You'll pay the price for that later," Sue prophesied, joining them with a plastic box filled with salad. "Don't go believing all those celebrity pictures you see of new mums getting their figures back within days. I was a size eight before I had kids and now look at me."

Rachel nodded, but looked dubious at Sue's claim. "Your body will certainly never be the same again after having a baby."

"It's true, Claire," Sue said. "Your body will change in all sorts of ways that people rarely tell you about. I mean, they'll tell you about the seven pound baby, but they never warn you about the ten pound haemorrhoid that comes along with it. And if you have an episiotomy or tear and end up having stitches, you'd be well advised to have your first couple of pees in a nice warm bath. Pack some ice packs in your hospital bag, you might need them to sit on. After giving birth, you'll feel like one of those monkeys you see on TV. You know the ones, they stick their bottoms out with those grossly enlarged, purple genitals..."

Megan was pretty sure the horror on Claire's face was mirrored in her own. Why anyone had more than one baby was beyond her. To put yourself through that more than once must be madness. Then she noticed Nick's expression: a picture of embarrassment and revulsion. He eyed his ham sandwich with his mouth turned down at the corners, then dropped it back into his sandwich box. Poor man – it must be torture working with so many women.

Rachel, on the other hand, was laughing. "You can kiss goodbye to perky boobs, for another thing. Do you know, I was reading the other day that if you can hold a pencil under your boob without it falling out, your bust is too droopy! Maybe if I'd never had kids I'd still be able to do that."

Sue scoffed at this idea. "A pencil? Ha! I could probably hold a pencil case under mine, never mind a single pencil."

They all chuckled.

Megan, sitting closest to Nick, was the only one who heard him mutter behind his newspaper: "You could fit a whole bloody stationery shop under those." The effort of trying not to laugh nearly made her spill what remained of her soup, and set off another coughing fit.

"Anyway, what's all this I've been hearing about you, Megan?" Claire asked, slapping her on the back to relieve the coughing.

"I've no idea. What have you been hearing?"

"A little bird tells me you were dancing with Tom Field at the Christmas party, and then you were spotted snogging him in the car park."

"I heard they were snogging in the lift," Sue said.

Rachel laughed. "Judging by that cheeky grin, I'd say it was both."

Megan had no intention of either confirming or denying the gossip. "You can draw your own conclusions. I couldn't possibly comment."

Claire persisted. "So are you involved with him, or was it just an embarrassing office party snog?"

"I told you, I had 'flu in the holidays, so it didn't go any further. Why? Would there be an issue if I did get involved with him?"

"Just be careful with him, that's all. I wouldn't want you to get hurt."

Sue raised her eyebrows. "Claire, you can't just leave us dangling with that kind of remark. If there's something Megan needs to know, you should tell her. The last thing we need is a star-crossed romance causing tears in the staffroom at break-times."

Megan eyed Rachel for any clues, but her bemused shrug made it clear she didn't know what Claire was talking about either.

"Alright. Spill the beans, Claire," Meg said. "What's the gossip?"

"Well… I know someone who's friendly with Erica, his ex," she began.

"Hang on - when you say 'ex', are we talking ex-wife? Ex-girlfriend?"

"Ex-partner, I suppose. They lived together for a few years. Although – no, actually, now I come to think of it - she must have been his fiancée. I'm sure my friend said they were engaged."

It would hardly be reasonable to expect him not to have had previous partners, but Claire seemed genuinely concerned. Better to find out now if he had some sort of shady past. "Go on," Megan said.

"He broke up with her last summer, pretty much out of the blue. Everyone was gobsmacked: one minute they were love's young dream and the next minute it had turned into her worst nightmare. Apparently he decided he'd had enough, packed all her stuff into bin bags and dumped it outside their front door. She begged him to let her stay but he took her keys off her and she had to move back in with her parents." Claire paused for emphasis, then added: "I also heard that she was so devastated, she tried to kill herself."

"Bloody hell." Rachel almost dropped her tangerine peel into her yogurt. "That sounds a bit melodramatic."

"Yes, well – if you think that was bad, it gets worse. Apparently she cut her wrists in the bath and had to be carted off to hospital in an ambulance. Her mum phoned Tom from the hospital and pleaded with him to visit her, but he refused point blank to go."

They all sat in silence, taken aback.

"That's why I thought I'd better put you in the picture. What kind of man lives with a woman for three years, kicks her out without warning and then refuses to visit her in hospital when she's tried to top herself over him? Bastard."

Megan gazed into the dregs of her soup. It did sound pretty bad when you put it like that. Disappointing. He had seemed so amusing and charming up to now.

"Might I interject in this fascinating debate?" Nick eyed them all above his newspaper, his bushy white eyebrows drawn together in a frown. Megan looked up in surprise, having forgotten that he was able to hear their conversation. "In the interests of fairness – not that I know anything about this particular case -   I'd like to point out that a man is innocent until proven guilty, and that there are always two sides to every argument. You women take tittle-tattle as gospel truth and use it to condemn a chap without bothering to find out his side of the story. Honestly, it's the same every lunchtime. If it isn't someone's love-life, it's your pets or your kids or your hairstyles or your weight. Can't you think of anything interesting to talk about and stop disturbing the equilibrium of my lunch break with tedious prattle?"

He shook his newspaper vigorously, folded it up and stuffed it into his bag before stalking off, presumably in search of somewhere more peaceful.

"Oooh – I don't know what's rattled his cage. That was a bit off… So anyway, Megan – what are you going to do? Are you planning to go out with Tom again?" Rachel asked.

A dilemma. Should she admit that they had arranged to go out on Friday? She wasn't sure after Claire's revelations whether to cancel on him after all. Damn it – why couldn't her love life ever be straightforward?

"I doubt it," she lied as nonchalantly as she could. "I've no plans to get seriously involved with anyone, so you can rest easy, Sue. Treat 'em mean and keep 'em keen, that's my motto: I'm looking for rom-com, not tragedy. As far as I'm concerned, no man is worth slitting your wrists for. I'm the one leaving the trail of broken hearts behind: I haven't been dumped yet, I always get in there first when I can see the writing on the wall."

There was no need to feel guilty about the initial white lie because the last bit was true. Bethan had told her off more than once for her habit of dating men who turned out to have little more than their looks in their favour. Generally all they wanted from a woman was an unpaid maid willing to offer sexual services. It wasn't a role she was interested in playing: Megan was no domestic goddess, as the shabby state of her flat would attest. If Tom turned out to be another shallow or heartless idiot, he'd be just another in a long line.

"Good girl. You concentrate on having fun. Now, Rachel – I need to speak to you about the risk assessment for the Year Ten visit to Stratford…" Sue rose to her feet, ready to head back to her classroom.

Megan forced her lips into a bright smile for Claire's benefit and got up to carry her bowl and spoon to the sink.

"I mean it, Meggie. Be careful if he asks you out again. It might be safer not to get involved."

Chapter Six

January 2005
Cardiff

In the end, Megan decided life was too short to waste time worrying. If nothing else, she'd hopefully have a pleasant meal on Friday evening without having to cook or wash up, and if it turned out that she didn't like Tom she need never see him again. Going by past experience, any relationship that might developed would more than likely be short-lived, in any case. It wasn't as if she was seeking a long-term partner, just a bit of fun. As Tom had told her himself, he was as free as a bird; and eligible, attractive men with good manners and a sense of humour don't come along every day. Claire's words of caution were worth bearing in mind, but there was also wisdom in Nick's advice. It seemed only fair to give Tom a chance.

So, when he arrived at her door just a couple of minutes after seven o'clock on Friday evening, she was ready. She had thought carefully about what to wear, not wanting to seem overdressed for a meal in a pub, but on the other hand not wanting to appear as if she hadn't bothered to make an effort. She'd fussed over her hair, straightening it as she usually did but leaving it loose down her back. He'd seemed to like it that way at the Christmas party.

The spark of admiration in his eyes when she opened her door suggested she'd got the balance right.

"You look sensational."

It may not have been a poetic or original line, but said with sincerity it was still gratifying.

"You don't look bad yourself. Proper clothes suit you so much better than tracksuits."

"Thanks – I think."   He put the car into gear and set off. "Maybe you should see me in my cycling shorts. I've been told I look quite fetching in Lycra."

"Hmmm. You obviously meet some very strange or desperate characters at the gym. Give me a sharp-dressed man any time. I'm afraid I associate tracksuits with the old 1980s shell suits, or Jimmy Saville with his nasty cigar."

"Dear me. If that's the case I'd better make sure our paths don't cross at work again, unless I'm all dressed up for a parents' evening. I'm surprised you agreed to come out with me tonight after seeing me in my trackies on Monday."

"That's because you made me laugh. I was prepared to overlook the sportswear in favour of the sense of humour."

"So would you go out with pretty much anyone, if they cracked a few jokes?"

"I don't know. It would depend if they had blue eyes and knew how to dance."

She liked the way his eyes crinkled at the corners when she made him smile.

"And it isn't about the ability to tell a few jokes, anyway," she continued. "I wouldn't be interested in a date with a man who told me sexist jokes – which would put Garin out of the running - or anyone who thinks it's funny to crack jokes about farts or immigrants or mothers-in-law."

"Hmph. I'm as amused by a bit of toilet humour as most men. But I'm definitely not a racist, and I've never had a mother-in-law to joke about."

It was an irresistible opportunity to fish for information about his rumoured ex-fiancée. "No? Have you never been tempted to get married, then?"

"No. Have you?"

"Good heavens, no. I'm too young to get married. I'll wait until I'm at least thirty."

"Does that make me past it, then, at thirty-three?"

"Positively on the shelf, I would say. I'm twenty-eight, in case you were wondering."

"Still plenty of time to meet The One before you hit your deadline, then."

His lips twitched. Actually, now that she'd noticed, it made her focus on what a very nice mouth he had. She'd been too distracted by the eyes before to notice. Bottom lip soft and full, almost like a permanent pout. She felt a warm rush as she remembered kissing him. Pull yourself together, she thought… staring at him like that was way too obvious.

"Where are we off to?" she asked, realizing that they had reached the outskirts of the city.

"A little country pub I know. They don't usually take bookings but the landlord happens to belong to the rugby club so I asked him to reserve a table for us."

"Most impressive, Mr Field. So in addition to your ability to quote Latin mottoes, you're a man of influence?"

"I aim to please, Miss Parry."

The glance he cast in her direction suggested he didn't only mean his ability to secure table reservations.

The pub was cosy and inviting, with a flagstone floor and low ceilings with beams that appeared authentically old. It was simply and tastefully decorated, with not a horse brass, sticky carpet or bowl of faded pot pourri in evidence. Just the sort of place she liked on a winter's evening.

Tom led the way to a secluded corner, its table for two within sight of the log fire but not so close that they would swelter. It was perfect. While he headed off to fetch her a glass of wine she arranged her jacket on the back of her chair and scanned the menu.

"Here I am guzzling while you're on soft drinks again," she said as he took his seat opposite hers. "I promise not to get quite so inebriated this time, though. I'll never touch Bacardi again after the headache it gave me last time."

"That's a shame. I seem to remember rather liking you when you were drunk."

"I hope I didn't give you the impression that I make a habit of pouncing on men I've only just met."

"We'd known each other at least half an hour; surely that's plenty of time to get acquainted? And it was an act of mercy, really - all in the interests of therapy."

"Did it have a therapeutic effect, then?"

"It had all sorts of effects."

That look in his eyes could leave her needing therapy herself. "What are you fancying?" she asked, struggling to focus on the menu.

He leaned back in his chair. "Despite laying off the Bacardi tonight, you're asking leading questions again. If I answer truthfully you might be shocked."

She tutted with mock disapproval. "What would you recommend to eat, then?"

He suggested a few dishes that he had tried in the past, none of which really appealed, so she chose something completely different. During the meal, their conversation seemed to flow effortlessly, covering all manner of subjects. His company was pleasantly agreeable, with none of the stilted awkwardness she sometimes felt on first dates. He was properly grown up, not like some of the men she'd known, who were fun to dance with but boring to talk to, and who expected her to behave like a whore in the bedroom and then mother them by cooking and picking up their dirty pants. Tom seemed to have a real sense of who he was. He had travelled and had interesting stories to tell, but also took the time to listen and seemed genuinely curious to find out more about her. He laughed at her anecdotes about her previous job in an inner-city London school, and asked her opinion about various topics – something she'd found a lot of men didn't bother to do. Claire's warning lingered in the back of her mind, but so far there hadn't been anything in his manner or his words to suggest he was selfish, cruel or unfeeling.

At half past nine, to her annoyance, Megan's mobile phone rang, shrilly interrupting their absorption in one another.

"It's my sister. Do you mind if I take it?"

At his nod she flipped the handset open to answer the call.

"What's up?"

Bethan chuckled on the other end of the line. "There's no need to sound so cross. I'm just checking whether you need me to invent a very sick auntie who needs us at her hospital bedside, to get you out of your evening with the man who drives women to suicide."

"No thanks. I was having a very nice time until you interrupted us."

She rolled her eyes and he headed discreetly to the bar to buy another round of drinks.

"He's not too bad, then? Hasn't threatened to abandon you in a dark country lane, or anything?"

"Not as yet, thanks. I'm going now, Bethan. I'll speak to you tomorrow."

She heard her sister's laughter as she hung up.

"Sorry about that," she said when Tom returned.

"I expect she wanted to check whether you need rescuing from Bluebeard? Very sensible."

"Hmm, something along those lines. My sister can be quite protective. She makes fun of me and loves nothing better than to wind me up, but she's always there for me when I need her. When I had 'flu, she came over every day: it made me realise how much I'd missed her when I lived in London. She's almost like a second mother to me, in a way. She and her husband have been told they'll probably never have children, so I suppose I'm the nearest thing she's got. Sad, really, to think of all that maternal instinct going to waste."

"It must have been a terrible blow for them, to want something so desperately, only to be told that it isn't possible. My brother and his wife tried for a while, I think, but they were lucky. I'm going to be an uncle in a few months – I can't wait."

She was tempted to ask if he wanted children himself, but didn't dare. That kind of question on a first date would probably send him running for the hills.

Closing time came all too quickly, and he got up to settle their bill at the bar.

"I'll pay for mine," she offered, reaching for her purse; but he wouldn't hear of it.

"We'll go Dutch," she insisted. "I don't expect you to pay for me."

"I invited you out, so you're my guest. I don't expect my guests to pay for their own food and drink."

He stalked off, wallet in hand, without engaging in any further discussion. She didn't know whether to be pleased or irritated by this traditional gallantry.

"I'll pay next time. You can be my guest," she said when he returned.

"Next time? Are we going out again, then?"

Her stomach curled. Had she assumed too much? But no, the warmth of his smile told her he was pleased she wanted to see him again.

"If you don't want to, then obviously that's fine."

"I think you know I want to."

She took a step closer and fixed her gaze upon his mouth in a blatant invitation that was rewarded when he stooped to kiss her. Unlike their passionate encounter in the lift, this kiss was soft and unhurried. Its gentleness made her legs weak. Gripping the lapels of his coat, she leaned against him, lost in the taste of him and the light pressure of his hand on the small of her back.

"As much as I don't want this evening to end, I really should take you home," he murmured when at last he pulled away.

It was bitterly cold outside, with a layer of frost sparkling on the ground, and he took her hand as they hastened to the car. She felt an almost childlike pleasure at the feeling of her hand in his larger, stronger one. Once again, he held the car door for her; she wasn't sure if she'd ever get used to those impeccable manners.

"What made you decide to become a teacher?" he asked as he negotiated the narrow lanes on their way back towards the city.

"Oh, I don't know. A lack of imagination, if I'm honest. I enjoyed English Literature at school, so I decided to study that at university. I had some vague notions of going into publishing or journalism or PR, but those all seemed very competitive somehow, and it made me feel a bit daunted. My mum suggested teaching, mostly because the training wouldn't cost anything; and it seemed a good way to earn money using the subject I love. I enjoy it more than I ever expected to, in fact. Particularly A level: I get a real kick from teaching the older students who have chosen the subject."

"I know what you mean. With the A level students, there's a sense that you are on a similar wavelength. They have a genuine interest in the subject, and because they're older there's more freedom to be yourself and to enjoy a bit of banter."

She nodded. "Yes, that's exactly what I find. Teaching can be such a performance at times, can't it?"

"You mean pretending to be nastier than you really are in the hope of scaring the crap out of them so they'll behave better? Or acting calmly when some fifteen year-old oik has told you to fuck off and what you really want to do is throw him against a wall and thump him till he's picking bits of his face up off the floor?"

She laughed. She'd had her fair share of those moments.

"What made you become a teacher, then?" she asked.

"Funnily enough, it was my mum who suggested it, too." They both smiled at the pleasure of discovering more common ground. "My parents excelled at school, and were both very ambitious. They met while studying medicine at Oxford. They hoped for a similar type of path for me, but I wasn't really into the academic subjects. Doing sport at university was a compromise, and teaching meant I could follow my sport in a professional career. Unfortunately my mum died before I qualified."

"Oh Tom, I'm so sorry to hear that."

She didn't know what to say. Her instinct was to reach out; she touched his thigh, and his quick glance told her he liked it, so she left her palm resting there as he drove, feeling his thigh muscle flexing under her hand whenever he changed gear.

As he brought the car to a halt in the Victorian terraced street where she lived, she finally asked him the question she had known all evening she would ask.

"Would you like to come in for a coffee?"

He didn't hesitate to accept her invitation.

She led him past the assortment of pushbikes in the shared hallway and up the stairs, apologising automatically for the mess, though by her standards it wasn't too bad. She had made an effort to tidy up, anticipating that he might accept an invitation to come in.

As she lit the lamp and hung their jackets on the pegs near the door, she was conscious of the shabby state of her flat. Hopefully he would be fooled by the subtle lighting and think it homely and inviting, rather than dingy and tatty. It wasn't all bad: there were a few original features to lend character, even if these had been half obscured by thick layers of impersonal magnolia paint, and she had dotted some bright cushions and pictures about to cheer it up. She scooped a couple of piles of books off the sofa and tossed them into a corner to allow Tom enough space to sit down.

"What can I get you to drink?"

"Coffee: white, but no sugar please." He had ignored the space she had cleared on the sofa and followed her into the tiny kitchenette.

In the confined area of the kitchen, she felt very aware of him. This is what they call chemistry, she thought: that feeling of knowing exactly how far away he is, even when I'm not actually looking at him.

The delicious anticipation of wondering if he will touch me, of hoping he will while pretending I'm only concerned about filling the kettle.

She hadn't brought any of her recent dates back to this flat, and Tom seemed oddly masculine and solid, almost filling the space between her and the doorway. Trying to conceal how flustered she suddenly felt, she rummaged about for some mugs that weren't either chipped or stained. She really must take them to Bethan's one of these days and run them through her dishwasher to get rid of the brown rings.

Water sloshed onto the counter as she set the kettle down.

As she spooned the coffee into the mugs, her hair swung down to obscure her face and she almost jumped when he reached out to sweep it back over her shoulder. His thumb brushed against her cheek; with her mouth suddenly dry, she moved a shade closer.

In an instant she was in his arms, the coffee entirely forgotten as he covered her lips with his and pulled her against him. Her response was equally passionate as she lifted her hands to clutch at his shoulders. His hands felt warm through the thin fabric of her blouse; the fingers he threaded through her hair making her scalp come alive. Tugging at his shirt to free it from under his belt, her hands sought the heat of his skin. As his lips scorched a trail across her neck and into her shoulder, she raked her nails lightly across his back.

"Have you any idea how gorgeous you are?" he murmured, his breath warm as he nuzzled her earlobe.

Her lips found his throat, taking in his warm, male scent, and she brushed her thumb brazenly across one of his nipples. A quiver ran through him as it peaked under her hand.

He lifted her up and sat her on the edge of the kitchen counter, reducing the disparity in their height and enabling him to continue his exploration of her neck and shoulder more comfortably. The kettle rumbled and clicked, coming to the boil unnoticed. She pushed herself against him, stirred to boldness by the obvious signs of his arousal, and wrapped her legs around his hips. He caressed her thighs through the tight denim of her jeans.

"Oh, Mr Field," she whispered. "You've got me all wet."

He groaned and kissed her again, daring this time to seek out her skin under her blouse.

"No, really - I'm soaked. You put me down in a puddle. I spilled water on the worktop when I filled the kettle."

She wriggled even closer, amused by his wry expression.

"Feel," she invited him; sure enough, a caress betrayed her soaking wet behind.

Ignoring her squeal of surprise, he scooped her up and carried her, laughing and clinging to his neck, across the living room to the sofa. Dropping her onto the cushions, he was over her in an instant, resting his weight on his forearms. She wrapped her legs around him again and unbuttoned his shirt to expose his skin to her touch.

"You're a minx," he growled, and fiddled with the buttons of her blouse to reveal the lacy fabric of her bra.

She swallowed sharply. He was probably into really sporty women with athletic figures. Maybe he wouldn't like what he was seeing. Although his expression didn't suggest displeasure.

"At the risk of sounding like Garin, I could die happy in there," he said, gazing down at her. "Have you any idea how irresistible you are?"

He kissed her collarbones before moving lower, making her skin blaze. She arched her back and surrendered to pleasure as he moved on to tease her breasts through her bra.

"Oh God, hang on a minute," she gasped, and writhed beneath him.

"Is all this wriggling some kind of bizarre seduction technique?"

"No. Sorry." She squirmed some more, then pulled a couple of paperbacks triumphantly out from under her shoulders and tossed them onto the floor. "They were digging into me."

"Lucky books," he murmured, making her giggle.

She stroked his buttocks through his trousers as he pushed her bra strap down to kiss the skin beneath.

"I want you," he whispered against the heat of her skin.

"I want you, too." She really did, hadn't felt like this in ages. But as he bent fervent lips to hers again, she lifted a regretful hand to stop him. "Wait."

"What is it?" he asked. "Are the Complete Works of Shakespeare digging into you now as well?"

"Only if that's what you've got in your trousers… Look, I'm really sorry but we can't take it any further tonight."

He drew back and she hastened to reassure him.

"I want to. I really, really want to."

She pushed her hips towards him again for emphasis, and he groaned.

"I can get us some protection if you haven't got any here," he offered.

"No, it's not that."

She waited for him to guess what she meant, but his expression was more confused than ever. Better explain. "This is a bit awkward... The thing is, my period started this morning."

"Shit. That's what I call bad timing." The disappointment on his face was almost comical.

"I know. I'm sorry, I didn't intend to lead you on. I wasn't expecting things to go quite this fast..."

Reaching up, she brushed a finger against his pouting bottom lip. He kissed her, more gently this time, then drew back slightly with a gleam in his eye.

"Looking on the bright side, I suppose I was lucky to miss the PMT this week. And you could console me by giving me a blow job."

"Ha ha, cheeky. I'm happy to just cwtch for now, thanks."

He had lived in Wales long enough to know that a cwtch is a cuddle, and to understand the word's deeper nuances, conveying a sense of safety, security and heartfelt affection. It was obvious that he'd rather be in bed with her than cuddling on the sofa, but his wry smile suggested he could accept a cwtch as second best for the time being.

"This would never happen in a movie," he grumbled. "You never see Brad Pitt or Tom Cruise in a love scene being interrupted by an inconvenient menstrual cycle, do you? Renée Zellweger didn't say to Jerry Maguire 'you had me at hello, but I'm afraid Aunt Flo just arrived for her monthly visit'. Kate Winslet didn't say 'draw me like one of your French girls, but leave my sanitary towel out of the picture.'"

"No, that's true. But then, if this was a movie I'd be living in a New York loft apartment instead of a scummy rented flat in Splott. And you'd be filthy rich, and I'd be impossibly beautiful."

"Ah well. One out of three isn't bad."

Her eyes goggled. "What? You're telling me you're rich?"

"No, sorry to disappoint. And this is most definitely Splott."

"So…?" It took her a moment to understand that he meant she was beautiful. Luckily she was already lying down, as the smile he gave her before kissing her again was enough to make her knees give out.

For now, Claire's warning was forgotten.

Chapter Seven

January 2005
Cardiff

Tom left Megan's flat some time after two in the morning. They had spent hours talking, getting to know one another better, and when he finally got home and went to bed, euphoria kept him awake most of the night. It had been months – no, years – since a woman had made him feel so good about himself.

They had made arrangements to go to the cinema the following evening, and he invited her to choose the film. Which may have been a mistake, as she opted to watch the recently released *Vanity Fair*. Something with a bit of action would have been more his cup of tea, but it would have been ungentlemanly to insist, so he went along with it. Once again she made a fuss about paying her share, so to avoid the embarrassment of a public argument he agreed to allow her to buy the popcorn if she would let him pay for their tickets.

"Oh, God," she complained. "I think I've ended up with the wrong end of the bargain. Last time I bought popcorn and pick 'n' mix at the cinema I thought I would have to take out a bank loan to pay for them."

Tom enjoyed the film more than he had expected to, despite her frequent interruptions to hiss "That didn't happen in the book!" or "Thackeray will be turning in his grave!" into his ear. He had to stop himself laughing more than once, not at the film but at her exasperated response to it. Going out with her was certainly entertaining, even if she had devoured the lion's share of the popcorn before the film even started. At times he found himself watching her more than he watched the screen: now and again she would catch him, smile knowingly and squeeze his thigh with her hand.

After the film, they strolled hand in hand down the open stretch of the Roald Dahl Plass towards Cardiff's waterfront area, past the towering illuminated water fountain and the newly opened Millennium Centre.

"Isn't it amazing?" She was full of enthusiasm for the new building with its striking architecture. "I do love it down here. I can't wait to see it all when it's finished. With the lights twinkling as they reflect on the water, and all the people gathered down here for the evening to enjoy themselves, it makes me feel happy."

He loved it too, despite shivering with the cold as they huddled together to admire the Bay. He unbuttoned his coat and pulled her towards him to enfold her in its warmth. She nestled close, snug against the freezing January air.

"I'd love to live near the sea," he said. "There's something magical about being near water, I think. One day I'd like to have a house right next to the beach. I'll have a couple of Labradors and in the mornings I'll get up early to take them for a walk along the beach."

"Is it a sandy beach or a pebbly beach in your fantasy?"

"I don't care. Either would do. I'll let the dogs out and we'll see what the tide has brought in each day. In the afternoons I'll swim and maybe learn to surf while the kids picnic on the beach and hunt for crabs in the rock pools; and in the evenings I'll sit behind my double glazed windows, snug and warm while the wind howls outside."

"Kids? How many do you plan to have?"

It should be strange talking about his dreams with her. Maybe she didn't want children, and would be put off by his admission that he did. But what the hell – better for her to dump him now than later on.

"I think two should be plenty. A boy and a girl to keep it even."

"Mmm, it sounds idyllic. But you'll probably need a lottery win to buy a house like that; it's not likely to happen on a teacher's salary."

"Hush. Stop being practical; a man needs his dreams."   He gave her a crushing hug and smiled. She hadn't pooh-poohed his ideas completely. "Come on, I don't know about you but I need a hot chocolate to warm me up."

They made their way back to his car, walking awkwardly as their arms remained entwined and her hip bumped against his thigh. I'm happy, he thought. I'm actually happy enough to have noticed that I'm happy. It had been so long since he'd felt that way, he'd almost forgotten what it was like to experience that glow of pleasure, the thrill of realising that the person who had ignited feelings in him seemed to be feeling the same way.

A week later, he arrived early at the restaurant where they had arranged to meet, and settled at a table in the corner where he had a view of the door ready to catch Megan's eye with a wave when she arrived. He was famished, needed something to fill him up after a busy day. Spaghetti alle vongole? No, too garlicky. He wanted to knock Megan out with the strength of his charm, not his breath. Steak, then. Keep it simple. He put the menu down and leaned back, satisfied with his decision. Idly, he scanned the other tables.

A familiar face was watching him from the other side of the room. Still attractive for her age, with intense dark eyes like her daughter's. Stylishly dressed, as always.

Shit. Of all the people he could have run into while waiting for Megan. He picked up the menu again and made a show of studying it. She didn't take the hint, but picked up her bag, ignoring the restraining hand of the man seated beside her, and picked her way carefully between the tables to stand before him.

"Tom. You look well."

He put down the menu, reluctant to engage in conversation but not prepared to be rude. Hopefully she would say whatever it was she had to say before Megan arrived.

"Daphne. I suppose it was inevitable that we would run into each other at some point. How are you and Bob?"

"We're fine, thank you. Which is more than can be said for Erica."

He was damned if he was going to ask after her. There was an uncomfortable pause. "I'm waiting for someone, actually," he said at last, hoping she would take the hint.

"Really? So are we. We're waiting for Erica, in fact. She's joining us shortly to celebrate my birthday."

The evening suddenly looked much less promising. "Ah. Well, then - happy birthday."

"It would be a lot happier if I knew my daughter was happy, but that seems too much to ask since you... Well, since things ended between you. You do realise, I suppose, that the baby would have been due about now?"

As if he needed her to remind him of that. A spark of anger rose in him, quickly suppressed as he turned away to gaze out of the window. Ignore her; focus on the rain on the glass, and pray that Megan doesn't arrive in the middle of this... But it seemed she hadn't finished.

"She hasn't been the same since you broke up – she's constantly miserable, thinner than ever, and hardly even goes out. I worry about her. She misses you, despite everything. And I honestly believe that even after all this time, if you would only swallow your pride and apologise..."

"Apologise?" he spat, finally losing patience. "You really haven't the faintest idea what you're talking about. I have no interest whatsoever in your daughter, and I have no intention of ever – *ever* – apologising to her over what happened. If she misses me, then I'm afraid that's her problem. I can truthfully say that since we split up I haven't missed her once. She needs to move on, as I have. Now, if you don't mind, I think I mentioned that I'm waiting for someone."

His guts churned with the urge to escape her reproachful gaze. *Just go, just go, just go. Leave it alone and move on.*

At last she sighed. "Well. You've made your position clear. I hope you understand that I had to try."

The ball of tension in his chest deflated. "I bear you no ill will, Daphne. You were always kind to me. I genuinely hope you enjoy the rest of your evening."

But as she moved to go back to her own table, his relief turned to dismay. Megan stood behind her, white-faced as she moved aside to allow Daphne to pass. Out of habit he stood and pulled out a chair for her. She sat down looking anything but relaxed.

"Sorry I'm late," she said.

"Don't worry about it." He cleared his throat. "I've already had a look at the menu." He passed it to her, but she didn't open it.

"Who was that woman?"

"Daphne. My ex-girlfriend's mother. Of all the gin joints in all the world, she had to be in this one."

The joke fell flat. How much of the conversation had she heard?

"I see. And are you going to tell me what all that was about?"

He reached out across the table to touch her hand, but she put hers back in her lap. Presumably she had heard at least some of what was said, then. She had never been so wary around him before. As much as he didn't want to rake up the past, he supposed she deserved an explanation.

"I will tell you. But not here; it's too public. We'll talk about it later, after we've eaten."

They ordered their meal, but it was clear that her heart wasn't in it. She barely spoke, answering his attempts to start conversation as briefly as she could without being openly rude.

Their meal arrived at last, providing a welcome distraction. He attacked his steak grimly, with a peculiar feeling of satisfaction when the blood oozed out as he cut in. Megan only picked at her food. His senses were on high alert: he jumped whenever the restaurant door opened to let a customer in.

When Erica arrived, the meat turned to sawdust in his mouth. He chewed mechanically, unable to enjoy the flavour. She sat with her parents and he tried to pretend he wasn't aware of every look she cast towards their table.

At last, they finished eating. Neither cleared their plate, but he had had enough. The evening had turned into a disaster. Might as well give up and move on somewhere they could talk without Erica watching.

He called for the bill, and Megan got up to make her way to the ladies' room. Usually she insisted on paying half, but not tonight. Not that he minded paying, but it was a sure sign something was wrong. And then things got worse, because in the corner of his eye, while he fumbled in his pocket for cash for a tip, he noticed Erica stand and snake past the other tables. With the waitress in the way, he could hardly get up and stop her. Before he could do or say anything, she had slipped through the doorway to the ladies' room, and was out of reach.

∞ ∞ ∞

Megan was washing her hands when the other woman slipped quietly in through the doorway and stood, apparently waiting.

"It's okay – there's no queue," Megan said. She flicked her hands over the basin before moving to collect a paper towel. Funny how one paper towel is never enough, she thought: why don't they just invent a slightly bigger towel so that you can dry your hands properly without having to take two?

That was strange, though - the other woman hadn't moved. She was watching her from the doorway with a haughty look that made Megan feel uncomfortable.

"So you're Tom's new girlfriend," she said at last.

This was unexpected. Carefully, Megan finished drying her hands and dropped the towel into the bin.

"It starts out wonderfully, doesn't it?" the woman continued. "He's so very charming and amusing, and such delightful company. Such fun to be with, so attentive in the bedroom; and he has such beautiful manners, paying for everything and holding your chair for you to sit down and insisting on walking on the outside of the pavement. Quite the perfect gentleman. But I'm afraid you should be aware that one day you'll find he isn't any more, and when that happens, which it will, suddenly you'll find yourself completely out in the cold. He turns, and you don't see it coming. So I thought I'd better warn you, before he dazzles you and you get yourself in too deep."

Megan said nothing, unsure how her voice would sound past the tightness in her throat. This was Erica, then. It made sense: there was a marked resemblance between her tall, slender frame and her mother's. Short, dark hair framed her face perfectly, emphasising the hollows under her cheekbones. It was only the thinly veiled desperation in her voice that marred the outward display of confidence and made Megan feel the teeniest twinge of sympathy.

"Thank you for the warning, but I can look after myself."

"We all say that in the beginning. I must say, you're not his usual type. When my mother told me he'd be meeting someone here, I wasn't expecting someone ginger and dumpy. Not to worry, though. If anyone can help you shift a few pounds it's Tom."

Now, that was nasty and uncalled-for. Any sympathy she had felt evaporated.

"Who knows what attracted him to either of us," Megan said coldly. "In your case, it certainly can't have been the warmth of your personality, or your looks. Maybe he's just realised what he'd been missing out on for so long."

She shoved past, not caring when the door bumped against Erica's arm hard enough to leave a bruise. The bitch should have got out of the way sooner. Tom hovered near the door, a look of dread on his face, like a little boy awaiting a telling-off. She glared at him: she'd get to the bottom of all this nonsense if it killed her.

In the car, she fumed silently. She'd almost been taken in by Erica's speech at first, had felt a chill of anxiety clutch at her stomach when the other woman described Tom's manner so perfectly. She'd been enjoying her time with him so much, had begun to hope this might at last be a relationship that could go the distance. And as much as she despised Erica's bitchiness, her warning, combined with Claire's words, had made her begin to doubt her own judgement. But if she was cross with herself, she was furious with Tom.

She had overheard Daphne urging him to apologise to Erica, and his rebuttal. What had he done when he "turned", as Erica described it? As if breaking her heart by throwing her out and failing to visit her in hospital wasn't enough, had he perhaps done something even worse? There had been a baby. Daphne said something about it being due about now. How could he not have stood by her if Erica had lost his baby?

God only knew where they were going. She'd taken the bus into the city to meet him, on the understanding that he would drive her home. But they weren't heading towards her flat. Looking out of the car window, she saw that he was taking her towards the coast, following signposts towards the seaside town of Barry.

"Going to the funfair, are we?" she said, unable to resist resorting to sarcasm. "Are you planning to tell me all about it on the Log Flume?"

"No; you'll have to wait and see."

Finally he drew to a halt away from the busy parts of town, in a quiet car park overlooking the sea. It was too dark to make out much of the beach, but the rain had stopped and the break in the cloud revealed a multitude of stars. Through the windscreen they had an unhindered view towards the water. The coloured lights of occasional aeroplanes passed overhead, coming in to land at the airport nearby.

Tom turned the key and the engine stilled.

"This is Cold Knap. It's quiet here; we can talk without being disturbed."

She frowned. Cold Knap? She'd heard of it, read a poem once about the place. The poem had been quite disturbing, if she remembered rightly, about a child drowning in a lake.

Moonlight gleamed on the waves.

"Daphne told you to apologise to Erica," she said at last, and was taken aback to hear him laugh softly.

"Well, Erica would probably love that." He faced her, his expression serious.

Now, perhaps, she'd find out what the hell had gone on. And once she knew, she'd decide what to do. Keep seeing him, or take Erica's advice and get out before she was inextricably involved.

"We were together for four years. We lived together for three of those, and I suppose we assumed we would get married eventually. She certainly assumed we would. She used to tell people she was my fiancée, even though I hadn't ever actually proposed to her." He rubbed his hand through his hair.

Meg waited. So far his story tallied with what Claire had told her, although it was interesting that they weren't in fact engaged.

"What's she like?" She had formed her own opinion, but wanted to know what he thought.

"She's nothing like you. Very athletic; very sporty. She was obsessively tidy…"

Megan sniffed: so far, Erica sounded like a paragon.

"She was difficult to live with, at times. She liked to have her own way. We all do, I suppose. But it was only towards the end that I realised how manipulative she was."

He fidgeted with the gearstick, pushing it in and out of neutral. She wished he'd stop: his nervous energy put her even more on edge.

"It must have been about February or March last year when she started to seem different. She always went to the gym a lot, but she started staying out later than before. It wasn't a problem, I wasn't out to keep tabs on her; but when I think back, that was when things changed. And she started taking a lot more interest in her appearance, getting her nails done, her eyelashes, fake tan and so on. She hadn't really ever bothered to that extent before."

"It's hardly a crime to visit a beauty salon."

He rubbed his brow and frowned, apparently frustrated that she hadn't understood his meaning.

"No, I realise that. One day in July I came home from work and found her in the bathroom. She was in a terrible state, sobbing hysterically. I couldn't get any sense out of her at first. She kept saying she was sorry, but I couldn't work out what she was sorry for. I threatened to call her mother, and that's when she told me. She'd had an abortion."

"Oh, God – the poor girl!" Megan's hand flew to her mouth. No wonder Erica was bitter: she'd been so unhappy with Tom's suspicious and jealous behaviour, she'd felt unable to go ahead with her pregnancy. Going through that would be bound to screw with anyone's head.

"I couldn't understand why she'd done it. If I'd known she was pregnant it wouldn't have been a problem: I'd have been pleased, for God's sake. We'd been together a long time; we were settled. Money wasn't an issue, we both had decent jobs. I had my flat, and if it wasn't big enough for three of us we could have sold up and bought a house together instead. I just couldn't get my head round it."

"Why do you think she did it, then?" Had he honestly not understood how controlling he had been, disapproving of her taking a bit of pride in her appearance by working out a bit more and having a few beauty treatments?

His expression hardened.

"I put her to bed with a hot drink and some painkillers. I gave her some time to herself, figuring she'd be better off without my clumsy attempts to offer comfort. She was too overwrought to talk, anyway - it made sense to leave it until morning. I sat in the kitchen for hours. I kept thinking that she'd gone off and killed our baby without telling me, without even giving me a chance to support them. I couldn't understand why she hadn't said anything, why she hadn't trusted me to be a father. In the end, I spent what was left of the night on the sofa. And then, in the morning, I picked up her mobile phone to contact her boss and let him know she would be off sick."

Meg frowned. How was that relevant?

"There was a text message on her phone from a friend of mine, Paul. If you don't mind, I'd rather not tell you what it said."

She bit her lip, unsure how to respond. What did this Paul fellow have to do with it?

"It didn't take a genius to work out why she'd had the abortion," he concluded bitterly. "It turned out she'd been seeing Paul behind my back for months. He would have run a mile at the prospect of fatherhood, and she wasn't sure she could get away with passing the baby off as mine. For all I know, Paul was the father, not me. But I still wonder sometimes. It would have been due about now."

She stared at him, speechless.

"You have to understand," he went on, a catch in his voice. "I couldn't forgive her. For me, it's no different from putting a gun against a kid's head – *my* kid's head, I thought at the time - and blowing its brains out. It need never have happened. And once I knew she'd been unfaithful, it was as if a switch had been flicked off inside me. Anything I had ever felt for her died."

"Surely you can't just turn your feelings off like that? Not after four years together."

"I can't explain it. But that's exactly what happened. I didn't even hate her, although I despised what she had done. I hated Paul, I must admit: I wanted to kill him. But I felt completely cold towards her: if I felt anything at all after the initial shock, it was indifference. That was what she found hardest to handle. I think she'd expected me to plead with her to stay with me, that I'd beg her not go off with that prick. She thought I'd feel sorry for her because of the abortion. It floored her when I didn't do any of that. I packed her stuff into black bags and threw her out."

"That was harsh." She swallowed hard. Her muscles felt frozen, despite the warmth of the car.

"I don't regret what I did. She didn't deserve any sympathy from me. And things can't have been that great between us because I haven't missed her. Fuck it, I had a lucky escape. Paul used to chase anything in a skirt: I had to go to the STD clinic in case she'd caught something from him and passed it on to me. Fortunately, I was clear."

Alright, so he had been treated badly, but this uncompromising attitude of his was hard to stomach.

"Where did she go when you threw her out?" She dreaded the next part of the story, remembering what Claire had told her, but she wanted to hear it from his own lips.

"Paul didn't want her once she was free: the last thing he wanted was to have to look after her. So she went back home to her mother with a sob story. The next day she waited until she knew Daphne was due to get home, and cut her wrists in the bath. But, as you know because you've seen her alive and kicking, there was no real cause for concern. She didn't do it properly."

She felt sick. A colder, harder side of Tom had been revealed, and she didn't like it. He went on, obviously feeling he had to justify his unsympathetic attitude.

"Meg, it was a classic attention-seeking gesture. Her mother tried to get me to go and see her, but there was no way I wanted to be involved any further. You need to understand that Erica is very manipulative. Her so-called suicide attempt was a last-ditch effort to make me feel guilt or sympathy and back me into a corner. Don't waste your sympathy on her. It's bad enough that she's got Daphne thinking I should have her back. Ha! One of these days I'll have to ask them what I'm supposed to apologise for."

"Not visiting her in hospital, perhaps? She'd tried to kill herself over you, surely it was the least you could do?"

His knuckles whitened on the steering wheel.

"I told you, she didn't really try to kill herself. And what purpose would it have served? If I'd visited, it would have raised her hopes for no good reason. There was nothing – absolutely *nothing* she could have said that would have altered my feelings towards her. It was fairer just to make a clean break."

Megan sat quietly, suddenly weary. It had been a hell of a night. It was a relief, in a way, to have heard his explanation: she felt instinctively that he had been truthful. Claire's warning had lurked in the shadows behind her for a couple of weeks, despite her attempts to forget it. A shame it hadn't turned out to be untrue: even though the reasons for Tom's behaviour were now clearer, the story didn't reflect well on him. He clearly felt he had good reason to act as he did, but Megan couldn't help feeling sorry for any woman who had gone through the trauma of an unwanted pregnancy, an abortion, relationship breakdown and homelessness, all because of a foolish mistake.

"Would you mind taking me home now?" she asked, not meeting his gaze. "I need some time to think about everything you've told me."

He didn't answer, but clicked his seatbelt back on and started the engine.

∞ ∞ ∞

Face grim, jaw set, Tom drove back towards Cardiff. It was obvious that Megan hadn't understood the depth of his sense of betrayal. Perhaps he should have said more about what it had been like for him: how, for instance, he had spent the next couple of weeks in a blur of grief and bitterness that made him drive like a man with a death-wish. For a man who habitually avoided conflict, the almost overwhelming desire to pound Paul's handsome face to a bloody pulp had been both shameful and frightening. And for months the sight of a couple with a baby had made him clench his fists until his nails cut into his palms.

Perhaps he should tell her how his brother had been moved to drive to Cardiff from Gloucester one night to talk him out of his self-destructive, furious drinking. How his truest friends had invented excuses to stay at his flat, to ensure he didn't do anything stupid in a fit of anger or self-pity. How his newly single status had cost him several friendships, when cosy couples sided with Erica or didn't know what to do with him at parties. How he hadn't been interested in getting involved with a woman for months, until he met Megan and had dared to hope she was different. Erica's treachery had left him crushed and humiliated, only too aware that many people would assume she had been driven to stray by some inadequacy on his part. He had felt like a failure, unable to trust himself to love again, until Megan's vivacity and passionate kisses at the Christmas party undermined his defences.

The words froze in his throat with every stolen glance at her wooden expression. He couldn't understand why she had so completely failed to comprehend his feelings. He felt powerless, unable to summon any words that might change her mind.

Finally, as they reached the outskirts of the city, he took refuge in anger. If she didn't get it, then so be it. He had thought her values would be in line with his own; if she thought Erica's behaviour was acceptable, he had clearly misjudged her.

When he turned the car into her street, she picked up her bag, obviously eager to get away.

"Thank you for explaining it all to me. I realize it must have been painful for you," she said, as if wearied by the effort of being polite.

He pulled the car into a space and waited. She stared at the bag in her lap.

"I'll be off, then. See you," she said.

As he leaned to kiss her, she flinched away and reached for the door handle.

The moment she closed the door, he shoved the car back into gear and roared away. Remarkably strange, he thought, how the coldness of women could stoke such a burning in his chest and throat. He had no idea whether he'd see her again. No idea whether he even wanted to.

Chapter Eight

January 2005
Cardiff

Megan slept fitfully that night. In the small hours, she dreamed of Tom. He was half-reclined against a stack of pillows in a hospital bed. As she hung back on the threshold of his room, he saw her.

His face was ghastly white, his eyes red-rimmed and shadowy with pain and reproach. She stood mute in the doorway, unsure what to do, then noticed a curious stain appearing on his chest: small at first, like a strawberry mark. He looked down at it, unsurprised, as if such a wound was to be expected. Under their gaze it increased in size, spreading out from his heart and saturating his hospital gown in scarlet. As it grew larger, his eyes became fearful, and he reached out in agitation towards Megan with fingers that were waxy and white. She felt she should offer him something – her hand, perhaps, for comfort; or a handkerchief to staunch the crimson flow; but instead a cowardly instinct made her run away down the corridor. As she fled, she heard him cry out after her, and she knew she had lost him before they had really begun.

She awoke with a start, disconcerted by the powerful dream, and gulped down tears. Although it was still early, not yet dawn, she threw off her duvet and padded around her flat to root herself back in reality. Gradually her heart rate slowed back to normal, and she felt she could breathe again. Finally, refreshed by a long drink of water, she crept back to bed and curled into a ball, her thoughts too muddled to allow her to sleep.

When Tom had confided in her, she had felt more sympathy for his ex-girlfriend than she had for him. However upset he was about the affair and the baby, he should have given Erica a chance to try to make it up to him, shouldn't have turned his back so easily on the woman he had shared his life with for four years. He seemed so unbending, so unprepared to see things from Erica's point of view. And Megan knew the hurt that could be caused by a man walking away from a relationship, had spent her formative years witnessing the bitter effect of abandonment on her own mother.

Her own relationship with Tom had seemed so promising up to now, but it was clear that if she ever made a mistake she could expect no forgiveness from him. Could Erica and Claire's warnings have been right? Was it wise to establish a bond with a man who was so lacking in compassion towards a woman he was supposed to love?

Now that she had calmed down, her dream seemed melodramatic and absurd. It was ridiculous to see Tom as some sort of wounded victim. But on the other hand, it didn't take a genius to work out what it had meant. He had revealed his heartbreak to her, and what had she done? Instead of seeing his point of view, she had created a mental picture of a desperate, pitiable fallen woman. Erica, the tall brunette: so slender, so fit, so elegant, neat and fastidious; so everything Megan would never be.

On the other hand, she had seen for herself what a bitch Erica could be. "Ginger and dumpy"? The memory of their encounter made her fizz with anger. She tussled with her pillow, unable to get comfortable. No, Erica wasn't some helpless victim. She had shaped her own destiny. Did her mother even know about Paul, and the possibility that the baby wasn't Tom's?

Cutting off all contact with Erica must have been the only way Tom could reassert control over his situation and gather up what remained of his pride. He had clearly felt betrayed and humiliated by the realisation that his girlfriend had turned to his friend for an affair and thus exposed him to the risk of a sexually transmitted infection. No wonder he was bitter. Maybe her own reaction had been a bit lacking in compassion. Maybe she should speak to him tomorrow, explain that she felt differently now that she had had time to reflect.

When she summoned the courage to telephone him the following afternoon, however, he didn't answer. Perhaps, after the way he had roared away in his car last night, he was still in a temper and didn't want to speak to her. She left a voicemail, hesitant and awkward.

"Hi, Tom. It's me. Megan, that is... I've been thinking about what you told me and - erm... I think we should discuss it rather than just leave things as they stood last night. Perhaps you could call me back?"

At midnight she gave up waiting for him to call, and flopped into bed. He obviously wasn't willing to speak to her. It was silly to be upset: they hadn't been going out for long. She couldn't claim to have been seriously involved with him. None of her friends had even known she was seeing him. But she had enjoyed his company, had allowed herself to hope they might take things further, until Erica and her mother threw a spanner in the works. Tears squeezed out onto her pillow.

The night dragged on into a miserable Monday morning. Back at work, she stumbled through the first two lessons, struggling to concentrate. When Claire came to her classroom to borrow a text book at break time, she remarked on Megan's glum mood at once and refused to accept her insistence that there was nothing wrong.

"Something's definitely up with you," Claire said. "You're not your usual bubbly self at all today. You might as well tell me: I'll only go on and on about it until you do. I'll wear you down eventually." Claire stood with her arms folded over her bump, clearly determined not to leave until Megan had provided an explanation for her sombre frame of mind.

Megan perched on the edge of her desk, feet swinging above the floor.

"You'll be cross with me if I tell you. In fact, you'll gloat and say 'I told you so'. And you'll be right: you did warn me. But I thought I knew better."

Understanding dawned in Claire's eyes.

"You've been seeing Tom Field! Alright: in that case, I told you so. Now, tell me what's happened."

"We had a few really nice dates. It was going really well: he's great in lots of ways. We seemed to be on the same wavelength. I thought he was lovely. He made me laugh. He's intelligent; interesting. He's charming."

"He's easy on the eye," Claire added.

"True. But then I met his ex. She was a bit catty, but the things she said about him made me wonder if I'd misjudged him. In the end I asked him about what had happened, and I… I kind of took her side."

"That's hardly surprising, given what he did. But then…" Claire's eyes had narrowed as she sensed from Megan's dejected expression that there was more to the story. "Did it happen the way my friend told me?"

"On the face of it, yes. But Tom sees things very differently. In his opinion, his actions were justified."

"Really? How could he hope to justify what he did?"

"You have to promise not to tell anyone. I wouldn't want him to think I've been gossiping," she insisted.

"Fair enough: I won't tell a soul. Now, spit it out." Claire sat down and rested her hands on her bump.

"She'd been sleeping with a friend of his, behind his back." Claire's eyes widened with surprise. "She got pregnant, and wasn't sure which of them was the father, so she had a termination. When Tom found out, he packed her stuff and threw her out. According to him, she didn't really try to kill herself. She timed it to make sure her mum would find her before any real harm was done. He sees it as an attempt to manipulate him into taking her back. That's why he wouldn't visit her in the hospital."

"What a godawful mess. I didn't know any of that. It explains why he wouldn't go and see her, and why he threw her out."

Megan picked at a ragged cuticle on her thumb. She pulled at it too hard, saw a bead of blood appear and sucked at it, the sharp, metallic taste assaulting her tongue. Damned stupid thing to do, she thought, cross with herself. Now her thumb would be sore for days.

"Doesn't this make things a lot better from your point of view, though?" Claire asked.

"What do you mean?"

"He's not just some heartless brute who kicks his girlfriends out without provocation."

"In a way, I suppose - but I hadn't realised there was such a hard-hearted side to him. He turned his back on a long-term relationship without a second glance. There isn't so much as an ounce of pity in him for a woman he had cared enough about to live with for three years. When he first told me, I kept imagining how devastated she must have been. In a short space of time she was made homeless, had an unwanted pregnancy terminated, and was rejected by two men. "

"Could you forgive that sort of betrayal?"

"No, I don't suppose I could. I know I should apologise for being unsympathetic, and I did leave a message on his voicemail, but he hasn't called me back. I don't think he wants to speak to me. It might be over, and I've realised I don't want it to be."

"Make him speak to you, then," Claire told her firmly. "If he's avoiding you, go and find him. He'll be supervising the gym club with Garin after school. Get him on his own and explain, and then perhaps we'll see that lovely big smile of yours again."

At the end of the school day, Megan headed across the campus to the fitness suite. She faltered at the threshold, smoothing down the long plait in her hair to ensure it was in place, before pushing the door open and stepping inside.

A number of pupils were making use of the exercise equipment, and the room smelled stale, with a pungent tang of adolescent sweat that made her want to hold her breath. Tom and Garin were at the back of the room, conferring with one of the sixth form boys. She squared her shoulders and started towards them.

Garin looked up with a wolfish smirk. "Miss Parry! To what do we owe the pleasure?"

Tom jumped as if he had been stung, met Megan's gaze for a tense moment, then turned abruptly to continue his conversation with the student.

She stepped forward, but Garin held up his hand.

"Sorry, Miss: we can't allow you in here with those shoes on."

Of course: kitten heels would mark the wooden floor. She reddened and pulled them off. She held her head high, trying to stand tall, self-conscious as Garin towered a full fourteen inches above her in his trainers, his eyes alight with amusement.

"I was hoping to speak to Mr Field about something."

Tom's back stiffened. "I'm busy," he said to Garin, and stalked away to speak to another boy.

Garin raised his eyebrows, then took her by the arm.

"Sorry about that," he said in a low voice, steering her towards the exit. "He's been a miserable sod all day. If I didn't know differently, I'd say he had woman trouble. But given that he's been as celibate as a monk since last summer, it obviously can't be that."

Her head jerked up. For the first time since she met him, his smile was kindly, rather than predatory. He had guessed, it seemed; and if he hadn't before, her flaming cheeks probably gave her away now.

"Shall I pass on a message for you?" he asked.

She slipped her shoes back on and bit her lip, hesitating. "Could you say that I've reconsidered my response to what we discussed recently...? I - well, I'd like to apologise to him." She paused; Garin waited. "That's it, really. If you wouldn't mind telling him. Thanks."

She set off down the corridor as if she couldn't wait to escape.

"I'll send him to your classroom in five minutes," he called after her. "Don't worry, just wait for him there and I'll make sure he comes over."

∞ ∞ ∞

Tom was as jumpy as a dog with fleas, still shocked by Megan's sudden appearance in the gym. What was she saying to Garin outside? The last thing he needed was for his colleague to realise his love life had suffered another setback.

He could guess what Megan had come to say. She'd tried to call him on the weekend, when he was pounding his disappointment into the pavement on a long, painful run. Heart sinking, he'd listened to her voicemail when he got back. It was obvious that she wanted to end their relationship, and was trying to do so politely.

"Hi, Tom. It's me. Megan, that is... I've been thinking about what you told me and - erm... I think we should discuss it rather than just leave things as they stood last night. Perhaps you could call me back?"

He'd played it through three times before deleting it. No point calling her back just to be dumped. Better to just leave it, pretend it hadn't mattered. He'd been hurt before, worse than this, and recovered... up to a point, anyway. At least this time it had ended before he'd let himself get too involved.

Garin was back. He headed straight for Tom, dragging him by the arm out of earshot of any pupils, fizzing with excitement.

"Time to get your head out of your arse and make your way over to the English department. And don't look like that: this is an opportunity not to be missed, something I've never seen or heard before. In fact, it's probably a world first. You could sell tickets if you didn't have to get over there so quickly." He paused for dramatic effect.

"Garin, what the hell are you talking about?"

"She wants to *apologise* to you, apparently. I can't believe it: I've never once heard a woman admit she was wrong – have you? So I've promised to send you over there within the next five minutes. And if you don't go, I will personally tie you to the wall bars and use you as a target for javelin practice. It shouldn't be hard to hit that big, fat head of yours."

For a long moment they faced one another, Garin unperturbed by Tom's scowl.

"I'll expect a full report later! What I wouldn't give to be a fly on the wall in that classroom..."

Tom marched away, ignoring him.

∞ ∞ ∞

Megan paced up and down at the front of her classroom, full of nervous energy. What to do while she was waiting? Would he even come? There was a stack of paperbacks on her desk: yes, put them away, it would keep her hands busy. She picked them up, ready to lift them onto the correct shelf, but startled as Tom thrust open the door without knocking. The books fell in a jumble on the floor.

Swearing under her breath, she ducked to gather them up, glad of the chance to hide her burning cheeks under the desk. He made no attempt to help, but closed the door and stood with his hand on the doorknob as if reluctant to stay for a moment longer than necessary. When she straightened and tossed the books back onto her desk, he finally spoke.

"Garin said you wanted to see me?"

Her heart sank as she read the expression on his face. His mouth was set in a tight line, his eyes cold. At first she thought he was angry, then she realised he was guarded, clearly reluctant to speak to her. She supposed she could hardly blame him.

"Yes, thanks for coming over. Do you want to sit down?"

"No, thanks. I can't stay long. I only came over to hear what you have to say."

She nodded. Better get it over with.

"I just wanted to say sorry. I should have been more understanding, last time we spoke, and tried harder to see things from your point of view. You were treated badly, and you deserved more sympathy. I was just - well, I was a bit taken aback at how quickly and decisively you ended things… If I'm honest, I suppose I found it hard to put myself in your shoes. It was easier to picture her as the victim, so I lost sight of the rejection and trauma you must have been feeling too."

His expression softened a fraction, and his hand dropped away from the door handle to be stuffed into his pocket; but he remained silent.

"I've never been in your situation myself. But I have experienced things from the other side, in a way." She took a ragged breath, unsure how to explain. Nothing for it but to dive straight in.

"When I was twenty, I thought I was pregnant. I was at university, and I'd been going out with a guy for a few weeks. I didn't even like him that much, to be honest. He was good looking; I was flattered that he'd asked me out because I knew loads of the girls on my course fancied him; and I suppose I admired his self-confidence. But it certainly didn't go any deeper than that between us. Then we were unlucky: the first time I slept with him, the condom broke; and a couple of weeks later my period was late."

His eyes had widened, but still he said nothing.

"It was the worst few days of my life. I was in the middle of exams. I was in no position to have a baby. I didn't have any kind of proper relationship with the father, and couldn't expect any kind of support from him, emotionally or financially. He'd already finished with me by then, in any case. A baby would have ruined everything I'd worked for. As it happened, it was a false alarm, thank God; but if it hadn't been, I'd already decided that I couldn't possibly go ahead with a pregnancy. It wouldn't have felt like a baby, but more like a parasite, destroying me from the inside. So when you condemned Erica for what she did, I felt for her. I know, up to a point, how she might have felt."

He shook his head. "The situation is entirely different. She knew I would have supported her, if there had been no doubt that it was mine."

"I know it's not the same and I'm not trying to make excuses for her. I'm just trying to explain why I had some sympathy for her, and why it was easier for me to relate to her than to you. I'm sorry."

"I don't really know what to say."

"How about 'I accept your apology, let me take you out to dinner?'"

"Would you really have got rid of it, if you had been pregnant?"

She nodded. It seemed he wasn't going to accept her apology too readily.

"I don't think I'd have had much choice. My mother would have found out eventually, and she'd have frogmarched me straight to the Marie Stopes clinic telling me not to ruin my life."

"And now? What if it happened to you now that you're more mature, you're working, and in a position to look after a child? What would you do if the father was willing to offer support?"

They faced each other, his face stiff and hers defensive. She tutted, irritated.

"Are you seriously asking me to make decisions about us facing a hypothetical unwanted pregnancy when we haven't even slept together?"

"I know it probably sounds crazy to you. I get that. I just know I couldn't go through all that again." He made a helpless gesture with his hands.

She sank into a chair and pressed her palms to her temples, suddenly weary. "Look, Tom – until I'm in that situation, and I sincerely hope I never will be - I just don't know. We're not at the stage you were at with Erica. You're comparing me with someone you were with for four years, but we've been together for – what? Four weeks? I've never lived with any of my boyfriends, and I've certainly never been in a relationship that's lasted for four years. Eighteen months is about my record, to tell the truth. I'm lucky: no one has ever treated me as badly as Erica treated you…Well, apart from the time when I was seventeen and Ricky Williams dumped me for Tania Bitchface Brunnock. I was so upset I cried for a whole week afterwards…"

"Was that a double-barrelled name?" he asked.

"Sorry?"

"Bitchface-Brunnock. It has a certain ring to it."

"Oh. Well - no, obviously not. That was just what I called her. She was captain of the netball team. Her legs were probably longer than my entire body."

She gave her head a shake, trying to clear her thoughts.

"Look, Tom - all I'm trying to say is that I do understand how you must have felt, but I haven't experienced anything on the same level... Things usually just fizzle out with me. One or both of us gets bored, and we go our separate ways. Or I make a fool of myself and get the brush-off. Or, more often, he turns out to be a total prick and I blow him out of the water. Given my past history, it's much more likely that we'll break up because you'll get bored with me than that we'll have a baby together, planned or otherwise. I guarantee that within two months you'll start finding me tedious: you'll decide I talk too much; I'll go blank when you try to explain cricket to me; and you'll realise I'm not particularly domesticated. I find cleaning a dreadful bore, for a start; I leave mess behind me like a snail trail; and I can't even bake to find my way to your heart through your stomach... Look - you're making me nervous, just standing there so quietly. Will you please just accept our differing views on suppositious unplanned pregnancies, forgive me for Saturday night, and give me another chance?"

He swallowed, rubbing his jaw. Had she said too much, put him off with her confessions? His thoughtful expression definitely suggested he was thinking of a way to let her down gently.

"How about Friday?" he said.

"Pardon?" She blinked, unsure if she had understood him.

"I seem to remember you promised to drive next time we go out. Shall we say eight o'clock? I'll text you my address so you can pick me up."

"Oh!" Her chest thumped with relief. "Yes, great. See you on Friday, then."

The corners of his eyes crinkled and he regarded her with a warmth that lifted her spirits.

"It's a date. I'll look forward to it." He sounded almost as relieved as she was.

He turned in the doorway as he was about to leave. "Oh, just one other thing…"

"Yes? What's that?"

"I wouldn't want you to get the wrong idea about me. The thing is, I'm actually much more interested in your body and your conversation than your baking or cleaning skills. I don't need a woman for those - I'm quite capable of doing them myself."

Chapter Nine

February 2005
Cardiff

Friday evening finally came. Megan escaped from work at the earliest opportunity and sped home, determined to spend a couple of hours concentrating her efforts on making herself look fabulous.

Hoping that tonight would end more promisingly than their previous date, she ensured she was perfectly exfoliated, moisturised and perfumed. Legs, underarms and bikini line were shaved, eyebrows were plucked and teeth carefully flossed. Her make-up was immaculate. It was pouring with rain, so she didn't waste time straightening her hair: the minute she went outside it would only frizz up again anyway. Instead, she scrunch-dried it and allowed it to fall in its natural waves. By the time she left her flat, car keys in hand, she had every confidence that Tom would find her irresistible.

Huddled under her umbrella as she dashed up the street to her car, she prayed that the lashing rain wouldn't ruin her new shoes. She wiped the condensation off the inside of the windscreen of her Mini with a rag she kept for the purpose, then checked her street map one last time before setting off towards the address Tom had given her. It was only twenty to eight, so she expected to get there with time to spare.

Unfortunately, she had reckoned without getting a puncture. Halfway to Tom's address the car began pulling to one side, the steering wheel suddenly heavy under her hands. Alarmed, she drew up at the kerb, put her hazard warning lights on and clambered out with her umbrella to examine the wheels.

"Oh, bloody hell!" Her front tyre was flat. She dithered, deciding what to do.

She had no intention of standing pathetically at the side of the road waiting for a chivalrous stranger to stop and help, and she didn't have breakdown cover, so the only possible course of action was to remove the wheel and fit the spare herself. It would be fine: she knew exactly what to do. Matt had shown her once, when she first bought her Mini.

If only it wasn't such a bloody dreadful night. Tiptoeing through the puddles to unlock the car boot, it looked horribly like her attempts to save her new shoes from further damage would be in vain.

After tossing several bags, books and a broken umbrella from the boot into the back seat, she was finally able to get to the spare wheel. With a grunt, she hefted it out onto the kerb. It was surprisingly awkward, not to mention dirty. Holding both the wheel and the umbrella proved impossible; soon her hair would look pretty much as it had when she stepped out of the shower.

Still, at least this tyre had air in it. Hunting in the boot again, she found the jack and wheel wrench. As she lifted them out, a car drove past and splashed her legs with dirty rainwater. The shock of the cold water made her squeal and almost drop the tools before she made it to the pavement.

A glance at her wristwatch: it was approaching eight o'clock now, and Tom would soon be wondering where she was. She reached into the car and dashed off a quick text message: *Got a puncture halfway over, will be with you once I've finished changing the wheel.*

Within a few moments she had prised the wheel trim off the car with a screwdriver and pitched it into the boot, getting her hands filthy with brake dust and road dirt in the process. She positioned the jack under the jacking point and turned the handle a couple of times to take the weight of the car off the wheel, the rain trickling down the back of her neck and soaking her through her clothes. Her carefully styled hair was now plastered to her head and she didn't even dare to contemplate how her shoes must be faring as she applied the head of the slippery, wet wheel brace to the first wheel nut. Despite heaving with all her might, the nut refused to move.

"What the hell? – stupid, bloody, bastard thing!" she cursed, purple-faced, completely unable to shift the nut. Then she remembered she had once seen someone bounce up and down on the handle of a brace to dislodge wheel nuts. Maybe that would work. Clinging to the front wing of the Mini for balance, she tried standing on the handle and bouncing up and down. Still it refused to budge. Admittedly, three and a half inch heels were probably not the safest choice of footwear for balancing on a wet metal bar, but her flatties were in the passenger foot well and it seemed a bit late to get them out now.

"Bollocks!"

She was about to step down onto the pavement when a familiar VW Golf pulled in behind her car. Oh God, she thought. He couldn't see her like this – she looked like someone who had just been rescued from drowning.

Tom stepped out onto the pavement, holding up his coat collar against the freezing cold rain and looking none too pleased.

"What the hell do you think you're doing? You'll break your ankles jumping up and down on there."

"Well, I'm not painting my nails, am I?" she snapped. "What does it look like I'm doing? I can't get the bloody wheel nuts undone. The stupid bloody garage must have used the air gun on them and tightened them too hard."

He gaped at her.

"Right, I can see that you're a strong and independent woman: it's understood, Megan, you don't need to prove it to me. Now, if you'll swallow your pride and get down off that wheel brace, I'll have a go at loosening the nuts off. You need a longer wheel brace to get better leverage. I've got one in my car."

After a moment's stubborn hesitation, and a final vain attempt to push down on the brace, she surrendered to the inevitable. Looking daggers at him, she stepped down onto the kerb.

"Get into my car," he said more gently, having retrieved a much longer wheel brace from his boot. "You're drenched. Haven't you got any breakdown cover, for goodness' sake?"

She fled to the warmth of his car, her teeth chattering. There was nothing she hated more than appearing foolish: she fumed now at being cast as the damsel in distress who needed a knight in shining armour to ride to her rescue. She knew exactly how to change a wheel, and it was infuriating to be unable to do it without help.

As she watched, Tom stamped on the wheel brace and wrenched it round, loosening the nuts before quickly pumping at the handle of the jack to lift the car up. His wet trousers clung to his leg and her eyes were drawn to the muscles of his thigh. As much as she hated having to admit defeat and let him take over, his display of physical strength was impressive. When he removed the useless, deflated wheel and slung it into the boot, he made it look maddeningly easy.

Now he was getting soaked, too, and he'd be bound to be angry with her for getting him into this situation. She fought the urge to stamp her feet in frustration.

She risked a peep into his passenger vanity mirror and immediately wished she hadn't, slapping the visor back up to the roof of the car. Her hair was a mess, her nose was red and her mascara had smudged, giving her panda eyes. She wouldn't be going out anywhere with him tonight. It was pretty certain that he wouldn't be in a hurry to go anywhere, either – by the time he had finished attaching her spare wheel and had lowered the car off the jack he was drenched.

Surprisingly, his eyes twinkled with good humour as he opened the door and got in. His hair was darkened and tousled, and rainwater tracked down his face and his coat.

"Right, Miss Have-a-go Hero. Job done. Jump back into your car and follow me back to my place so we can dry off. I think we'll have to give the bright city lights a miss this evening." Shaking his head, he added: "I still can't believe you haven't got breakdown cover."

She pouted, defiant. "My car is only five years old, and I have it serviced regularly. I didn't think I'd need it."

"Even a brand new car can get a puncture."

"If the wheel nuts hadn't been so tight I could have dealt with it myself." His sceptical expression made her fume.

"Why on earth doesn't your dad insist that you have breakdown cover, a woman driving around a city on your own?"

She laughed derisively. "My dad? I haven't seen him in twenty-five years. He walked out on the three of us and as far as I know he hasn't been in touch since."

Tom stared at her, obviously taken aback. "Well... That explains why you've never mentioned him. How could he do that?"

"He obviously didn't care for us very much, did he?" She tried to keep her tone light, but a tinge of bitterness crept into her voice.

He touched the back of her hand, his own fingers still wet and cold. A droplet of water swelled and fell onto it from a wavy tendril of her hair. His voice was soft, his expression intent.

"If you were mine, I would never walk out on you," he said.

He genuinely meant it. How were her defences supposed to cope with that? It was too much. What with the cold, the rain, her ruined hair and make-up, her humiliating failure to solve her own problem with the car, and now this unexpected tenderness: it was as if a bubble of tension inside her abruptly popped, leaving her vulnerable. She wiped away a raindrop that was trickling down to her jaw.

"You do my head in, you do," she blurted out.

He drew back his hand. "Why on earth do you say that?"

"With other men, I've always run a mile - or they've got fed up with me before I could start to feel much for them. But you, damn you…" She shook her head, furiously brushing away the prickle of imminent tears. "Your ability to get under my skin scares the hell out of me."

Gently, he swept a tear from the corner of her eye with his thumb, and she leant her cheek against the comforting warmth of his hand. Her words came out in a rush.

"The trouble with you is you're funny: I love the way you can laugh at yourself. You make me laugh when you tease me, the way you can stay poker-faced when you're joking so I have to look twice to check whether that twinkle is there in your eyes… You constantly surprise me - like when you swept me off my feet on the dance floor, or with your Latin quotations, or the way you looked so full of compassion when I told you about Bethan and Matt not being able to have children. On the one hand you're this hard rugby player, showing off your preposterous biceps by posing in my classroom doorway, or riding to the rescue like the fourth bloody emergency service… Then, on the other hand, you're practically hyperventilating because you're stuck in a lift for a few minutes. You make me want you when that expression comes into your eyes… Yes, that one, that makes the blue so beguiling, and the corners go crinkly…

"When you weren't speaking to me last weekend, I missed you so much it hurt. It's ridiculous, of course, because I hardly know you, but I really feel I *do* know you already. You're a good man, a moral and principled man – almost to a fault, because I can't say I agree with all your views; but there's also that deliciously naughty side to you that I find hard to resist. When you kiss me, it throws me completely off balance. I've never had that feeling in my stomach so strongly before with anyone else. It's like a heat; it drives me until I want nothing else but to be consumed by it, and make it consume you. You're exciting… Being with you is like being high. Or like freefalling. I'm mixing my metaphors, but that's how it feels.

"But then, Tom - what you told me last weekend… You set a very high standard, and I don't honestly know if I can live up to it. You want whole-hearted devotion, and until now I've never wanted to give anyone that. If I risk committing to you so completely, how do I know I won't upset you one day and be cut off without so much as a backward glance? I mean, obviously I'll try my best not to do anything to hurt you. I've done it once without meaning to, and you could barely bring yourself to look at me when I came to set things right. I never want to see you look at me like that again."

There was a part of her that cringed at herself, wanting to take back the torrent of words that had revealed so much of her feelings. She had only known him a matter of weeks: what kind of fool was she to leave herself so exposed?

"I'm making a fool of myself, throwing myself at you again, aren't I, like I did in the lift?"

"Hmm, yes. But I like your impulsiveness. You talk like you kiss: obeying an urge, without worrying too far ahead about the consequences."

She laughed softly. "That may be true. Unfortunately, I eat like that, too, so I'll never be skinny like Erica."

"Trust me, I couldn't be gladder that you're not like Erica. You've given me more to feel good about in the past four minutes than she did in four years."

"Okay. Well, that's good. Tell me, then, if I was to obey the urge I'm feeling now, to kiss you again, what would be the consequences of that?"

"I suspect I'd find it difficult to ignore urges of my own."

She swallowed hard, her mouth suddenly dry.

He spoke quietly, wry humour gone. "I don't really ask for that much, you know. I do ask for faithfulness. I'm a one-woman man – it's the way I'm made, and I'm insecure enough to need a woman who's made the same way... And I do demand honesty. But as far as I can tell, Megan, you've been completely direct and open with me since the moment we met. You've never tried to disguise your feelings or pretend to be something you're not. It seems to me that you would struggle to be anything but honest."

She nodded her thanks, eyes brimming again, and shuddered as much from emotion as from the cold.

"You're shivering!" he exclaimed. His voice became abruptly authoritative as he sat back in his seat and buckled his seatbelt. "Come on, we'll go back to my place and find you something dry to put on."

She smiled at his sudden use of his firm teacher voice. "Yes, sir," she said, with a mock salute that made his eyes gleam again.

She ran back to her Mini, new shoes squelching uncomfortably in the freezing puddles. With her teeth chattering, she started the engine and wiped the mist of condensation off the inside of the screen again. As soon as she could see reasonably clearly through the glass, she set off, keeping close to the tail of his Golf all the way.

They parked outside a modern block of flats and he led the way inside. It was all glass and chrome here, with polished floors and white walls: a far cry from the tired woodchip wallpaper and threadbare, patterned nylon carpet where she lived.

"I need a shower," she said, dripping in the hallway and stooping to remove her sodden, filthy shoes. "I know how to change a wheel, but I never realised it was such a dirty job."

"Hmph. It is when you're standing in the gutter in the pouring rain."

"Which floor do you live on?" she asked, starting up the stairs behind him, shoes in one hand and handbag in the other. She felt brighter now that she was indoors, intrigued at the prospect of seeing his home.

"Fourth."

She gaped, unable to keep up as he bounded up the steps.

"You live in a fourth floor flat when you're scared of lifts? Are you nuts? Hang on, slow down a minute: your legs are a lot longer than mine, remember."

His casual shrug acknowledged her assessment of his choice of home.

"I suppose it does seem a bit odd. I think you'll see why when you get there, though. And climbing four flights of stairs every day helps to keep me fit, especially when I've got stuff to bring up."

She was puffing by the time she reached his front door. Stepping inside, the first item to greet her was a signed Liverpool football shirt hanging in a frame next to the front door. Dropping her shoes into a corner, she grimaced slightly: this was obviously going to be some boyish bachelor pad. Half expecting to find a room filled with dusty black furniture dotted with empty beer cans, sweaty sports kit and porno magazines, she followed him along the narrow hallway.

Contrary to her preconceptions, the living room was light, neat and welcoming. There was a comfortably inviting sofa and a leather armchair; a cream rug that was clean enough to suggest that he wasn't in the habit of wearing muddy trainers indoors; and a dust-free coffee table on which three remote control handsets lay side by side like lines on a tally chart.

"Wow. You were right when you said you were capable of doing your own cleaning. Unless you were fibbing and the Help has just left, of course. You've got me wondering now if you've baked me a nice Victoria Sponge?"

"Why, is it your birthday?"

"Not until October, but we could always pretend."

"Scones are more my thing, anyway. I've got a nice, light touch."

She cast her eyes around the room, trying not to think about what his touch felt like. "You'll have to show me how to bake one of these days. We could be like Demi Moore and Patrick Swayze in *Ghost*, only with flour and butter instead of clay."

A long oak shelving unit stood against one wall, bedecked with orderly rows of books and DVDs. Such was the impression of neatness, she wondered if they had been ordered alphabetically, and was absurdly relieved when an inquisitive glance revealed that they weren't. To her surprise, the television and sound system didn't dominate the room, and there seemed to be no sign of a games console. She had been expecting an enormous home cinema system with a fifty inch plasma screen and an X-Box.

A huge seascape on canvas faced the door, above the sofa. Its deep blues, greens and greys, depicting wind and waves in tumultuous abandon, contributed a sense of drama to the otherwise measured simplicity of the room.

Venturing further in, she saw at once why he had chosen his fourth floor flat. French doors led out onto a tiny balcony, edged by glass panels. The long voile curtains were parted, revealing a magnificent view over the city.

"That's fantastic!" She marvelled at the vista, pressing her nose against the cold pane of glass. "I can see the Millennium Stadium and the Bay from here."

Tom emerged from another room with an armful of towels.

"I thought you'd like it. You can see a lot more in daylight. It's not close enough to get a bird's eye view of the rugby matches, unfortunately – but still, it's not bad. Shall I take your coat?"

She peeled it off her wet shoulders, teeth chattering again. Her top clung to her skin, leaving little to the imagination. His adam's apple bobbed as he swaddled her in a towel.

"You need to get out of those wet things," he murmured, kissing her forehead.

"I've nothing to change into… And I'll be worried if you've got a stash of women's clothes in your wardrobe."

The mischievous glint she liked so much lit his eyes. "None of my dresses would fit you," he said.

Heading back down the hallway into the bathroom, he set the shower going and came out carrying a towelling bathrobe.

"I know this will be too big as well, but at least you'll be warm. Go and have your shower. If you pass your wet things out, I'll put them in the drier."

She did as she was told, for once. She had had such a soaking from the torrential rain, even her knickers were wet. She had to smile at the irony of him handling her carefully chosen underwear like this. She had planned to be wearing it when he glimpsed it for the first time.

"Don't put my bra in the tumble drier, will you?" she called from the bathroom as she tossed her damp clothes out. "The underwiring might come out and clog up the mechanism."

By the time she emerged from the bathroom she felt warm and clean, but self-conscious without her makeup. She had failed to find any conditioner in his bathroom, despite hunting nosily through the cupboard, and consequently had struggled to force her comb through her tangled hair.

A glance in the mirror had reminded her, disappointingly, that her skin was too pale and freckly without a mask of foundation and blusher, her lashes too fair without mascara. Perhaps he wouldn't be so keen on her now, seeing her like this. She sighed and snuggled into his bathrobe, rolling up the sleeves to find her hands. It smelled faintly of aftershave: wrapping herself in it felt surprisingly intimate.

Tom came out of the small kitchen carrying a mug of tea. He had taken off his wet clothes and pulled on some jeans, draping her bra over a radiator and throwing the rest of their wet things into the washer-drier, but he hadn't yet put on a clean shirt.

Transfixed by his chest, she barely noticed the hot drink, and forgot all about her lack of make-up. When experiencing that strong torso up close, she hadn't realised how good it would look unclothed. He was muscular, but not pumped up. There was a fine scattering of fair hair across his chest, darkening as it trailed downwards over his flat stomach towards his belt. No wonder they call it a happy trail, she thought. She'd be downright ecstatic if she could track her way down there.

"I didn't know if you take milk or sugar, so I just made ordinary builder's tea."

"Thanks, that's perfect."

She tore her gaze upwards to meet his eyes. The expression she saw there did nothing to alleviate the flush spreading across her cheeks and throat. To cover her sudden awkwardness, she took refuge in banter.

"I didn't use any of your shower gel. I didn't think V6 Turbo Diesel Boy Racer Sport, or whatever it was, would be my kind of fragrance."

"It's a man thing," he replied, leaning comfortably against the door jamb cradling his mug of tea. "We like to smell sporty; women like to make themselves smell of flowers or food. I've never understood, personally, why anyone would want to step out of the shower smelling of strawberry milkshake or lemon meringue."

She perched on the arm of the sofa, watching him as she blew softly across the steaming mug of tea.

"Don't you like your women to be fruity?" she asked with mock nonchalance, feeling the little buzz of enjoyment she always felt when she made him smile.

"Believe me, Meg: you don't need to smother yourself in lemon or strawberry to be good enough to eat."

She melted a little under the warm appreciation in his gaze. She was first to look away, pleased with his flirtatious response.

"Have you got a hairdryer I could use?"

"A hairdryer?" he repeated blankly.

"Yes. It's a small hand-held electrical device that blows out hot air."

"I know what it is, but do I look like someone who needs one?" He rubbed a hand through his short hair, making it stick up. It was almost dry already.

"Actually, I'm quite pleased that you don't," she said. "My last boyfriend used to take longer getting ready to go out than I did. He had a hairdryer, straighteners, mousse, gel, everything."

"Oh? So you generally go for men who spend ages on their hair… Is that a subtle way of telling me I'm not your type?"

"Let's just say my taste seems to be improving."

He put down his mug with the merest hint of a smile and strode out of the front door barefoot. She followed as far as the doorway, ducking back inside when she saw him chatting to a woman in a flat across the landing. She couldn't hear much, and didn't want to be seen wet-haired and huddled into a bathrobe that was several sizes too big for her, so went back inside the flat and put her empty mug down on the coffee table. He had little mats to protect the surface, she noted, making sure to use one.

A moment later he was back, a hairdryer in his hand.

"I'm surprised she didn't drag you inside and keep you there as her sex slave, going over there with no shirt on like that."

He paused, clearly tickled by the suggestion. "She'd be more likely to drag you in there, actually. I wouldn't be to her taste at all."

Megan shrugged. Gay or straight, only a corpse could remain unmoved by that torso.

While Tom was in the bathroom, Megan roughly finger-dried her hair, noting the neatness and sparse, modern style of his flat – quite the opposite of her own junkshop clutter. Her place resembled student digs, complete with text books, although these days she had ditched the joss sticks and empty pizza boxes. When he emerged, still barefoot and with his hair damp and tousled, but now dressed in jeans and a simple white shirt, she was perusing his CD collection.

"Ah, do I pass muster in the CD department? A man's musical taste is like a mirror into his soul. Maybe even more than his choice of curry."

"You have quite eclectic taste, don't you? Everything from rock to classical to Britpop to indie – even a bit of folk. And it's nice to see that you like some of the Welsh bands…" She traced along the shelves with her finger. "Catatonia, the Manics, the Stereophonics… I'm glad it's not all Iron Maiden and Metallica, or something."

"Hmmm, no. They had to go to make room for my Barry Manilow collection."

She chuckled. There were no Barry Manilow CDs on the shelf. She moved along to examine his DVDs, and he folded his arms, apparently awaiting her verdict.

"Your DVD collection is more disappointing. Lots of action movies…Sci-fi…"

"What were you expecting? *Beaches*? *Steel Magnolias*?"

"There's no need to be facetious. Did you know, by the way, that facetious is one of only a few English words containing all the vowels in the correct order…?" She ignored his grin and continued to survey his DVDs. "Good Lord – you need to get out more. How many documentaries about great goals and terrific tries can one man watch?"

"I promise you, it's impossible to have too many. There are some epic tries on those discs: I particularly like it when the England team scores against Wales."

"Hmmm…. You should be careful, I'll go off you if you make too many comments like that. Still, it seems your interests aren't limited to films and sport. You've got a few nature documentaries here, too."

"I find animals very interesting. Particularly their mating habits. Did you know, male dolphins ejaculate in only twelve seconds?"

"I once had a boyfriend like that. I wouldn't look to dolphins for a role model, if I were you."

"Don't worry. I can last – oh, at least twice as long as a dolphin."

She was getting used to his sense of humour: the glint in his eye belied his poker face.

"Twenty-four seconds? It's lucky you went into teaching, not PR or marketing, Mr Field. You're not selling yourself very well."

He seemed to be trying very hard to keep a straight face as she twitched back the edge of the curtain to admire the view.

"Rest assured, Miss Parry. It's athletes who think it's good to be fast. I'm a Rugby Union man: I can keep going for the whole eighty minutes plus extra time."

"As long as you get a ten minute break in the middle, presumably?"

He padded over to stand behind her at the window and slid his arms around her. As he nuzzled against her ear, she felt a hot jolt of excitement.

"With you, I'd never want to stop. Not even for a minute," he murmured against her neck.

Her pulse quickened as she absorbed his words. He wasn't joking now. He continued, his voice soft and deep near her ear.

"You know, your hair is gorgeous, all mussed up like that. It's always beautiful, even when it's tied back; but I do love your curls. They looked like that the first time we kissed."

"Did they? Perhaps you should remind me what that was like?" Turning within the circle of his arms, she pressed herself against him and tilted her face upwards for his kiss.

He bent eagerly to oblige. As their kisses soon grew more passionate he dropped to the floor and pulled her down to join him.

"That's better," he said. "I don't want to be distracted by my neck aching."

"I've been called a pain in the neck before," she said. Hungry for more of him, she tugged his shirt out of his waistband and deftly undid the buttons. "It was hardly worth you putting this on…"

"I disagree. It was definitely worth it, to have you take it off."

With his chest bare again, she pushed at him until he yielded and lay on his back, then leaned over him, exploring his exposed skin with her hands and mouth, relishing her power to make him groan and close his eyes. Soon they dispensed with clothes altogether, and he tipped her back onto the carpet to carry out intoxicating explorations of his own.

"Will you think badly of me for making sure there was a packet of condoms in my handbag tonight?" she asked, only half joking.

He gasped, pretending to be shocked. "How many did you get?"

She frowned, puzzled. "Three, why?"

"Only three? Disgraceful. In fact, you should be ashamed of yourself, young lady. I bought twelve."

"Twelve! You're planning a busy evening." With a saucy grin she unfastened his belt. "Better get cracking, then."

They made love right there, on the floor of the lamp-lit room with the panorama of city lights twinkling outside in the cold January air. Afterwards they lay like spoons in a drawer, legs entwined and with Tom's arm draped around her. Contentment enfolded her like a warm blanket, making her throw caution to the winds.

"I know it's probably much too soon to tell you this… but what the hell, I suspect you've worked it out already. I've fallen in love with you, Tom Field," she said.

She had more or less admitted it earlier, in any case. Perhaps it was reckless to say the words aloud, but she couldn't help but acknowledge the strength of her emotions. No one else had ever made her feel such longing, or such completeness. The first time with a new man was so often a disappointment; she hadn't expected this time to feel so different.

It took him a while to respond, making her heartbeat quicken again. Had she said too much? But eventually he spoke, murmuring the words into her hair.

"I think I'm falling for you, too."

There was hesitancy in his words, but also honesty. It was enough for now, she decided, from this man whose heart had been broken only months before. She kissed him again.

"I think I've got carpet burns on my knees," he said. "They're really sore. So is my back, where you dug your nails in. I'm glad you indulge your urges - I've reaped the benefits this evening. But now I'm realising there's a price to be paid."

He shifted slightly to ease his weight onto a less tender area of skin.

"You can't be a wimp if you want to be with me. Toughen up, Field. Anyway, I can match you for carpet burns: I've got a big one on my back. I'll let you kiss it better later... Maybe we should try the bed next time?"

He nodded, obviously struggling to keep his face serious. "Doing it standing up should be safe. In the shower, for instance. Or against the wall."

"We never did manage to do it on the kitchen counter. It would be a shame not to try that."

"How about on the sofa?"

"Great. How about all of the above? We've got fourteen more goes before one of us has to run to the chemist."

"Mmmm. Let's get started. You can rub ointment onto my wounds later."

He jumped up decisively, making her giggle by yanking her to her feet. As he dragged her by the hand to the bedroom and pulled her down on top of him on the bed, she felt a surge of delight.

Being with Tom promised to be a lot of fun.

∞ ∞ ∞

Waking the next morning, Tom was thirsty and ravenously hungry but reluctant to unwrap himself from the delightful warmth of Megan's body. He kissed her hair softly, revelling in the clean scent of it. He marvelled that she was here, in his bed, and that sex with her had been so good.

In his previous relationships there had always been a piece of the jigsaw missing, and yet he hadn't even realised it until now. With Megan, that piece had suddenly and surprisingly slotted perfectly into place. He couldn't define what it was that made the difference, whether it was her vivacity or her honesty, her determination to be strong or her sense of humour. She made him feel good about himself again, that he had something to offer. It wasn't only the way she responded to his touch, as if he'd turned her to jelly, but the way she looked at him, the way she gave as good as she got when he teased her.   Was it wise to let her into his life and his heart? He had a funny feeling it was already too late to ask himself that. But part of him was scared. He didn't know how he would cope if she should reject him as Erica did.

As he lay watching her, she stirred and her eyes opened, widening when she saw him.

"Hello there," she murmured happily against his chest.

"Hello, you. Did you sleep well?"

"Mmmm." She rolled over in the crook of his arm, feeling for his feet with hers. "I did sleep well, thanks – apart from being woken up in the middle of the night by a sex-crazed maniac."

"Really?"

For a moment, he wondered if his nocturnal advances had offended her. She had been more than willing at the time, he remembered, had responded pretty enthusiastically in fact.

He covered his sudden attack of doubt with a joke. "Lucky you. That must have been quite an experience."

"It was. Fortunately, he was rather good at it so I let him carry on."

With her face hidden against his arm, he couldn't read her expression.

"Any regrets?" he asked.

"Plenty."

Shit. That didn't sound good. Maybe one night would be all they'd have. He felt suddenly cold.

She stretched out like a cat, allowing the duvet to slip from her breasts. "Not eating last night, and not bringing a toothbrush, for a start. I'm starving, and I bet my breath is rank this morning."

Thank God for that. He cupped an exposed breast in his hand and kissed her deeply to prove her wrong.

"Ooh, hello." Her sleepy eyes widened as her hip touched him. "Seems you'll be pole-vaulting out of bed this morning."

He glanced up from the trail of soft kisses he had begun to drop between her ear and throat. "I am a sportsman, after all. Pole vaulting is only one of my many athletic talents."

"Hmmmm…. You're clearly ready for more action, Mr Field. Does this foreplay mean we're going for a personal best of four times in twelve hours?"

"I'm game if you are," he said huskily against her nipple, making it harden in anticipation.

With a shove, she pushed him back onto the mattress and straddled him, the wildness of her long, uncombed hair giving her a wanton appearance that made him desire her all the more.

"So, Mr Sportsman. If three times makes you a Hat-Trick Hero, what would four times make you?" She slid her hips a little lower, teasing him.

His eyes gleamed as she bent to kiss him again. "I believe the technical term for that is 'the luckiest man in Cardiff'."

Chapter Ten

Diamond Jubilee Bank Holiday:
Tuesday 5ᵗʰ June 2012
Saunton, North Devon

How was it possible, Megan wondered, for a relationship to slide from magic to misery in only a few years? Her anger at Tom's desertion ebbed away as she waited in his beloved van, remembering how they had been in the early days. Now, she felt an acute sense of loss: they had been so perfect together back at the beginning. He had been considerate, exciting, funny and sensual.

He was an unselfish lover, more intent upon giving pleasure than receiving it. Her skin had thrilled at the anticipation of his touch. Sometimes he teased her, pinning her down easily and hovering his mouth just above her eager flesh, taunting her with his breath. He enjoyed nothing more than provoking her until she writhed from his grip and dug in her nails, pleading for more. She was always well rewarded: he made her pleasure his mission.

In those early days, she had loved exploring him, discovering which sensations aroused him: the places he liked to be nuzzled; the times when a feather-light touch would make him beg or push her off to punish her with kisses. The times when a scratch or gentle bite would leave him groaning helplessly. She had never before had a lover who devoted so much energy to making their time together so mutually pleasurable.

Where had that irresistible man gone? How had he been replaced by the morose and uncommunicative figure whose desires now seemed like just another domestic chore making unreasonable demands upon her?

He had demanded fidelity and honesty. He had promised never to walk out on her. Yet he had gone, that curt and neutral note he left against the kettle his only attempt at honest communication. He hadn't felt able to speak to her about why he needed to "get his head together". Was it her? Was it the baby? Was it work? Worse, was it because he had found someone else? It would go against everything he had ever promised her if it was.

Why hadn't she listened while she had the chance? Perhaps she had let things slide into resentment and antagonism for too long. Perhaps his will to attempt to open the lines of communication with her had been sapped by her rejections.

Hot, frightened tears sprang to her eyes. She tried to concentrate on the view from the window, gulping them back, but that just made her nose run and soon she was sobbing and fumbling blindly in her bag for a tissue as her chest ached from so much pent-up emotion.

If he had been miserable enough to leave her and the girls, maybe he would never come back. Her children would grow up as she and Bethan had, without a father to nurture and protect them. There was still a defiant part of her that said she didn't need him: her mother had coped and so could they. But her memories of the man Tom had been made her want that man back, if there was any way to make it happen.

They'd had disputes even in the early days, like the time when he had told her about Erica's betrayal. Even then he had done his best to avoid face-to-face confrontation, preferring to avoid her altogether rather than run the risk of an argument; but back then she had been able to win him round.

This time was different. There'd been a kind of steady antipathy growing between them for months. But she couldn't identify anything in particular that could have triggered his sudden desertion. If this was conflict avoidance, then it was on a drastic scale.

Her greatest fear was that it might be too late to save their marriage. He had turned his back on a woman he had ceased to love before, so it wasn't beyond his capability if he no longer loved his wife. What if he cut her off as he had Erica?

They had already been engaged when she first fell pregnant accidentally: Alys had been born only four months after their wedding. And now this third baby had been an accident too, the result of Megan getting heartily drunk on her thirty-fifth birthday and forgetting to take her contraceptive pill. Maybe he felt trapped, that his life hadn't followed the course he had planned for it to take?

When she thought about it, her birthday in October had probably been the last time they had really been passionate with one another. He had tried to initiate sex many times since then, but tiredness had been an issue for her in this pregnancy and she had found it beyond her to respond in anything but the most perfunctory way. For the past five or six months, she hadn't even bothered to do that, but had spurned his advances and accused him of being selfish and oversexed.

One such occasion came to mind.

"It's as if a tap has turned off in you, or a switch has been flicked," he complained, clicking his fingers to illustrate the point. "You've gone from being pretty much constantly up for it, to being completely disinterested. You can't blame me for finding it hard to turn off my feelings just like that. You should be pleased that I want you so much."

He had tried to caress her cheek, but she'd brushed his hand away impatiently, focussing on the many tasks she had to do instead of hearing him out. His desire, which once had excited her and made her feel cherished and confident in her own allure, now seemed like an irritant, even a burden. She had treated him like a pest, rather than trying to meet him halfway. Perhaps, she now wondered, if she had made more effort to hold him, to listen to him, they could have worked through this phase with more understanding of each other's needs?

Regret roused a fresh flow of tears and more tissues were pressed into service as the floodgates of emotion opened. Eyes puffy, throat painful from crying, in one of those lulls that intersperses bouts of weeping, she gazed out across the car park towards the path to the beach.

The afternoon had worn on. Several families headed back to their cars with their deckchairs and picnic bags; their young children would need their tea soon. One couple towed a toddler along in a little red wagon stacked high with buckets, spades, towels and mats. The wheels were clogged up with sand and pulling it along seemed like heavy work for the boy's father, who was also laden with a brightly-striped windbreak folded under one arm. Although she couldn't hear them from inside the van, it was obvious that the little boy was grizzling at having to leave the beach, while his father remained grim-faced and his mother tried vainly to reason with him. Megan sympathised: she'd had her own fair share of toddler tantrums to deal with. In another eighteen months or so she'd no doubt be fending off a few more.

She stroked her bump at the thought: as if answering her, she felt the prod of an elbow or foot under her hand, and her belly rose and shifted as the baby moved. As always, the movement reassured her: the baby had been quiet that afternoon.

Up the path came an elderly couple, hobbling slowly along, hand in hand. The man looked almost comical, his long socks and smart shirt incongruous with his shorts and sandals, while his companion seemed to have trouble with her legs or hips, as she winced with every step. But his patient glances and supportive hand under her elbow made his devotion clear. Megan's eyes pricked again. Would she and Tom be able to sustain their marriage into old age?

Another couple had come strolling up from the beach, barefoot. Each carried a long surfboard under one arm, and their wetsuits had been rolled down to hang from their waists. The young woman was tanned, long-limbed and blonde with a gorgeous figure: slim, and clearly very fit. The triangles of her bikini top, exposed by the removal of the top half of her wetsuit, left little to the imagination. Even from this distance Megan observed several men casting admiring glances in her direction, clearly envious of her partner. She only had eyes for her companion, though: she kept touching his arm, brushing against him as if by accident, and smiling.

Only half paying attention, Megan glanced to see what he was like. He had been looking down at his feet when she first noticed them; now he was looking away, towards something in the shop or café, so she couldn't tell if he was as attractive as the girl. He was neither as deeply tanned nor as bright-haired, but he looked pretty fit: he had just the kind of strong chest and shoulders Meg liked. Not too hairy; a nice, flat stomach. No wonder the girl was so interested. He turned his head back towards the car park and although he was squinting into the sun she knew at once that his eyes would be a bright shade of aquamarine. She knew that face better than she knew her own.

Tom.

Megan swallowed hard, the hairs rising on her arms as if a chilly wind had blasted across her path. Her face reddened and froze, mask-like, as her brain struggled to process what she was seeing.

Was this young blonde the reason Tom had come to Devon without his wife and children? If so, it would be completely out of character and contrary to all the values that he normally stood for.

But then, leaving as he had was also uncharacteristic. Perhaps anything was possible.

With the moment of meeting him now imminent, she was suddenly gripped with anxiety. Would he be angry with her for following him to Devon? Would he be embarrassed at his heavily pregnant wife turning up to cramp his style, interrupting his fun like a middle-aged mother hounding a delinquent teenager? Would he make a scene? Would he choose the flirtatious blonde over his wife and children? Might he tell her it was over?

She was torn. Should she prepare to fight for her man like a wildcat, or step back and give him the freedom he seemed to crave? She couldn't hope to compete against the blonde's looks and sportiness. She could only hope that six years of marriage meant something to him.

It was too late to regret coming all the way down here now: there could be no going back, no avoiding whatever decision he might choose to make with regard to their future. She wiped her face with a tissue, quickly checked in a mirror that it wasn't too ravaged by weeping, and clambered out of the camper van. With her hands cradled protectively under her bump, Megan waited beside Greta for her husband and the girl at his side to approach.

Chapter Eleven

The previous day: Monday 4th June

2012

Saunton, North Devon

Tom had spent the whole day on the beach, and his body ached from the battering of the waves by the time the surf school wrapped up for the day. His surfing skills had improved immeasurably in the few days he had spent at Saunton. He had a sportsman's natural strength, grace and balance, and these had helped him learn the techniques required to paddle out, then pop-up to a standing position to ride the breakers in towards the shore. He had learned about water safety, surfing etiquette, currents and rip tides; he had been taught about the features of the board such as the fin, rails and leash. He had learned how to turn his board and was beginning to understand the characteristics of different waves, though this would no doubt take much longer to master. Most importantly, he was learning to judge which waves would give him the best chance of getting upright and riding in towards the shore, the ones which would be powerful enough and break at the right time.

Garin had been right about surfing: it was both exhausting and exhilarating. Tom fell off far more than he succeeded, but the drive to improve spurred him on to keep practicing and to get back out into deeper water, time and time again, to catch yet another wave. He felt a rush of adrenalin when he managed to stand and keep his balance to ride a wave, however briefly: the level of focus and concentration required to stay steady on the unstable board banished all other thoughts and concerns from his mind.

The physical and mental challenges surfing presented were a remarkably effective stress-buster. He had laughed this week more than he had in months, mostly at himself and his failed attempts to ride the board. He had pushed himself to take on the new challenge, and felt his physical strength improving even while his muscles ached. He returned to Greta each night tired out, just about able to manage the short drive back to the farm where he was staying, to grab a bite to eat and then sit outside, enjoying the tranquillity and expanse of Devon sky.

He had spent most of his evenings alone, glad of the solitude back at the farm. Garin had recommended it as a place to camp cheaply. It had only the most basic facilities, but Tom wasn't troubled by the lack of amenities: as long as he could park up on a level spot of land and get a shower to wash the sand and salt out of his ears at the end of each day, he was content. Away from the city, without the street lighting, cars and buildings that crowded him, the multitude of stars punctuating the darkness helped him gain a sense of the smallness of his troubles compared with the vastness of the sky.

Time on his own gave him the opportunity he needed to reflect on the feelings that had driven him to flee reality and head towards the coast. He had even played his guitar a few times: the concentration required to make his unpractised fingers co-operate was a welcome distraction from other thoughts. Alone in the field in the clear twilight, he felt none of the self-consciousness that he would have felt playing in front of someone else. He picked out old, familiar tracks and new songs that he had recently heard, occasionally sipping his bottle of beer, finding in the pleasure of making music an outlet for the emotions that had been building in him over the preceding months.

Fresh air and exercise made him so exhausted that by the time he set up the double bed in the van each night, he barely had the energy to climb into his sleeping bag before falling asleep. It was so peaceful not being disturbed by the girls, or by Megan sitting bolt upright in the middle of the night yelling with cramp, waking him with a jolt to beg him to rub her calf or push against her foot to ease the symptoms. Usually he hated sleeping alone, and struggled to settle without Megan's warm body against his back; but here his slumber, although punctuated with strange dreams, was deeper and more refreshing than the sleep he had been getting at home of late.

Lounging in his canvas chair in the cool evening air, watching the pale blue of the sky deepen to twilight grey, his thoughts would turn to Megan.

They had been married for six of the seven years they had been together, and in the early days it had been wonderful. He had counted himself the luckiest man alive to have found a wife who excited him, desired him, made him laugh and restored his belief in himself after Erica's betrayal. Megan was lively, intelligent, funny and passionate. He had been in awe of her strength of spirit and her indefatigable determination and resilience: although she was physically small, she was as stubborn as a mule and in some ways much stronger than he. He adored her feistiness and vivacity. He loved catching her off guard and making her laugh. He loved seeing desire in her eyes. The speed with which he fell in love with her had astounded him.

Within weeks of their first meeting, he knew that being with her was different. He had been in love before, more than once, but his feelings for Megan were on an entirely new plane. He had been with Erica for four years without ever feeling ready to propose marriage to her. But he knew almost from the very beginning with Megan that he wanted to cement their relationship with a deeper level of commitment.

He thought about her constantly, missing her when they couldn't be together, lonely the moment they said goodbye. They regularly stayed overnight at each other's flats almost from the start: not officially moving in together, but unwilling to be apart for a moment longer than necessary. He craved the smell of her, the sight of her and the warm softness of her skin. To detach himself felt like a wound, as if a chunk of his flesh had been gouged away.

Initially she was more cautious than he, despite having been the first to declare her feelings. She assumed that he would eventually tire of her, so insisted on arriving at work separately. She was concerned to maintain a professional demeanour and to avoid staffroom gossip, even though rumours of their relationship had spread like a bush fire among both teachers and pupils at St Dyfrig's High.

Ironically, the more she asserted her separateness and ability to fend for herself, the more he wanted to look after her. She was fiercely proud, continuing to baulk at allowing him to pay for her meals or drinks.

He recalled when, several months after their relationship began, the time had come to renew the annual lease on her rented flat. She mentioned it one evening in passing, not anticipating that he would seize the chance to try to persuade her to move in with him.

She had been reluctant to agree to this proposition at first.

"What will happen when you get bored with me? I'll have nowhere to live."

"Meg, are you serious? I can't imagine ever being bored with you. Exhausted, perhaps; but never bored."

Still unconvinced, her brow creased in a frown. "We've only been together for six months. People will think we're mad."

Abruptly, he put down his knife and fork and leaned closer across the table to command her full attention.

"I *am* mad about you, in case you hadn't noticed. Six months has been too long to wait already: don't make me wait even longer. Even though you hog the duvet, I want you in my bed every night. Even though you're evil until you've had your first cup of coffee, I want to wake up with you every morning. I want to see your toothbrush in the beaker next to mine and your toiletries in the bathroom cabinet, instead of that hideous pink toilet bag constantly cluttering up my window sill. I want to have to make space in the wardrobe for your clothes, and I want to grumble about how your shoes are taking over the flat. I want to have to go to Ikea with you to buy shelf units for all those Penguin Classics of yours, and then stand back while you insist on building them without any help. I want to argue over the remote control with you and fight over whose turn it is to unload the dishwasher, instead of us constantly feeling like visitors in each other's homes. I want my home to be yours... No, actually, that's wrong. I want it to be ours."

She had been staring as he spoke, the fervency of his words apparently making her forget to chew. She swallowed her mouthful of steak in a lump and put down her fork, thoughtful. He could accept that for her, moving in together felt like a huge step, taking their relationship onto a new level; but they spent almost every minute of spare time together anyway. Moving in would save the forward planning of wondering what to take to her place each evening, to ensure he had everything he needed for work the next day. One of them usually ended up forgetting something, when staying with the other. Having to dash home for his razor or a clean shirt on the way to work was an infernal nuisance. Moving in together made perfect sense.

"I'll pay you rent," she said at last.

He shrugged, focussing on twirling spaghetti around his fork to avoid revealing the elation in his eyes. "I expected no less."

"We'll split the housework equally between us," she insisted.

He pondered her suggestion for a moment as he chewed. "Hmmm. Why don't we just agree for now that whoever gets home first should make a start on dinner? The whole cleaning rota thing is a bit too much like student flatmates."

"Okay." But having agreed, she looked flustered. "I'll keep the place tidy, not clutter it up with too much of my stuff."

He paused, fork halfway to his mouth, and stared at her. "Let's not be unrealistic about this. I don't expect you to make any promises you won't be able to keep – ouch! That was uncalled-for." He rubbed his shin under the table, laughing.

"Look, are you really sure you want me messing up your place? My stuff getting in your way? Long hairs in the plug hole and my undies drying on all the radiators? Paperbacks and scented candles dotted around the bathroom?"

Knowing how much she loved his eyes, he exploited them shamelessly now, sending a look of intense desire across the table.

"For the chance to cuddle up with you on the sofa every evening, make love with you every night and wake up with you in my arms every morning? I think I could put up with anything to have that."

She would have needed a heart of granite to resist him in those days. Within a fortnight she had moved in.

Time passed, and he had been thrilled at the news of her first pregnancy. Although it had happened earlier than they had intended, they were already engaged, and he was overjoyed at the knowledge that he would be a father. No secret termination this time around, and no doubt over his role in the creation of this child. He felt such pride in being able to provide a secure home and family for Meg and their little daughter, there were times when he thought he might burst with it.

Three year-old Nia had been very much planned. When Megan suspected that she was pregnant that second time, they watched together as the blue line appeared in the window of the pregnancy test stick and hugged each other in delight and awe.

Now there would be a new baby arriving soon, and while Tom had come to accept the idea, he couldn't help but worry about how they would cope with three small children. He had made a decision, not yet discussed with Megan, to take steps to ensure that this baby would be his last. He was too old now to ever want to face the prospect of new fatherhood again, and in any case, two accidental pregnancies was more than enough for any couple. She would just have to accept that this baby would complete their family.

It was sad to think how far their relationship had deteriorated. He knew he must shoulder a great deal of the blame for being morose in recent months, not the cheerful man Megan had married. But in fairness, she shared some responsibility for the change in him. Their sexual relationship had ground to a standstill some eight months earlier, when she first started making excuses to avoid any physical intimacy. He'd heard them all: she was tired; she had had a stressful day at work; she'd had enough to do attending to the girls' needs all day without attending to his. Looking back, it was easy to ascribe her tiredness and moods to her pregnancy, but he hadn't known she was pregnant for the first few months.

As much as he had tried to be understanding, respectful and patient, he had come to feel a painful sense of rejection. For him, making love was an affirmation of his desirability and a way to connect intimately with her. It was a way to confirm and be reassured of their continuing love and mutual attraction. He could have been content without sex if they had been able to maintain some level of physical intimacy, but she interpreted any approach on his part as an attempt to initiate intercourse, and accused him of being insensitive and obsessed with sex. He couldn't even put his arm around her these days without her making an excuse to shrug it off.

Without any positive response from her, he withdrew for fear of being rebuffed. He was cautious around her, giving less of himself, wary of her moods. He tried to be sympathetic to how she must be feeling; but, finding his own needs and feelings dismissed over the course of months, he came to feel frustrated and insecure. The scars left by Erica's infidelity, which he had believed were long healed, reopened and in his darkest moments he even asked himself if Megan could be having an affair.

Ironically, he never found her so beautiful as when she was pregnant. Each time, the ripe fullness of her curves seemed to him exquisitely erotic. The tight smoothness of the skin over her belly and the swollen magnificence of her breasts seemed so gorgeous, so tactile. Her flesh was hotter, her hair more glorious, her senses so readily stimulated. During her first two pregnancies, he had loved nothing more than stroking and massaging her skin, kneading the knotted muscles in her aching back, kissing her belly and whispering to the baby within. But this time, she had been so different. This time they were like duelling battleships, launching salvos of spite targeted to strike at the heart.

They had been arguing frequently, and had both engaged in periods of sulking, barely speaking to one another. She had lost none of her feistiness over the years. In the early days he had found it a charming trait, but now, without the outlet of their mutual passion to help them resolve their disputes, he often found her exasperating. They snapped at each other where once they would have encouraged one another. He guessed that she now thought him a sour old curmudgeon, and he found himself living up to her expectations.

"Have you always been grumpy, Daddy?" Nia had asked him innocently a few weeks ago during their evening meal. He laughed it off, but noted the scornful twist to Megan's lips and resented it. No, I haven't always been grumpy, he thought: you can blame your mother for that, in part. He didn't say the words aloud, but she had made it obvious that the coolness of his expression infuriated her.

Remembering this now, Tom felt the return of the despondency that had driven him to flee to Devon in the first place. He thought he had shaken it off, but it seemed it had only been lurking in the background, waiting for a setback to pull him down again.

He would be the first to admit that in all the most important ways he was truly blessed. Yet he had begun to feel he was experiencing life through a grey veil of melancholy that sapped his spirit and made it difficult to experience any real pleasure or delight in anything. It felt almost as if some part of him inside was dying: there was an emptiness in him that nothing seemed to fill: neither fatherhood, his wife's love, friendships, nor work.

There were too many people and things demanding a piece of him, too many worries causing him sleepless nights. He was disappointed in himself for succumbing to despondency when he had so much to be thankful for. Guiltily, he felt he couldn't live up to other people's expectations of him as a manager, husband, father or son. The stress of so many demanding roles had robbed him of his former easy confidence.

It was a downward spiral: the gloomier he became, the more conscious he was that he wasn't much fun anymore. The more aware of this he became, the lower his self-esteem sank. In work, he had to maintain a professional demeanour. And he kept up a jolly façade for his daughters' benefit, finding it easier with them to pretend that everything was as it should be.

He was like an actor, playing the part of the man he felt he should be. With his father it was impossible to break a lifetime's habit of filial duty, and he didn't feel he could burden the old man by telling him how he was feeling. So, unfortunately, it was only with Megan that he felt he could let his mask slip and allow his true state of mind to show.

How ironic: the person whose esteem he valued most had borne the brunt of his irritability. Poor Megan, contending with a busy and demanding life of her own, had been subjected to sarcasm, anger, impatience, resentment and bitterness. Thinking about it made his head feel hot with shame. He could only hope that this time in Devon would help him relax and feel more positive, so that he could be a better husband.

Earlier tonight he had made an effort to be more sociable, accepting the surfing instructors' invitation to join them for an evening barbecue on a local privately-owned beach. The idea of eating freshly caught mackerel cooked over a fire, and relaxing with a few beers in pleasant company, had been appealing. The beach was only about a mile and a half from his pitch at the farm, so he had no need to drive, but strolled with a couple of four-packs of beer in his hands and a fleece jacket over his shoulders to meet the rest of the group at around eight o-clock.

One of the instructors, Jess, was a young Australian blonde with a tanned beach body like something from a celebrity magazine. She was the first to greet him when he descended, following the glow of their fire from the cliff above.

"Hey, Tom! Down here!" she called, with a wide smile and a wave. She looked sensational, her cut-off Daisy Dukes showing off a pair of long, tanned legs that a film star might envy. He suspected she wasn't unaware of the sidelong glances from the men around the campfire as they struggled to keep their eyes off her pert behind.

"What took you so long?" she asked as he approached. "We've eaten all the fish already." Laughing at his uncertain expression, she pointed out some foil parcels nestling on stones at the edge of the fire. "Nah, just kidding. There's loads left. Dig in and help yourself. Are those beers cold? No? Swap them with some from the Esky."

She indicated a cool box full of cans, and he gratefully exchanged his beer for a cold one.

"Cheers," he said, cracking open the ring pull and nodding to the other surfers.

Settling down on a picnic rug, he sipped his lager and soaked up the banter around the fire. It seemed the other surf-school rookies were enjoying the lessons as much as he. A couple of the younger men were clearly infatuated with Jess, hardly taking their eyes off her while she laughed and dished out generous helpings of deliciously fresh fish and baked potatoes to everyone. They ate with their fingers, using squares of foil for plates, blowing on their fingertips in between mouthfuls of the steaming food. Finally, with their stomachs satisfied and everyone mellow, one of the guys played softly on a guitar. Another took out a tobacco tin and began rolling a joint.

Tom stretched out on his back on the tartan rug and gazed up at the stars. Let them carry on. He had no desire to spoil their fun, but couldn't have felt less interested in participating. They were a pleasant enough bunch of kids, but he had little in common with them beyond an interest in learning to surf. While they discussed their hopes for when they finished university, or their plans for the summer holidays, his thoughts were with Megan, Alys and Nia. Surrounded by young, friendly faces, he felt old and alone.

With the baby due in only three weeks' time, he knew his responsibilities were about to increase and there would soon be no time for self-indulgence. It was only right that they could have no understanding of the weight of obligation he felt as the main provider for his family. They had plenty of time and a myriad of opportunities open to them before they would begin to feel as he did. He'd lie here quietly, with the pungent aroma of weed and campfire drifting past his nostrils, and let them carry on in blissful ignorance of what responsibility meant.

At last he figured it was probably time to start heading back to the van. He lay in the dusky twilight after the golden-red glow of the sunset had filtered away, contemplating getting up as he gazed at the rising moon's brightness. The softly rushing waves at the beach, the insistent chirping of crickets in the dunes, and the gentle thrum of guitar and quiet conversation had lulled him. Then the sand beneath him gave slightly sideways. He turned his head. Jess knelt next to him on the rug.

"How're you going, alright?" she asked, sitting on her heels. "You're pretty quiet over here."

"I'm fine, thanks. Just lying here, enjoying the sky and listening in to the conversation."

"Hmmm. Mind if I join you? I like a bit of sky myself."

A small voice in Tom's head urged caution, but he moved over and Jess lay down on her back next to him. For a time he was tense, acutely aware of her presence at his side; but he kept his eyes on the heavens and she made no attempt to move closer.

"Stargazing's kind of weird here," she said and pointed towards the Great Bear. "That one there, like a saucepan – I don't see that back home. And I can't see the Southern Cross from here. Which figures, I guess, seeing as we're in the north."

She laughed softly. She had a generous mouth and his attention was caught by the flash of a piercing in her tongue. As he looked at the smooth silver ball in her mouth, a knowing smile lit her face. To his surprise, she poked out her tongue, then curled it back again. He was transfixed by the blatantly flirtatious gesture.

"How long are you planning to stay in Devon?" he asked, ignoring the heat rushing to his face and hoping small-talk might steer his thoughts into less dangerous territory. She was gorgeous, and she obviously knew it.

"I'll stay for the summer. I'll have a bit of a holiday then, see a bit of the Med, then head off to Austria to work with the snowboarders."

"It sounds like a great life," he said, wistful. It was the kind of lifestyle he might have aspired to once, if he had been braver.

"Oh, it is. I get to see the world and meet loads of really great people. Like you, for instance."

Tom had seen enough teenaged crushes at work to recognise admiring glances when he saw them. However, unlike the teenagers he taught, this girl was of age and eligible as well as interested.

He cleared his throat. Curious, he asked: "How old are you?"

She rolled over and cupped her chin in her hands. A strand of her long hair blew across his face, and his hand twitched to brush it away.

"I'm young enough not to mind being asked," she quipped. "Twenty-one, to be precise. Why, how old are you?"

He summoned the will to look away. "Old enough to be your dad."

"No, really?" She laughed and laid a hand unexpectedly on his stomach. "It's a good job I like older guys, then, isn't it?"

He opened his mouth to speak, his heart beginning to thump at the implied invitation and the intimacy of her warm hand through his t-shirt. His breath caught in his throat. The heat of her hand was electric, sending warmth skimming over his skin. It made the hairs on his arms rise, a familiar throbbing twitch in his groin. She shifted, moving subtly closer, and leant her cheek on her left hand. Under his gaze, her full lips parted slightly. She had long eyelashes, he saw; brown eyes - not green. He was used to looking into green ones. A miniature jewel sparkled in one nostril and a scattering of freckles dusted her tanned skin, gilded now by the glow of the fire. His senses prickled with the scent of her floral perfume over the smoky campfire smell in her hair, the faint warmth of her breath as she leaned towards him to touch her mouth to his, her left hand moving to ruffle his hair with her fingers while the right slid slyly down his stomach.

With a jolt, an instant before their lips made contact, he rolled onto his side and sat up, his back towards her. He scratched his head where she had touched it, wanting somehow to erase the sensation of her fingers in his hair. He could almost feel her lips on his. Unwilling to acknowledge how his stomach had lurched at the thought of kissing her, he fumed at his body's involuntary responses to her advances. What the hell had he been thinking, letting her think he wanted this?

"What's up?" She sounded amused. "It was just a friendly kiss."

He rose to his feet. "It can't just be a friendly kiss when one of you is married." He should have seen this coming, shouldn't have let it get this far. Angry with himself, he swept up his fleece jacket and began shaking the sand off it.

"Married?" To his surprise, she chuckled.

"Yes, married. I have a wife. And two children. And a baby due in a few weeks."

She raised a sardonic eyebrow, peeping up at him from her position on the rug. "Well then, what are you doing here, doing such a great impression of a single guy?"

He said nothing, but started back up the beach towards the path. He was beginning to ask himself that very question.

"Oh, come on, Tom – don't be such a wowser. What Wifey doesn't know won't hurt her – and I won't tell if you don't."

He threw a glare back at her without breaking his stride, digging in his pocket for his torch.

"See you in the morning," she called after him, not in the least bit perturbed.

"See you, Tom!" he heard one of the others call out to him. He waved without looking back.

He didn't know if he wanted to surf with them again tomorrow. He'd been so bloody stupid – stupid to join the group for the evening, stupid to let Jess get the wrong impression, stupid to come so close to giving in temptation.

Eight months, he thought bitterly. Eight interminable months since a woman had wanted him, but it wasn't the woman he wanted. The unfairness of it rankled.

Adrenalin spurred him up the steep path back towards the farm at a run, muscles straining at the pace. He wanted to roar with frustration; to stamp, to kick, to punch, to shout, to break something. He contented himself by pausing some distance along the cliff path and grasping a pebble from the edge of the path. It felt smooth and heavy in his palm. Checking first that there was nothing in the way, he hurled it into the air towards the sea. It soared upwards, dimly visible in the dusky half-light, and he felt absurdly satisfied as it finally dropped with a splash into the water.

By the time he slid Greta's side door open, his leg muscles were aching from the brisk pace of his climb inland, but his tension had begun to ease. Cracking open another can of beer, he sank down onto the step, his thoughts turning again to Megan. He had missed her on previous evenings; tonight, she had never seemed so far away. His body's dangerous response to Jess's flirtation had brought home to him how much he missed physical intimacy. He ached with it, wanted to grind his teeth with desperation. He could only hope that she was missing him too.

He had thought when he left that she would probably manage well enough without him for a few days, but now he found himself wondering if he'd been right. Might she be struggling to cope without his help? He would make it up to her, he vowed to himself. Buying Greta; going away; being too cowardly to tell her his plans; putting himself in the path of temptation – he would make up for all of it.

If only he could pick up the phone and speak to her now; but his battery had failed during the first night. If he hadn't been drinking he could drive somewhere, find a phone box. But it was impossible. He'd call her in the morning, make sure she was okay.

He drained the last of the beer and sighed. It seemed a night for impossible wishes. Most of all, he wished he could turn the clock back six months.

Chapter Twelve

Six months earlier: December 2011
Cardiff

Christmas was approaching, and Tom was weary. Thank God there was only one week of term left before the holidays - he could hardly wait to have some time off. It had been a demanding few weeks at work, with interim reports to prepare, staff meetings, fixtures to organise, coursework to assess and a couple of particularly lengthy parents' evenings that dragged on past nine o'clock. He was getting too old for thirteen-hour working days.

There had been pastoral issues to contend with, too: incidents of low-level disruptive behaviour such as defiance, bullying and graffiti occurred on an almost daily basis. This week, kids had been caught bringing drugs into school to sell to their friends, and a boy was temporarily excluded for carrying a knife. A girl with a particularly dysfunctional background had completely lost control and tried to strip off her clothes in full view of other children: she was wrestled to the floor by a couple of support assistants before she could go so far as to remove her underwear, while Tom and other members of staff hastened to usher the audience of gawping teenagers away. He'd broken up a fight; investigated which prankster had set off the fire alarm in the gymnasium; and comforted a boy who broke down in tears over a particularly acrimonious family split.

He should never have allowed himself to be persuaded to apply for the head of department job when the previous incumbent retired. Megan had insisted it was a perfect opportunity for him to advance his career, and with two children and a burdensome mortgage to support he couldn't deny that the extra money was useful. She had used some clever arguments to press her case: if he didn't go for the job, someone from another school might get it and keep all the most enjoyable classes for themselves. A newcomer might want to make their mark and change the way the department operated even where change wasn't needed. For Tom, this had worked even more persuasively than the financial argument. His favourite classes were with the most senior pupils: he would hate to see those groups cherry-picked by someone else.

Still, now that the job was his, a part of him hankered after the days when he had less responsibility and a small flat, instead of a demanding job and a four-bedroomed between-the-wars semi that seemed to require endless maintenance. Spending hours on paperwork for a forthcoming school inspection gave him no job satisfaction, but plenty of sleepless nights.

His fortieth birthday loomed, and he anticipated it with a growing feeling of dread. His best years were in the past. He'd given up playing rugby after injuring his shoulder, and years of sport had taken their toll on his knees. Some mornings he awoke full of niggling aches and pains that hadn't been there ten years ago. He felt particularly sore after those nights when little Nia clambered into their bed and spread herself out like a starfish between him and Megan.

As much as he adored their daughters, it wasn't much fun spending most nights balanced on the edge of his mattress like an imposter in his own bed, with tiny restless hands fiddling with his ear, or sprawling feet kicking him in the kidneys. Nia wriggled like a tub of maggots: she was never still, even when she was asleep. Occasionally, both Alys and Nia would want to get into bed with them, seeking comfort after disturbing dreams, or warmth after kicking off the duvet. I'm a man on the edge, he thought sometimes, and he didn't only mean the edge of the bed. Aggrieved, he would give up any pretence of being able to rest in his own bed and head for the sofa or tussle through the mound of soft toys for space in Alys' single bed.

When he looked in the bathroom mirror these days, he saw his father's face looking back. A kind person might say he was craggy or rugged. Tom thought he looked haggard. There were dark shadows under his eyes, and lines like drainage ditches around his eyes and mouth. Only recently Nia had poked his forehead and asked why Daddy had so many "crinkles", when Mummy had none. Megan had laughed gleefully, but he had felt a pang at leaving the prime of his life behind.

His hair was still reassuringly thick, but there were signs of silver at the temples, and his hairline had retreated a little higher than in his youth. Even his chest displayed a few white hairs. Megan said she didn't mind his new "distinguished" appearance, but Tom was less than enthusiastic about these obvious signs of ageing. His eyebrows had started sprouting long, wiry hairs like spiders' legs. They needed regular trimming if he didn't want to end up resembling Leonid Brezhnev or Dennis Healey. To his horror, Megan had given him a nasal hair trimmer as a novelty gift the previous Christmas: what really upset him was that he was actually starting to find it useful. It would only be a matter of time, he thought resentfully, before he'd have hairs growing out of his ears as well.

He was still fit and lean, but it was getting harder to stay that way, especially with so much of his time taken up by work and family commitments. The days of living in a smart little flat with only himself to please and four flights of stairs to climb each day to keep him fit seemed a lifetime ago.

It wasn't that he regretted marriage and fatherhood: his two little girls were, in a sense, his proudest achievement. There was no better feeling in the world than spending time with Alys and Nia, seeing them reach their milestones and having them chatter to him or ask him impossible questions like "Daddy, is a giant bigger than a dragon?" He loved their childish wonder at the things adults take for granted: they prompted him to pause and consider the world afresh.

But having young children gave him more concern about the future and what it might hold for them. He wasn't convinced that a city was a healthy environment for children, despite Megan's enthusiasm for the opportunities for activities and culture. At heart, Tom was a country boy. He still cherished his dream of living near the sea, but even making time to get to the beach for a paddle with the kids seemed like hard work, needing to be co-ordinated like a military operation around everyone's activities, commitments and domestic chores.

As if his home and work responsibilities weren't enough to worry about, his father had become a matter of concern. Though still in relatively good shape, Hugh Field was ageing and considering selling his large house to move somewhere smaller. His hip gave him trouble, and his back frequently pained him, so that getting in and out of the car was difficult. Auntie Jean had become forgetful and frail, and struggled to manage the stairs or to keep up the standards she would have liked to maintain around the house. Tom felt guilty that he wasn't more immediately available to help. Living eighty miles away would soon inevitably mean an increasing amount of time spent travelling to ensure Dad and Jean's needs were met. If Hugh did decide to downsize, it would mean hours of work for Tom and Rob to sort through and dispose of many years' worth of accumulated possessions and decorate the house ready to put it on the market.

When he wasn't being expected to take on more and more at work, he was needed to fix and maintain things around the house. On the weekends, he'd often travel to Ludlow, or shuttle the girls between a relentless round of tedious children's parties and activities. While he knew Megan was busy too, teaching part-time and taking on the lion's share of the domestic chores including co-ordinating all these activities for the whole family, there was sometimes a resentful voice inside his head. At least Megan had a little time to herself, when Alys was at school and Nia in playgroup, to meet up with friends for a coffee and a chat. It wasn't that he begrudged her those opportunities: on the contrary, he was glad she was keeping up with friends. But he had no room to do the same. He spent each working day counting down to the weekend; each week of term counting down to the next school holiday; and the bulk of the holidays either planning for the following term or doing things for other people.

Life had lost its sparkle, and impending middle age seemed a daunting prospect. So Tom devised a plan. He had been saving a small allowance out of their joint incomes, and had built up a little nest egg of nearly fifteen hundred pounds. He knew exactly what to do with it.

Garin, of all people, gave him the idea. As much as Garin was a prize idiot in many respects, he was no fool when it came to enjoying life. An obsessive surfer, he spent every weekend in the spring and summer, and plenty in the winter too, riding the waves in the Gower, Pembrokeshire or occasionally further afield in North Devon and Cornwall. After work, if he could possibly manage it, he headed off to catch an hour or two on the water. With no regular partner or children to factor into his plans, he could indulge his passion to his heart's content.

He had been trying for a couple of years to convince Tom to take up surfing himself, and with his little pot of savings, Tom planned to splash out and buy himself an old camper van. He wouldn't get a trendy one for that amount of money, but he should be able to find a tatty 1980s van to use as a mobile changing room and for storing a surfboard and wetsuit. He'd take Megan and the two girls with him to the beach in the van on sunny days, and they could picnic together. Meg could read and watch over the girls while he spent a couple of hours in the water. If they wanted to stay overnight, they could throw a mattress in the back and rough it once in a while. It was a perfect plan.

Tom had a soft spot for Volkswagens: at the age of seventeen his very first car had been a battered old Beetle, named Bessie by his girlfriend at the time. He'd long admired Garin's ancient VW camper, imported from America with most of the paint blasted off by the desert heat and winds. Garin insisted that its weather-beaten paint work was a definite point in its favour, assuring Tom that the "rat look" was very fashionable. It had cost a small fortune. But by setting his sights lower, Tom was sure he could pick up a bargain.

Apart from buying a van, Tom intended his fortieth birthday the following week to pass with as little fuss as possible. He had avoided any mention of it at work, hoping that the milestone would pass unnoticed in the hectic period just before Christmas. To her disappointment, he had expressly forbidden Megan to arrange any kind of party, had insisted in the most forceful terms that he would hate to be the centre of attention at any such event. It was alright for her: she was five years younger, still in her prime. His only concession was to agree to a simple family celebration. A quiet meal in a restaurant with their extended families would be a perfectly adequate way to mark the beginning of middle age.

His birthday fell on a Friday, the last day of term before Christmas. As he had feared, it didn't go unmarked in school. His colleagues in the P.E. department knew all about it and decorated his tiny office with sparkly helium balloons and banners proclaiming his age to everyone.

He was taken out to the nearby pub for lunch and made to wear an enormous badge decorated with a large and luminous "40". He was touched by the card from his colleagues, and by their presents of wine, cufflinks and a Liverpool FC birthday cake from the local supermarket which he promptly shared out. He was less touched by the gift bag containing haemorrhoid ointment and anti-wrinkle cream, or by the inflatable Zimmer frame.

When he arrived home, immensely relieved that term was over, Alys leapt at him to wish him a happy birthday, and Nia dashed down the hallway to greet him, beaming and with arms outstretched. Carrying them both to the kitchen, blowing raspberries on their giggly cheeks, he laughed as Alys stumbled over her words in her haste to tell him about her day in school. It seemed she had particularly enjoyed having a Christmas party and watching cartoons in class.

"You wouldn't get to watch DVDs in my lessons," he said, shaking his head. "Kids go to school to work, not to have fun! My class get all the fun they need learning about the respiratory system."

Megan sent a smirk over her shoulder as she reached to load two brightly coloured beakers into the dishwasher. "The respiratory system? Well, what could possibly be more fun than that?"

He raised an eyebrow. "How about the reproductive system? That's a real hoot. Especially the practical aspects. Although after six weeks of enforced celibacy, I'm so out of practice I doubt I could teach it. The students probably know more than I do."

She flashed him a warning glare, then composed her features as if he hadn't spoken. "The kettle's hot, if you want a cuppa. I'm going upstairs to get ready. Come on, girls – let's find those party dresses!"

Picking up a knife, he slit open an envelope from the pile of mail on the kitchen table as if disembowelling it, then shook the letter open. Ah - a generous offer of a savings plan to cover his funeral expenses. Tossing it straight into the recycling bag, he made for the stairs. Hopefully a hot shower would help him start to unwind.

By a quarter to seven they were all ready to head to the restaurant where they planned to meet up with the rest of the family. Hopefully Nia wouldn't misbehave, being out this close to bedtime. There was a bag of toys in the boot to keep her occupied while they waited for their food.

"We need to pop in to the rugby club on the way, just for a couple of minutes," Megan said.

He was instantly suspicious. "Why? Won't it make us late?"

"No, it'll be fine. I asked Maureen to make your birthday cake and I need to go to pick it up. I've warned the others we might be delayed by a couple of minutes, but I doubt it will take long."

"Couldn't you have sorted it out with her earlier? Alright, but I'll wait in the car with the girls, to save time."

"That would be a bit ungrateful, don't you think? You know what Maureen's cakes are like: it's bound to be fabulous. She'll have spent hours on it; it would be rude of you not to go in and thank her. And if she doesn't get to say hello to the girls she'll never forgive me."

His eyes narrowed. He smelled a rat, but Megan was a picture of nonchalant innocence. Alright – he'd call in to the club for no more than two minutes. She busied herself with unstrapping Nia from her car seat while Tom held Alys' hand to take her inside.

"You go first," she said, hoisting Nia onto her hip and taking the car keys from him to bleep the central locking.

He should have seen it coming, of course. As he swung open the door to enter the building, there was a great roar of "Surprise!" and he was faced by the beaming faces of just about everyone he knew. Behind him, Megan laughed triumphantly.

"I told you I didn't want a party," he muttered as they were swamped by family and friends offering handshakes, hugs and kisses. He did his best to appear pleased, but this was overwhelming. He had been looking forward to a quiet meal in a restaurant with their respective families, and now here he was in the thick of a crowd, many of whom had, touchingly, travelled a long way to be there on his birthday. Knowing it would be churlish to appear ungrateful, he cranked his unwilling cheeks into a smile and greeted everyone with as much enthusiasm as he could muster. The drinks that were quickly pressed upon him helped him relax a little, but inside he was fuming that his wife had so deliberately ignored his wishes.

To give her credit, she had obviously put a lot of effort into organising it. There was a buffet of monumental proportions; the promised cake was shaped like a rugby ball with the English rose piped onto it. A disco blasted out songs from his youth and the room was festooned with *Happy 40th* balloons, banners and sparkly confetti, intermingled with Christmas decorations. A flipchart displayed photographs of Tom, some dating back to his infancy, with the title "This is Your Life". Sticky notes were provided for the addition of amusing captions. He suspected Garin had supplied the rudest ones.

He mingled for a time, catching up with everyone. Megan seemed to have invited just about everyone in their address book: old friends from university, work colleagues, cousins they hadn't seen since their wedding day or Nia's christening. He didn't enjoy the buffet as much as he would have enjoyed the restaurant meal he had been expecting, but he made the best of it and sidled along the table with his paper plate, shoulder to shoulder with Auntie Jean, who marvelled and cooed over the vol-au-vents and sausage rolls as if she had never seen party food before.

"Tommo! You flanker!" Garin greeted him later, pint glass in hand. He made Tom's old rugby position sound like an insult.

"Gaz, you old hooker," Tom responded in kind. "You might have warned me about all this, you bastard."

Garin laughed derisively. "And spoil your surprise? Megan would have had my bollocks for a bookmark if I'd dared."

"How long have you known about it?"

"About six months. She booked the date with everyone well in advance, to make sure Christmas plans didn't get in the way."

Tom groaned and swore under his breath. Clearly he had expressed his wishes far too late.

"What's up? Don't you like being the centre of attention?" Garin's eyes gleamed wickedly: he knew full well Tom didn't. "Cheer up, now. Try not to be a grumpy old fucker. Some of these people have come a long way to celebrate you entering your dotage."

There was a pause in the music, and an announcement that made Tom's heart sink.

"If the Birthday Boy could come up here, please, and join his lovely lady wife, she'd like to say a few words."

Shit. He made his way self-consciously to the microphone to join Megan. She was beaming at him, radiant with excitement. Everyone laughed good-naturedly as she fiddled with the microphone, adjusting it downwards to allow for her diminutive stature.

"First of all I'd like to thank you all for coming along tonight to celebrate Tom's fortieth birthday with us," she began. "Some of you have travelled a long way to be here, at a busy time of year, and it really is wonderful to be able to share this special event with the people who mean most to us."

He nodded his thanks as everyone applauded.

"I'd also like to thank you for keeping it a secret." she laughed, casting an arch sideways look up at Tom. "He honestly didn't know a thing about it. I've never told so many lies in my life – and the day he told me he didn't want a party for his birthday I seriously considered cancelling the whole thing! But now that it's out in the open I'm very glad I didn't, because I wanted today to be special - and having you all here is most definitely the icing on the cake."

He eyed her ruefully, and she took his hand. Hopefully she would finish soon, and he could get his own speech over with. It was a funny thing: he could address an assembly of several hundred teenagers without a moment's anxiety; yet in front of a group of adults his throat wanted to close up.

"What Tom doesn't realise yet is that there's actually another surprise in store for him."

He tried in vain to read her expression. Exasperating and wayward though she was, she looked particularly lovely. There was an aura of exultant happiness about her; but a frisson of nervousness, too. What on earth was she about to say?

"Actually, this has come as something of a surprise to me, too. I only found out for sure at the end of last week," she said, stepping closer to him.

The assembled family and friends waited. Some glanced speculatively at one another, obviously making their own silent guesses at what she might be about to say. At the edge of the crowd, Bethan and Matt linked hands.

"I was going to tell you as soon as I found out," she said to him, the lilting cadence of her Welsh accent magnified by the microphone. "But then I thought it would make a perfect extra birthday surprise." She paused for effect, then handed him a piece of paper she had been hiding in her pocket. Her eyes were huge, watching his face.

It seemed everyone held their breath as he looked down to examine the piece of paper.

It took a moment or two for him to register its significance, even though he had seen a few just like it before. A grainy picture, printed on shiny computer paper: fuzzy, pale blobs on a dark background. Towards the top, a white splodge, clearly edged with a snub-nosed profile. A head: out of proportion to the body, with big eye sockets, like an alien from a science fiction movie. A light grey bean shape sprouting little buds of arms. A leg kicking out; the curve of a spine.

Along the top of the picture, in block capitals, a name: MEGAN PARRY FIELD. A date. Three days had passed since the picture was taken.

Tom swallowed hard as her next words to the audience confirmed what the picture had already told him.

"I'm very excited to be able to tell you all that in June next year, Alys and Nia will have a new baby brother or sister. Happy birthday, Tom."

Chapter Thirteen

December 2011

Cardiff

Ahs, whoops and cheers burst from the delighted throng of well-wishers. Tom took Megan in his arms, hiding his face in her hair to conceal his confusion. Holding her in front of everyone, feeling her excitement in the trembling of her limbs, he felt shaken to the core. They hadn't been trying to conceive: she had been taking the pill as regularly as clockwork, as far as he knew. Had she got pregnant deliberately, without asking him what he wanted? He was so stunned he hardly knew what to think.

Garin called out: "Bloody hell, mun! Haven't you got a telly in your house? You need to stop making your own entertainment!"

A chorus of other voices in the audience demanded he make a speech. It couldn't be avoided, however much he wanted to whisk Megan outside and demand to know exactly what the hell she was playing at. He fumbled to re-adjust the height of the microphone. Don't look anyone in the eye. And definitely don't look at Dad or Rob. If anyone would discern the panic in his eyes, they would.

Afterwards, he could hardly recall what he had said. Something about it being a night for surprises, and how he was going to have to watch his wife more carefully in future as she was a bit of a dark horse and clearly more cunning than he had ever realised.

They stood together, arm in arm in front of the DJ's flashing coloured lights, and received the warmest possible congratulations from everyone; and all he felt was cold shock and a clutching, griping fear twisting his stomach. He still held the picture, in a hand that now shook. How in God's name were they going to cope with another child, when they were already financially stretched, rushed off their feet and sleep-deprived?

Dazed, he stood and nodded his gratitude at the good wishes everyone heaped upon them. Garin handed him a pint of bitter with a wink, saying: "Still got lead in your pencil, then, old man! Here, I got you a pint of Skull Attack to help you drown your sorrows."

"Thanks. Do me a favour and get me a whisky chaser."

Garin's jaw dropped with surprise at the speed with which Tom downed the beer. It was renowned locally for being stronger than it seemed: hence its nickname of "Skull Attack", referring to the hangover likely to result from drinking it. The whisky went down even faster, so strong it made Tom shudder.

Megan's mother appeared, and he took in a deep breath, trying to head off the instant prickle of irritation that she invariably aroused in him. In the seven years he had known her, they had never hit it off, behaving with tolerable politeness around one another only for Megan's sake.

"Going for a boy this time, are you?" she asked, puckering her lips and reaching up to bestow a cold peck on his cheek. He leaned down to receive it, resisting the childish urge to wipe his face with his hand afterwards.

"I always had a feeling you'd want to try again, Tom, to get yourself a little rugby player or footballer," she said in the acid tone she so often used when addressing him. "So typical of a man, to want a son and heir: a little mini-me."

"The thought honestly hadn't occurred to me, Olwen," he told her perfectly truthfully. The icy glare he flashed at her was at odds with his upturned mouth.

"At least you can see from the picture that it isn't twins."

He hadn't thought of that possibility. The suggestion of it made his head swim.

"Of course, they do say that if you've already got two of one sex, the third is likely to be the same. You'll probably end up surrounded by women!"

"Well now, there's a thought." He started another beer. Please, just leave me alone, he pleaded with her in his head.

"Imagine in a few years if they're all pre-menstrual at the same time!" Olwen cackled maliciously, making the chunky beads on her bosom rattle. "They do say that when women live together, their cycles coincide. Do you remember, Megan, when you and Bethan still lived at home? For one week of every month we were all absolutely evil!"

Olwen was pretty evil throughout the month, as far as Tom was concerned, but he pressed his lips together to stop the words. The momentary satisfaction of telling her what he really thought wouldn't be worth the prolonged punishment that would inevitably ensue. As soon as he could politely get away, he headed to the gents' toilets.

It wasn't just the alcohol making his head spin and his stomach twist. Checking that he was alone, he shut himself in a cubicle and sank down onto the wonky lid of the toilet, head in his hands. He hated surprises. Megan of all people should know that. Yet tonight she had hit him with two in the space of a few hours.

Organising the party was perhaps forgivable: while insensitive to his wishes, he accepted that she had genuinely believed he would enjoy having all these people around him to celebrate an occasion he would have preferred to ignore.

But to tell him in front of an audience that he was to be a father again? Surely that was a moment for privacy, an intimate thing for a man and his wife to share? At least she hadn't asked him yet how he felt about the baby. She had forced him into a position of pretending to be thrilled in front of pretty much everyone they knew, when he actually felt shell-shocked. He wasn't ready to be excited. Quite honestly, he wanted to throw up.

The door opened, but Tom was retching too violently into the ammonia-scented, brown-stained toilet pan to hear it.

"Thomas, is that you?" Hugh's voice exclaimed from outside the cubicle. "Are you alright?"

Oh, God. Dad. Tom lurched to his feet and grabbed some tissue to wipe his mouth. His stomach seemed to have finished emptying itself at last: he felt dizzy, strangely light and hollow. He rasped out an indistinct response and, pulling the flush, unlocked the door to stagger outside.

"You look ghastly," Hugh said.

"Hmmm. Bad pint." A peek into the dusty mirror proved his father's words were an accurate assessment. Quickly, he washed his trembling hands and swilled his face.

It was a poor excuse, and Hugh obviously wasn't fooled for a moment.

"I take it you had no idea about the baby." It wasn't a question.

"No. It came as a bit of a surprise." He gazed despondently into the basin, trying to make his eyes and brain focus.

"You never did like surprises, even as a little boy." Hugh hesitated, then added wryly: "And yet here I am, about to supply another."

"Bloody hell, Dad – are you serious? I don't know if I can take any more tonight." He leaned on the basin and watched his father with anxious, blurry eyes.

"Well, this surprise at least should be a little more welcome than the last two." Whatever he saw in his son's face at that, Hugh discreetly back-pedalled: "Not that the baby isn't welcome, of course. Just – well, a little unexpected… You'll manage. Where there's a will, there's a way, and all that." Hugh patted his arm.

Tom straightened and adjusted his cuffs. His face was still bleak and green from the nausea, but he understood the message his father was sending him. He should probably make an effort to smarten himself up.

"Now, then," Hugh announced more briskly. "I haven't yet given you your birthday present. I hadn't planned to do it in the gents' toilets, but this is the first time all evening that I've had an opportunity to speak to you on your own."

He reached into the inside pocket of his blazer and pulled out a piece of paper that looked suspiciously like a folded cheque.

"Now, then. Your birthday present. And it is for you, my boy. Not for the family: I must emphasise that it's for *you*. I want you to use it to do something or buy something that enriches your life – in whatever way you think best."

Tom swallowed, his mouth still foul with beer and bile. Hugh thrust the paper at him again. At last, with some reluctance, he took it and unfolded it. Reading it, his eyes widened in shock.

"Fuck!" he exclaimed, then remembered who he was speaking to. "Sorry, Dad. But honestly, fuck – this is a cheque for ten thousand pounds!" He stared at his father in bewilderment.

"I'm aware of that, Thomas; I wrote it."

"I can't possibly accept it," he protested, pushing it back. But his father calmly folded his arms.

"I can afford it. And besides, it's only fair: I gave Robert the same on his fortieth birthday."

"Did you?"

"Yes, and he was no more keen to take it than you are. Ungrateful buggers, the pair of you." There was a twinkle in his watery pale blue eyes. "I've no idea what he did with the money," he continued. "Knowing him, he made a nice, safe, tax-free investment. But I don't want you to do that. I want you to enjoy it. I want you to use it to…" He hesitated and grasped Tom's shoulder to emphasise his point. "Well, use it to *live*."

Tom was taken aback by the sudden urgency of his father's tone. His face must have betrayed his confusion, for Hugh patted his shoulder gently.

"Do you remember how old your mother was when the cancer was first diagnosed?"

The question took Tom by surprise. His mother's illness was something they rarely spoke about.

"I'm not sure exactly – I know she fought it for a long time before she died."

"She was forty-three."

The words hit Tom like a punch in the jaw.

"Only three years older than you are now." Hugh's voice had become husky; he cleared his throat self-consciously. "We had two teenaged sons to think about: Robert was about to sit his 'O' levels at the time. She was desperate to see you both grow up; I honestly think that having you two boys helped to keep her going for those eight years. One thing it taught us was the vital importance of making the most of your life while you can."

Tom's heart went out to his father, who now smiled warmly.

"As tonight has demonstrated, Thomas – you never know what's around the corner. And, trust me, sometimes it's a good job you don't. So use the money in whatever way helps to make your life fuller and richer and more satisfying. Use it in any way that blesses you. Don't be afraid to be selfish with it, if necessary. If you're happier, then the family will be happier. I trust your judgment, my boy: I have every faith that you will use the money well."

Tom enveloped his father in a hug, speech failing him at the old man's uncharacteristically emotional words. They patted each other's backs, pulling apart abruptly when one of Tom's friends from his university days came in to make use of the urinal. Pausing only to acknowledge his friend, Tom tucked the cheque into his shirt pocket and followed his father back towards the noisy function room.

"Thank you," he whispered, as they swung open the door to be greeted by the blare of the disco and another friend bearing drinks. Hugh only smiled and disappeared into the crowd.

It was probably a mistake to drink more alcohol after his stomach's previous protests, but three emotionally charged shocks in one evening made him throw caution to the wind.

He would come to regret it, should have remembered that a late night doesn't necessarily make young children sleep in late the next morning. Nia woke as early as ever, lack of sleep making her grumpy. Whining, she burst into Tom and Megan's bedroom not long after six o'clock, and tried to shake Tom awake despite his groans of protest.

"Nia – no, darling…. Please go back to bed. Daddy isn't feeling well." He squeezed his eyes closed against the bedside lamp she had turned on. His head pounded, his stomach felt like a washing machine on a spin cycle, and his tongue tasted so bad, he wondered if it could have developed gangrene overnight.

"But I want breakfast," Nia complained. "I'm hungry, Daddy."

With such a crashing hangover, and after only five hours' sleep, the last thing he wanted was to have to get up and make breakfast.

"Megan…" he croaked, but she cut him off abruptly.

"I'm pregnant," she mumbled from her side of the bed, tugging the duvet more firmly around her. "I'm entitled to a lie-in."

Her words sliced through the alcohol-induced haze, reminding him with a jolt of the previous night's events.

"I want some toast, Daddy... Daddy, wake up!"

Tom groaned again as Nia tried knocking firmly on his head to get his attention. He reached for his dressing gown and stumbled downstairs, head throbbing, to settle her with some toast in front of the television. Hopefully she would be sufficiently distracted by cartoons to leave him alone for a while. He dragged himself back upstairs with a long drink of water and some painkillers. It was years since he had suffered from a hangover of this magnitude.

Carefully, trying not to cry out from the pain in his head that was exacerbated by even the slightest shift in position, he slipped back under the duvet.

"You should have seen your face last night," Megan said with a soft chuckle. She, of course, was tired but not hung over as she had accepted only soft drinks throughout the evening. "I never thought I'd manage to keep it a surprise from you; I'm quite proud of the way my plans came together."

He inhaled sharply. "Are you referring to the party or the baby?"

"The party, silly. It was months in the planning."

He paused, lying very still, eyes closed against the faint beginnings of the winter morning light, mouth grim and an arm draped across his forehead. This seemed as good a time as any to ask the question that had stung like nettle rash all through the previous evening, ever since her public announcement.

"Was the baby planned, too?"

"No, of course not." She rolled to face him, making the mattress wobble. The movement induced a wave of nausea: he swallowed it down and waited to hear her excuses.

"If you remember, I got rather drunk on my birthday. Nearly as drunk as you were last night. I was late taking my pill the next day, and I forgot that the mini-pill only gives a few hours leeway. I didn't get the morning-after pill because I thought we'd still be safe but – well, obviously it didn't work out that way."

He couldn't speak.

"You do believe me?"

"If you say so."

"For goodness' sake, Tom! Why would I lie to you about something so important?"

Because she'd known he wouldn't want another child – it was so obvious, he couldn't even summon the will to say it out loud.

She tutted impatiently. "I can't believe you're being like this. I thought it would add to the atmosphere of the evening to wait until your birthday to tell you. I expected you to be thrilled. You couldn't have been more excited when I was expecting Alys and Nia." When he still didn't respond, she huffed and muttered: "I should have listened to Bethan, obviously."

"Why should you have listened to Bethan?" His silky tone belied the danger behind his words.

"Oh, nothing." She squirmed, trying to brush the words aside, and rolled back to face the other way. "Let's get some more sleep before Alys wakes up."

He raised himself onto his elbow, squinting against the resulting pain in his head. "What did Bethan say?" he demanded. With his free hand, he pulled her shoulder so that she had to face him. She wouldn't meet his gaze.

"She said you might not like being told in front of everyone," she mumbled, pouting.

Tom's pulse throbbed in his head.

"You told your sister we were having a baby before you told me?"

"Only because I needed her to have the girls while I went to the hospital for the scan."

"And why, might I ask, wasn't I told that my wife needed to go to the hospital?"

She spluttered an attempt at a coherent explanation: "Well, I wasn't sure that I was pregnant, and I wasn't sure how you would feel about it, or how I felt about it for that matter; so I thought if it turned out that I wasn't, there wouldn't have been any point in worrying you. So I saw the GP on my own, and she suggested I should go to the assessment unit, and I thought if I just went there on my own as well, I'd get everything checked without you needing to take any time off, and then I could tell you afterwards. But then of course, it turned out that I was – I am… And it was thrilling once I got over the initial shock, and that's when I thought how nice it would be to surprise you at your party. I couldn't think of a more exciting way to tell you, and it was only a couple of days away, so it's not as if I kept it from you for long."

"Fucking hell, Megan!" He practically exploded out of the bed, one hand clutching his head as he did so. She shrank away into the middle of the bed.

"I didn't want the fucking party in the first place!" he roared.

"Mind your language! The children…"

"I told you and told you," he growled, cutting off her words. "But did you listen? No! Did you think about what I wanted? No!" He cut off her attempts to argue, incandescent with rage. "You went your own sweet way, as you always do. I dread to think what it must have cost: the venue, the disco, the buffet, the cake, the decorations." He counted each item off on his fingers. "All for something you knew I didn't want. And then, you didn't think it would be right for me to know before anyone else that we're having another child together, but went gossiping to your sister instead. I expect Matt knew before I did!"

Her guilty expression confirmed his suspicions.

"For fuck's sake! Did you tell your mother as well?"

She shook her head, clutching the duvet like a shield. The force of his anger had brought tears to her eyes.

"You say you were shocked when you first realised you were pregnant. How did you think I was going to feel, being told in front of all those people? Knowing it wasn't planned, knowing I thought our family was complete; knowing, Megan, that I was under the impression that you were taking your pill and we were safe. Not that we've been taking any risks lately – your birthday was probably the last time we had sex!"

On the defensive now, she snapped back. "No, it wasn't! We've done it at least once since then."

"Once! Since October! And I should be grateful for that, should I? For the crumbs from the mistress' table."

"Well, at least we know now why I haven't felt like it. It must have been my hormones. It explains why I've been so tired lately."

"Oh, spare me." He tugged his jeans on. "I'll ask you something else: did it not occur to you to consider how Beth and Matt might feel about your little titbit of news? Knowing that they've tried for a baby for years, and here you are falling pregnant accidentally, *again*?" Fully dressed, he headed towards the bedroom door.

"Where are you going?" Her guilty expression had been replaced by panic.

"Who knows? Anywhere I can get away from you and calm down." He glared at her from the bedroom doorway, face hardened by fury, making her cringe back in the bed. "You know, Megan, sometimes I really don't like you at all. It's hard to believe you spent four years at university and still came out so fucking stupid."

It was the most hurtful thing he had ever said to her. He heard her snivelling while he went to the bathroom; no doubt she expected him to come back and apologise after a couple of minutes to cool off.

He didn't. He pounded down the stairs and unlocked the front door before she could have time to get up and slip into her dressing gown. It banged as it slammed behind him, but he was already halfway down the driveway. He strode off down the avenue, thrusting his arms into his coat as he hastened to get away.

If his headache hadn't been so painful, he would have gone for a run, but a walk would have to suffice. Shoving his hands into his pockets against the cold December air, he headed towards the park, hardly aware of his surroundings at first. Upon reaching the dam that headed the lake, he finally slowed his pace and paused to gaze out over the water.

It was barely light: the shortest day of the year was less than a week away. The reflections of a few lights from nearby houses glowed softly on the lake. Most people were probably still asleep. An elderly man with a decrepit West Highland terrier hobbled slowly by, nodding politely as he passed. A couple of birds had begun calling to one another, and a jogger ran past, absorbed in whatever he was listening to through his headphones. Otherwise, the park was quiet.

It was funny: there was something about water that invariably drew him and imbued him with a sense of calm. He'd always dreamed of living near the sea. It wasn't ever likely to happen, especially now with another child on the way to postpone his freedom from responsibility. He'd be close to retirement age by the time this one would even begin to consider the possibility of leaving home.

He set off again, huddled into his coat as he shivered against the biting cold air. He remembered the beanie hat in his pocket and donned it gratefully while pondering practicalities. His head still throbbed, but at least now his ears were warmer.

Bedrooms, for a start. They had four, fortunately, but the smallest was used as a study, with a sofa bed for guests. They would have to think about whether to lose their valuable study space - so useful when there was school work to be done in the evenings - or whether to keep it and make Alys and Nia share a bedroom.

Then there was the issue of transporting a family of five. Megan had a nippy little car that was economical to run and perfect for city driving, but Tom doubted it would be possible to fit three child seats in the back. So if Megan was on her own with the children, one of them would have to go in the front passenger seat. The thought of it made him uncomfortable. His own hatchback was bigger, but he still couldn't imagine being able to transport two adults, three small children, a pram and a week's groceries in it. He'd have to start researching MPVs or other larger cars. If only the thought of driving around in a people carrier wasn't so dispiriting. He could kiss goodbye to his sporty "hot hatch". From now on, power would be less of a consideration than space; sound systems would be superseded by in-car DVDs blaring out cartoons or Disney films.

And then – what about holidays? They would also be trickier, he realised, as hotel rooms were generally geared up to cater for families of four. Food was packaged for smaller families, too. And they'd have less money while Megan was on maternity leave. She'd better not decide to reduce her working hours any further, because they needed her income, and day-care for Nia and the baby, plus childcare before and after school for Alys, was going to use up the bulk of her earnings. He envied those of his colleagues and friends who were able to rely on free childcare from grandparents, but it wasn't an option for them, with Hugh eighty miles away and Megan's mother in Carmarthenshire and still working full-time. Not that Tom would ever be happy to leave his daughters to be influenced by Olwen's poisonous views, even if she had lived next door to them. The less time they spent absorbing her venom, the better.

He'd have to venture up into the attic and check how much of the old baby equipment would still be useable. The old pram had outlived its usefulness and had been taken to the tip some time ago. How much would a new one cost? Hundreds of pounds, no doubt: Megan wasn't likely to settle for anything cheap and cheerful. He could look forward to months of being dragged around overpriced nursery suppliers in search of the perfect combination of colour, fabric, handle height, storage baskets, cup holders, weight, wheel configuration, seat positions, collapsibility and manoeuvrability. There would be internet reviews to consider, parenting forums to consult. From what he could remember, choosing their house had been less complicated than choosing their first pram.

The faint morning light grew a little stronger as he wandered along the path around the lake, lost in thought. In the distance, he heard the grating sound of a crying baby. The sound drew closer, and he saw a grim-faced man, well wrapped up against the cold, pushing a pram.

"Alright?" Tom nodded as the man approached.

"Bit of a sleepless night," the man said, clearly exhausted. "He's been fractious like this on and off since tea time yesterday.   I think we've only managed about three hours' sleep in total. Usually the motion helps to send him off, but it hasn't worked yet. I've brought him out so my wife can get a couple of hours' sleep." The baby's squalling increased in volume, drilling into Tom's aching head, and the man set off again with a rueful wave of his hand.

I hope I don't get one that does that, Tom thought, dismayed. Alys and Nia had never been quite that bad, had they? Perhaps they had, and he had blotted out the memory. Nature must have ways of playing tricks with parents' memories; otherwise surely no woman would want to give birth more than once?

He remembered Alys and Nia's births as if they were yesterday. Megan was in labour for about twenty-four hours with Alys, and was exhausted by the time she was born. He had been terrified that she would struggle, being so petite, but she had managed in the end. He remembered how proud he had felt, and how helpless, as she groaned and leaned on him through the hours of labour. He'd tried to mop her brow with a cool flannel and she shouted at him: "It's not my forehead that's hurting, you idiot!" He couldn't help smiling at the memory.

She'd actually bitten him while in labour with Nia: she'd been resting her face on his shoulder and had been so overwhelmed by the strength of one contraction that she sank her teeth in and gripped hard. They cried out in unison from the pain of that one; he remembered the midwife laughing at them. He remembered how guilty Megan had felt afterwards: the sight of his bruise had made her blush with shame. He had teased her about it for weeks.

His face softened in spite of his lingering headache as he recalled Alys and Nia as babies. Tiny, starfish hands curling around his finger, melting his heart. The irresistible rush of protective love he had felt. He knew without a moment's doubt or hesitation that he would be willing to fight for his children, lay down his life for them; even kill for them, if the situation ever required it.

They were demanding but utterly delightful: loving, cheeky, determined and comical. They sometimes fought like demons, and each exploited the other's insecurities and weaknesses to tease and torment. They questioned everything: even the most ordinary things fascinated them. He found their capacity to learn and absorb new experiences astounding.

His love for his two daughters was so great, it was almost impossible to imagine having any room in his heart for another child. But then, he had felt the same before Nia was born. He had realised then that love wasn't like a cake: once portions had been shared out, it hadn't gone. It grew. And with children, he believed love was the safest investment, with guaranteed returns. Remembering this helped. He wasn't sure yet how he and Megan would manage, but somehow he was just about beginning to believe that they could.

Life would be different, yes: but it didn't necessarily have to be worse. His child was growing, already formed in Megan's womb. They had time to make decisions, time to carry out whatever preparations they needed. And then all the time in the world to get to know the new little person who would soon be sharing their lives.

At last he headed for home, his thoughts turning to Megan. Whatever his opinion of her actions in the past week, he had the highest regard for her as a mother. Her patience with Alys and Nia as babies had been seemingly infinite. Even at her most exhausted, she had put the children's needs above her own. Anyone else waking her hourly through the night to demand her attention would get short shrift, but there was some primal ability in her to endure it for months from her babies without resentment.

Remembering Megan's better qualities made Tom feel more positive as he approached the street where they lived. Yes, she had been thoughtless in arranging the party, but there had been no malice in her intentions: she hadn't set out to ruin his evening with either the party or her announcement. Better not dwell on Bethan knowing about the baby first, as he still felt sore about that. His steps faltered when he thought about it. But, he thought as he put his key in the lock and pushed the front door open, even that wasn't necessarily unforgiveable.

He slipped his hat back into his pocket, shed his coat and shoes, and padded to the kitchen to make himself a mug of coffee. Hopefully some caffeine and more painkillers would clear what remained of his headache, and the hot drink would warm him up.

Megan was in the kitchen, wrapped in her dressing gown and loading breakfast dishes into the dishwasher. The atmosphere was heavy with her suppressed anger: he realised he should have expected it, as she wasn't someone who took kindly to being shouted at. She was determined to ignore him, it seemed. He flicked the switch on the kettle and briefly pondered whether to join in with the silent treatment or give in and apologise for his words earlier.

In the event, she broke the silence first.

"You're a fine one to criticise me for keeping secrets," she snapped, snatching up his dad's cheque and brandishing it under his nose. "When exactly were you planning to tell me about this?"

Typical of her to mount an attack instead of apologising for her own misjudgements. He lifted a mug down from the cupboard above the kettle.

"Are you having coffee?" he asked.

"I've had juice. Now, why didn't you tell me that your dad has given us ten thousand pounds? Or were you planning to keep that 'little titbit of news' to yourself?"

He inhaled sharply, realising she was using his own words against him. How he hated that tone of voice, when she felt herself to have the upper hand in an argument. Spooning the aromatic granules into the mug, he replied coolly: "He didn't give it to *us*. He gave it to *me*."

He turned, one eyebrow slightly raised, his better mood evaporating as quickly as the steam from the kettle. It wasn't usually in his nature to provoke a fight, but he was still smarting from last night and as far as he was concerned, she had no right to try to take the moral high ground.

She blanched, excepting patches of high colour on her cheekbones. He had intended to provoke her, but he saw at once, to his shame, that in fact his words had hurt. He reached out to touch her arm, meaning to explain, but she flinched and shook it off as if his touch was utterly repellent.

"I'm sorry." He held up his hands in surrender. "I didn't mean that the way it sounded: you just sounded so high-handed, I couldn't help myself."

"I see. So you're not in fact saying that what's mine is yours, but what's yours is your own?" She glared at him, expecting an explanation.

"Of course I don't mean that. We've always done everything jointly." He sighed, tired of the tension between them. "Let me make myself a drink and we'll sit down and talk about it."

She spun on her heel and stalked off to the living room. His head thumped again as he finished making his coffee; all the beneficial effects of his walk in the fresh air were gone.

Alys and Nia had gone upstairs to play, so they had a few minutes to themselves. Megan sat, stiffly upright, while Tom explained his dad's instructions.

"What are you going to do with it, then?" she asked, when he had finished.

"I don't know. I haven't decided yet. Obviously I planned to talk to you about it, but we didn't get a chance last night, and to be honest I'd forgotten all about it until you waved the cheque at me just now."

"So you *were* going to discuss it with me?"

His exasperated huff finally eroded some of the tension from her face.

"It's a lot of money," she said.

"Yes, it certainly is."

"I was thinking when I found it - perhaps we could take the children to Disneyland; but then I thought – it would be silly to do it now, with the baby on the way… It would be much better to go when they're all old enough to remember it." Her expression grew more animated as she expounded her ideas. "And then I thought: we could have the garden done – it would be lovely to have a proper outside area for entertaining, and with that kind of money we could get a garden designer in."

"But we don't really do any entertaining."

"Well no, but if we had a nice garden perhaps it would give us a bit of impetus to invite more people over. But then it occurred to me:

the best idea of all." She seemed brighter now, had cheered up visibly. Maybe, after all, he could relax.

"Go on."

"We could have a brand new kitchen."

No, no, no, no, no... He knew she had dreamed of having the kitchen refurbished for the four years they had lived in their house. As much as she loved living in a spacious old house with its high ceilings, picture rails and feature fireplaces, he knew that being forced to live with so much of the previous occupants' taste in décor needled her. They had spent as much time and money as they could stripping back and restoring parquet floors, sanding paintwork and carefully selecting pieces of art deco furniture and lighting to suit the character of the house. As far as Tom was concerned, they now had a home to be proud of. There was very little wrong with their kitchen as far as he could see, except that it was slightly dated.

She was so full of enthusiasm for her own plans that she hadn't seemed to notice Tom's stiff silence.

"It could be fantastic! For ten grand we could have the whole lot ripped out and start afresh. I could have a range cooker and one of those big American-style fridges that's plumbed into the mains so it makes ice cubes and cold water. One of the mums at playgroup has got one. And she's got the most gorgeous limestone tiles in her kitchen: I'd love something like that. And a quartz worktop, or maybe granite? I'm not sure which; we could go and have a look at them in some showrooms. I fancy oak doors with chrome handles, something quite plain; but if possible, we could try to incorporate some art deco elements in keeping with the house. Black and white tiles, maybe.

Something geometric. But I'm sure a kitchen designer could help us with that."

Trailing off, she frowned very slightly, as if she had finally noticed that he had not immediately agreed to her idea. "Well? What do you think?"

He scratched his head, making his hair stick up at the crown. He had no intention of going along with this idea, but the prospect of another argument this morning was just too exhausting.

"I'll think about it," he hedged, and escaped to find the girls.

Chapter Fourteen

Four months later: April 2012
Cardiff

Garin slid out from underneath the van with a screwdriver in his hand and a gratified smirk on his face.

"Not a sign of rust! It wouldn't stand a chance: there's more protective wax under there than in Shrek's ears."

Springing lightly to his feet, surfer-style, he directed his attention to the interior.

"Look, all the seatbelts you need in the back, and the roof on these Viking conversions is absolutely massive. Honestly, Tommo – it's like the Tardis. It's got everything: it will sleep six people; there's a fridge, a cooker, mains electric… This type of interior is really flexible, too. You can take individual seats out, if you don't need to use them all, or make this row face the other way when you're travelling. The cooker lifts out if you fancy cooking al fresco. And see here - there's even a bog under one of the seats."

He lifted the lid on one of the seats, revealing a plastic camping toilet. Obediently, Tom peered in.

"Every modern convenience," he agreed.

They were inspecting a bright orange Volkswagen camper van, owned by a friend of Garin's who planned to emigrate to Canada. Its interior was in excellent condition, a veritable palace of 1970s retro chic in beige vinyl with brown and cream checks.

"Out of all the British conversions, this was probably the most top-notch model. But best of all," Garin went on, "you can trust the history of this one. Jez restored it four years ago, and it was completely stripped back. He's got an album full of photos to prove it, but I can vouch for him in any case – I remember him doing it. It had a really top notch rebuild. This is no old banger, Tom: she's a cracking van, in really tidy, honest condition."

"What's it like mechanically?" Tom asked, cautiously excited. He knew very little about engines, and hated having to depend on someone else's judgment, but in this instance Garin genuinely was something of an expert.

They wandered slowly around the exterior of the vehicle, admiring the sheen of its smooth, flat panels.

"Sound as a pound," Garin told him. "The engine's a beaut'. The suspension's been lowered just enough to improve the ride without making it so low that you couldn't drive across a field. It's not as low as mine, obviously. Mine's lower than a Chihuahua's cock – it's bloody lush, but I'll admit it rattles your teeth out of your head on bumpy ground."

"Hmmm. I don't see that going down well with the wife," Tom remarked.

"No, you don't need yours slammed to the weeds like mine; you need one like this: practical, built for a family. Here, look - there's an envelope full of receipts..." Garin thumbed approvingly through the van's recent service history. "She's been well cared for by that garage I was telling you about. Jez wouldn't let just anybody touch his van. She's his pride and joy."

Tom peered over Garin's arm, unsure whether to be reassured or concerned by the amount Jez had spent on the van in recent years.

Garin lowered his voice and leaned confidingly towards his ear.

"What you've got to understand, Tom, is this: for Jez, selling his van is like selling one of his children. He'd rather shove wasps up his arse than part with her. But he doesn't have any choice. She has to go within six weeks because he doesn't want the hassle of exporting her to Canada. If you don't want her, someone else will snap her up, especially at that price. Twelve grand is a snip, believe you me. You'd pay fifteen or sixteen from a dealer for a van in this condition. And it's not like spending twelve thousand quid on a new car: these little beauties don't depreciate if you look after them. Keep the rust out and the chances are the value will go up, not down."

Tom knew he wasn't exaggerating: he'd been trawling the internet for the right van for months, without finding what he wanted within his budget.

He had had four months to reflect on what to do with the unexpected gift of ten thousand pounds from his father. Hugh had been very clear that Tom was to spend it on something to enrich his life, and to be selfish if necessary. Megan had been like a dog with a bone, refusing to give up her own ideas about what to do with it. She had started visiting kitchen showrooms on Boxing Day, and had become as devoted a worshipper of cabinets, handles and tiles as if she had converted to a bizarre culinary cult.

"We could get a lovely kitchen with that amount of money," she had told him repeatedly. "This one is so dated. It has to be at least fifteen years old."

Tom, trying to be fair, did cast a critical eye over their kitchen. However, he still saw no reason to change it. The cabinets were in good, solid condition. If the doors and worktops weren't in line with current fashions, well - they lived in an old house, so he didn't really see a need to keep up with new trends. While a shiny new kitchen would undoubtedly give Meg a great deal of satisfaction, it would do absolutely nothing for him. And he didn't accept her argument that it would add value to their house. Their tastes might not be in line with those of any potential purchaser; and besides, they had no intention of selling, so the value of the house was immaterial.

For once, he dug his heels in, and it had obviously come as something of an unwelcome shock to her. She was accustomed to him being ready to bend to her will in most things. She tried wheedling; she tried taking him to visit friends who had stylish, modern kitchens. She even resorted to a lingering tour of Ikea in the hope that a choice of cheaper units might sway him. She tried moaning and whingeing, finding fault with the slightest thing like a loose handle or a slightly wonky cupboard door. None of it had any effect other than to irritate him. He had even, once, accused her of paying more attention to their kitchen than she did to him.

He had explained his father's instructions to her. A kitchen would not enrich his existence. A kitchen would not bless him, however trendy the handles were, however gorgeous the slate or limestone or granite. A kitchen would in no way make his life feel fuller or more satisfying. And he was determined not to spend his birthday money on one.

No, he had his own plans. Instead of spending his savings on an old banger of a surf bus, as he had originally planned, he would add them to the money Hugh had given him, and buy a proper camper van. He could now afford a solid vehicle, provided he took advice from someone knowledgeable, and Garin was the perfect candidate with his connections in the classic VW scene. He had flirted with the idea of importing a rust-free van from the Arizona desert, as Garin had done; but now this van had come up for sale, and Garin was right: she was a beauty.

Its jolly orange paintwork and cleverly designed interior encouraged him to dream. He and the whole family could use it to enjoy quality time together, out in the fresh air in the countryside or near the sea. It would give them opportunities to go away for weekends and make the most of the school holidays. They could perhaps tour the UK – or even go abroad, into France and further afield. He had pored over blogs by families undertaking road trips into Europe and beyond, so he knew it could be done; with six weeks off work together each summer, it needn't be an unrealistic dream. It would be wonderful to be able to introduce the kids to different parts of the world.

Megan's idea of a perfect holiday, he knew, was a combination of indolence and sightseeing, preferably all-inclusive in a plush hotel with a spa and decent restaurant somewhere in the Mediterranean. Perhaps camping couldn't rival Campania or Capri, but he cherished the hope that being able to relax together away from the demands of real life, without the hassle of airports or timetables, would help them renew their passion for one another. A simpler style of holiday could free them to focus on what was really important: togetherness, and quality time with the children away from the distractions of the television or the telephone. No computer, no email, no diary, no work: it would be bliss. They could spend more time outdoors, walking, cycling or swimming; or, in a few years' time when the girls were older, taking up activities like surfing or climbing. Given time, he was sure he would be able to convince Megan to share his viewpoint. It all made such perfect sense.

There was something about the bright orange van that said "sunshine"; something about the nostalgic style of a 1970s VW that spoke of holidays, fun and relaxation. Even the simple act of sitting in the driver's seat made him feel more relaxed. This van had the advantage of being right-hand drive, which an imported van like Garin's wouldn't be. And there was a certain amount of truth in what Garin had said: he would be unlikely to lose money if he should ever decide to sell it.

"I wouldn't really go taking her above fifty-five or sixty miles per hour if I were you," Garin advised as they took her out for a test drive.

"She's an old lady: she needs treating with respect if you want her to last."

Tom raised his eyebrows at Garin's serious expression. "Gaz, when have you ever treated a lady with respect?"

His spirits lifted as soon as he turned the key and heard the distinctive rhythmic, raspy burble of the air-cooled engine. It took him back to the sound of his Beetle, in the days when he had first discovered girls and the delicious freedom of being able to drive to secluded lanes for thrilling, furtive petting in the back seat.

"God, I love the noise it makes," he said happily as he drove carefully up the street towards more open roads.

Garin grinned. "Sounds like a skeleton wanking in a biscuit tin, doesn't it?"

Driving along the dual carriageway, Tom didn't care that he was being overtaken by any number of faster, more modern vehicles. Let the Mercedes and BMW drivers carry on: he was content at a slower pace. Let them pursue their rat races and their deadlines; let them be controlled by their schedules and their satellite navigation systems.

"If you think this is slow, wait till you go up a hill," Garin warned him. "And allow yourself plenty of time for braking."

The leisurely pace was a revelation. Pootling along in the sunny orange leisure van made him feel he had all the time in the world. All he needed was a Beach Boys track on the radio to make the vision complete. The thought made him laugh aloud.

"You've got the bug, haven't you?" Garin wore a triumphant smile. "I knew you would. An air-cooled VW engine sounds and smells like nothing else. There really is something about these vans.

They make you feel free. You'll never be financially rich, owning one: you'll always be spending money to maintain it. But you'll be rich in the ways that matter. Adventure before dementia, that's what it's all about."

He bought the van, of course. Jez was glad to see his cherished van go to a fellow enthusiast. It was as if he was selling a puppy, not a vehicle, Tom thought, as Jez droned on about how he wanted her to go to a good home. He felt guilty driving away, seeing Jez struggling to hold back tears as he waved goodbye. It was astonishing to see how attached he had been to it.

Unfortunately Megan's reaction to his new purchase was less than positive when he pulled into their driveway, his face alight with excitement. Her green eyes were coldly accusing as he got out, her hostility palpable.

Nia and Alys, on the other hand, were elated. To them, it seemed like a Wendy House on wheels. Jez had included his camping equipment in the sale, not wanting to ship it all to Canada, and the girls ransacked the lockers and drawers, pulling out enamel plates, battered saucepans and a dented whistling kettle, exclaiming over them as if they were precious treasures.

"Be careful," Tom said, delighted by their enthusiasm. "We don't want to go breaking anything when she's only just arrived."

Megan's arms were folded frostily over the gentle swelling of her pregnancy bump. "Please tell me this is a wind-up. *Please* tell me you haven't gone insane and blown twelve thousand pounds on this ridiculous old rustbucket."

He remained calm, convinced of the sound reasoning that had underpinned his purchase. He stood beside her, hands in his pockets, admiring the van's paintwork.

"She's not a rustbucket. She's in very sound condition, actually. Yes, she cost twelve thousand pounds, but that was a bargain. She's probably worth a couple of thousand more. This is the perfect conversion for our family: there are bunks up in the roof for Alys and Nia, and the downstairs seats can be made up into an enormous bed with enough room for you, me and the baby. We can strap all three of them in safely when we're travelling. And look – there's an electric socket. You'll be able to take your hair straighteners on holiday."

Admittedly, this last point smacked of desperation. Still, even though it was obvious that she was entirely unmoved, he persisted in trying to persuade her of the merits of his plan.

"Believe it or not, Meg, I did think it through. This van fulfils everything my dad wanted for me. It will give me the chance to spend quality time with you all, to take the kids to new places on weekends or even just day trips. We don't need to go far: there are some lovely places along the coast in the Vale of Glamorgan. We could explore that new Welsh coastal path, for instance. Or we could head up into the Brecon Beacons, or the Forest of Dean. And what about the Cotswolds, Devon, the Gower, Pembrokeshire? They're all only an hour or two away. Think how much the girls will love spending time on the beach or in the countryside. We're lucky, living here, with so many great places to go within an easy distance." Seeing her mutinous face, he added softly: "This really will make our life richer, if you'll let it."

To judge by her scowl, she remained determinedly disbelieving. He gave up. Better to ignore her petulance for now. Hopefully she would come round, in time, to something approaching his way of thinking.

"Look at this, girls." He unclipped and raised the elevating roof. The canvas was huge, a great prism-shaped tent that extended beyond the side of the van, above the sliding door. He lifted them up to show them the bunks and they squealed gleefully.

"There's loads of space up here, isn't there? It will be like having your very own den. And you've got a window. We can put up some bed guards to make sure you don't roll out, so you'll be safe and sound. And we'll get you a sleeping bag each, to keep you snug and warm. Camping will be like an adventure."

"Can I choose my own sleeping bag?" Alys asked, enthusiastically bouncing up and down. "I want a Barbie one!"

Nia joined in. "I want Peppa Pig!"

"But where will you and Mummy sleep?"

"The seats down here turn into a big bed for me and Mummy."

"Actually, Mummy will be sleeping in her own bed at home," Megan cut in from outside.

Alys and Nia's faces crumpled with disappointment. Tom swallowed his annoyance.

"Will you have a sleeping bag too, Daddy?"

"Mummy and I will have a big sleeping bag to share. You can help us choose one when we go to the camping shop," he promised, giving each a kiss as he lifted them back down.

"Now, then: we need to give the van a name," he continued cheerily. "All camper vans should have names. What do you think we should call it?"

"Peppa!" Nia suggested the name of her favourite cartoon character, beaming.

"Don't be silly." The bossier Alys dismissed this idea. "We should call it a proper name, like Daisy or Poppy."

"Hmm, those are all good ideas. And you're right that it should be a girl's name. But this type of camper is called a Viking, so maybe it should have a Scandinavian name? Perhaps we should call her Helga…? Or maybe Hilda!"

Alys and Nia shook their heads and giggled at his suggestions.

"I'll give you a name for it," Megan said venomously. She had remained obstinately on the driveway. "Call it Greta, after Greta Garbo. Because in being so utterly selfish and ignoring my wishes, I can only assume that you 'want to be alone'."

He wouldn't give her the satisfaction of knowing she had annoyed him.

"Greta?" he pondered aloud, as if it had been a serious suggestion. "Yes, of course! That's an excellent idea. Greta Garbo was Scandinavian; she was beautiful, alluring; a true classic. Greta is a perfect name for her. Isn't Mummy clever, girls?"

They glared at one another above their daughters' strawberry blonde heads. The girls were oblivious, playing with the plunder they had found in the van's cupboards.

Tom took a step down from the van and stood with palms outspread in a vain appeal to Megan's more generous side. Perhaps poetry would do it: she was usually impressed by that.

"'I, being poor, have only my dreams,'" he pleaded. "I have spread my dreams under your feet, Meg; tread softly, because you tread on my dreams."

She spun on her heel and went back into the house without a word.

Chapter Fifteen

Diamond Jubilee Bank Holiday:
Tuesday 5th June 2012
Saunton, North Devon

On the morning after the camp fire, Tom's first act after getting dressed was to head to the payphone to call home. No one answered. Upon hearing the familiar recorded message, he hung up the receiver, but immediately regretted his cowardice and called back to leave a message. He hoped his voice sounded natural and friendly, not shifty and guilt-ridden.

"Hi everyone, it's me. I just wanted to let you know that I'm okay. Hope you're all okay too. I'll see you in a couple of days... Big hugs and kisses to all of you."

Making his way to the surf school van, he approached the male instructor first to collect his surfboard. He did his best to avoid making eye contact with Jess, but she was having none of it.

"No hard feelings, eh?" She handed him a wetsuit, a twinkle in her eye.

It would have been churlish not to nod, but to his dismay she took this as encouragement to behave as flirtatiously as before. For the rest of the day he took extra care to do nothing to encourage her attentions.

Walking back from the beach with her at the end of the afternoon, he told himself that she was only being playful when touching his arm and walking too close. She couldn't possibly mean anything by it, given the difference in their ages, especially after he had told her he was married. He kept his tone light and his body language detached, avoiding eye-contact again, hoping that she would get the message and turn her attentions to one of the younger lads who was practically drooling after her. As they strolled up the sand-strewn tarmac path towards the car park, surfboards under their arms, Jess chattered coquettishly, battling to get his full attention.

He nodded politely enough but his mind was on other things. He should really make another effort to contact Megan from the payphone, despite dreading the inevitable flak he would have to take if she answered the call. He hoped she was coping. At least she wouldn't have the stress of getting out to work in the mornings, now that her maternity leave had started. Nor would she have to get the girls off to school or playgroup, as it was half term. But he knew that looking after them on her own, twenty-four hours per day, would be tiring for her. Perhaps he should phone home again tonight and offer to cut his holiday short by a couple of days. If he went home on Thursday afternoon he would have a whole weekend to make things up to her before going back to work.

So engrossed was he in his thoughts, he didn't immediately notice the woman standing next to Greta. Then, all at once, her rounded stomach and long auburn hair caught his eye. He focussed on her dress – he had seen that bright, flowery print before.

He paused. Could it be Megan? But how would she have got here? She hadn't been driving for the past couple of weeks, with her growing bump so uncomfortably close to the steering wheel. He dismissed the idea as impossible. No, it couldn't possibly be her.

But as he stared, she lifted her arm to brush a loose strand of hair from her eyes and the familiarity of the gesture gave him a rush of certainty. It had to be her.

He dropped his surfboard and took to his heels, barely registering Jess's squeal behind him. Dodging the people lingering on the path, not thinking to pause and check for moving vehicles, he tore across the car park. Megan's tired, pink-rimmed eyes widened as he sprinted towards her and swept her into his arms.

She gasped as he crushed her to his chest and buried his face in her neck with a muffled cry of gladness. She smelled so good. He wanted to enfold her in his arms and never let her go. In that moment, none of their recent wrangles mattered. All that mattered was that she was his; she was here. He could almost have believed in that moment of recognition that he had conjured her by wishing. She must have been delivered to him by the wind or the sea.

"Megan! What are you doing here?" He loosened his grip a little in case he was hurting her in his delight at seeing her.

Her green eyes were sharp, their colour accentuated by the purple shadows like bruises below. The furrow in her brow deepened. "I thought I'd better find out why my husband left me," she said.

He blinked, puzzled. "What do you mean? I haven't *left* you. Didn't you read my note? I told you I'd be back at the end of the week. As a matter of fact, I was only thinking today that I'd probably come home sooner. I tried phoning you this morning, but there was no reply."

"Are you sure you haven't left me for a younger, taller, slimmer blonde?" She glared towards Jess, who had by now picked up Tom's surfboard and was crossing to the surf-school van, looking distinctly huffy.

"Who? Oh, you mean Jess? She's just one of the surfing instructors," he said, with as much nonchalance as he could muster. "She's young enough to be my daughter."

Megan faced him squarely. He was uncomfortably aware that he looked a mess, his hair sticking up, sand in his ears and several days' growth of grizzled stubble on his face.

"If she's got her hooks into you, I swear to you I'll tear her eyes out. If you've come down here to be with her, I'll-"

"Meg, I've been here for the surfing and the solitude, not to look for an affair. Besides, I haven't had sex for months, remember: I'd be of no use to an energetic young slip of a girl like that. I've probably forgotten what to do."

She bristled, probably thinking he was accusing her of rejecting him again, but the warmth in his smile seemed to reassure her a little.

"How did you get here, anyway?" he asked, steering the conversation away from Jess.

"On my broomstick," she drawled.

∞ ∞ ∞

Megan was gratified to hear Tom's startled laugh. She hadn't made him laugh without irony for a long time. But then, he hadn't held her like this for a long time, either. It felt good to be in his arms again. Even in this unfamiliar place, being in his embrace made her feel as if she had come home.

"Matt drove me here," she admitted, and as Tom glanced about for any sign of their brother-in-law, she explained that he had returned home to Bethan and their daughters.

"Are the girls alright? Have they missed me?" he asked.

She took a step back, leaving the circle of his arms.

"Well, what do you think? Of course they've missed you! But they're fine. Mind you, they're a bit miffed that you've gone on your first camping trip without them. They're looking forward to seeing you when you're ready to come home…" His relieved smile died as quickly as it had begun with her next words: "…That's if you still want to come home, of course. Don't feel you have to, if you don't want to."

The words burned her throat like acid and dried her mouth as she spoke. She felt it was only right to give him the option of leaving if that was what he wanted, but her offer of freedom still hurt her pride. Huskily, she cleared her throat and lifted her chin. She was determined not to cry in front of him, not in a public car park with that tall, leggy blonde watching. His desertion had hurt her, but she still had some vestiges of dignity.

He was staring at her.

"What are you talking about? Of course I want to come home. It's where I live."

So that answered her main concern: he wasn't really leaving her. But the initial relief ebbed quickly, allowing anger to resurface. She felt like a mother whose child had narrowly avoided a serious accident: her first instinct was to hug him in gladness that he was safe; her second was to give him a very hard slap for giving her such a fright.

Somehow, she managed to suppress the urge to hit him. "It was a bit difficult to be sure, Tom, given that you left without a word."

He gnawed at the corner of his lip, his brow creased in a frown.

"Alright. You've every right to be angry with me. I was a coward not to talk about it with you; but given the way things were between us, I couldn't face discussing it. Sometimes, Meg, it's easier to seek forgiveness than permission."

She blinked and opened her mouth to respond, deflated by his calm readiness to apologise; but he cut her off.

"Look - I don't know what you think, but it seems to me there are lots of things we need to discuss. I haven't been particularly happy over the past few months, and somehow I don't think you have been either. Maybe, in a funny sort of way, us being here – away from home, away from the kids…. it's a golden opportunity for us to talk, don't you think? How long are you planning to stay?"

Again, she was wrong-footed. She hadn't got as far as thinking about when or how she would get home.

"I haven't thought about it. I didn't really get any further in my mind than finding you and finding out whether we still had a marriage."

He nodded. "Stay tonight," he urged her softly, blue eyes unblinking. "We'll have the whole evening to talk things over. It's peaceful where I'm staying: there'll be nothing to disturb us. I'll cook something." He paused. "It'll be your first taste of camping," he pointed out, barely able to conceal his glee.

"I sort of assumed we would go back tonight, if we were still together."

He cocked an eyebrow and leaned his back against the van, his hands in his pockets. "I see. And what were you going to do if we *weren't* still together?"

"You would still have taken me back to Cardiff. Whether you still want to be married to me or not, you are not the sort of man who would make his pregnant wife walk a hundred and thirty miles home. And you'd have had no option but to drive me home, given that I'd refuse to catch a bus and you'd hate paying for a taxi to take me that far."

Their eyes locked: his faintly amused, hers mocking. They were interrupted by a shout from one of the young men from the surfing school, beckoning and pointing to his watch.

"Ah - I have to give back the wetsuit before they go. I won't be long." He eyed her again for a long moment before straightening up. It was the kind of intense regard that made her part her lips slightly, half expecting a kiss; but he turned away with what seemed like reluctance.

From her position in Greta's shadow, she watched him saunter over to the *Wipe Out! Surf School* van. His loose-limbed walk had always done something to her: it was graceful and masculine, with just a hint of a swagger. She supposed those broad shoulders, combined with his narrow hips, were what did it. She knew every inch of that smooth back: his birth mark; the scar he'd acquired by falling out of a tree as a boy; the muscles he liked her to knead when he ached. She'd rubbed sun tan lotion into it on holidays and massaged Ibuprofen gel onto it when he'd exercised too hard. She'd kissed every freckle and mole many times over the years, scratched it like a cat in the heat of passion.

It was strange, standing there gazing at him now, how the sight of his back brought so many memories to mind: some fond, many arousing. How long was it since she'd watched him and felt the stirrings of longing? How bizarre that it should happen now, when it hadn't happened for months and she was still angry with him. It was unexpected, given that her own back was aching so much, her muscles wound tight with tension. Perhaps he was right: being alone together, away from the demands and distractions of home for a night, would give them a chance to reconnect.

Seeing him talking to the surfing instructors and stripping off the bottom half of the wetsuit, she guessed he wouldn't be long, and took the opportunity to pop over to the facilities again, groaning inwardly as she waddled uncomfortably across the car park to the toilets. She couldn't wait to have this baby in her arms and off her sciatic nerve.

By the time she returned to Greta, he was inside and dressed in a t-shirt, cargo shorts and leather flip-flops. At her approach, he jumped out of the van and leaned against the door.

"I'm ravenous after all that surfing," he said. "And I'm too tired to drive home tonight. I need some food, a beer and one last evening under the stars, if you can bear to grant me the pleasure of your company. Then, if you still want to, we can drive home in the morning. I'm sure Bethan and Matt won't mind having the girls for one night."

She glowered at him, recognising that she had little choice but to accept his proposition. "If the bed in that van is as uncomfortable as I suspect it to be, I may well have murdered you by morning."

"As long as I die in your arms, I'll die happy," he declared, hand over his heart. "Ah, that's better. That's the first time you've laughed since you arrived."

In fact, it was the first time she'd done so since Friday evening, but he wasn't to know that.

He held the passenger door open and she hauled herself up with some difficulty, given her present ungainly state. Seeing her safely inside, he slid the side door shut and hopped into the driver's seat, buckling himself in and treating her to his most devastatingly charming smile.

"Welcome aboard."

"Don't push your luck."

She turned her head away. He drove with just one hand on the steering wheel, resting his right arm out of the window to enjoy the cool air trickling through his fingers. On the way to the farm, he stopped at the local convenience store to buy supplies while Megan stayed in the van to take advantage of a clear mobile phone signal.

"Has he shown up yet?" Bethan asked abruptly on picking up the phone, dispensing with any pleasantries. "Matt got back about two hours ago: he told me you found the van without too much trouble."

"Yes, he did show up eventually. And – well, we're talking, at least. He says he hasn't left me permanently. He hasn't actually apologised as such, but he has admitted that going off without a word was a cowardly thing to do..."

Bethan harrumphed at the other end of the line, unimpressed.

"Look, Beth - if it's alright with you, I'm going to stay here tonight. Would you mind keeping the girls until tomorrow? I know it's asking a lot after all that you and Matt have already done."

"Of course I will. Are you sure it's a good idea, though, to stay so far away from home in your condition?"

She sighed. "No, I don't necessarily think it's a good idea. But we need to talk, and maybe we can do that more easily here than at home. I can't say I'm looking forward to sleeping in the van tonight, but let's face it: now that I'm the size of a wartime barrage balloon, I wouldn't sleep very well at home either. The only difference is, I won't be able to get up in the middle of the night and go downstairs to watch TV like I usually do."

"Just make sure you let him know what a shitty thing he's done. He really should apologise profusely for the way he's treated you. I still can't believe he spent all that money on some stupid van and buggered off like that: there's a part of me that thinks you should really make him suffer for it. Make the dickhead grovel."

Meg's mouth twisted sourly. "Don't worry, he'll be left in no doubt that it can't happen again. But you can't blame me for wanting to give him a chance, Beth. He is my husband, and Alys and Nia should have their dad around - if I can bring myself to forgive him."

"I'm well aware of that. It's the only thing that's stopped me coming down there myself and lobbing a brick through his precious windscreen. I do hope you can work things out, but I have to say he's gone a long, long way down in my estimation."

Tom emerged from the shop with a carrier bag in one hand and a large bottle of spring water in the other.

"I'd better go: he's coming back to the van. Give the girls a kiss from me and tell them we'll be back tomorrow."

"Everything alright?" Tom asked as she slipped her mobile phone back into her bag.

"Yes. Bethan will look after the girls tonight but I've told her we'll be back tomorrow."

"The fellow in the shop says there's bad weather coming in tomorrow afternoon, so that's probably the best idea. I don't really fancy surfing in a force ten gale," he remarked.

She stared at him, eyes sharp and accusing, as he pulled away and continued their journey towards the farm. "I've just noticed - you're not wearing your wedding ring."

Had he been trying to worm his way in with that blonde surfing instructor after all, by pretending to be single?

"No, I know," he replied mildly, glancing at his left hand. "I didn't want to lose it. Being in cold water for hours on end, I was worried my fingers would shrink and I'd never find it again if it slipped off. It's in the glove compartment; I'll put it back on if you want."

The explanation sounded reasonable enough, but she had noticed something else. "And you're wearing a necklace. One of those silly leather things."

He grinned sheepishly and touched it lightly with his fingertips. "Ah. Yes. It seemed to go with the surfing. Helped me fit in when I was hanging loose with the dudes. I can even do the shaka."

He held out his fist, thumb and little finger extended, in the classic surfing gesture.

"Huh. There's no fool like an old fool, is there?"

He didn't respond.

"Still, I suppose it's different," she said, unable to resist the urge to snipe at him again.

He looked at her uncertainly. "What is?"

"Most people run away from home when they're in their rebellious teenage phase. But not you, Tom. Oh, no. You waited until you were a forty-year old father to do it."

They had left the village now and were puttering along a country lane, hemmed by hedgerows. At this time of year, after a typically damp British springtime, the fields were a vivid shade of emerald.

He said nothing, pressing his lips together as he always did when denying her the satisfaction of starting an argument. On arriving at the farm a few silent minutes later, she braced herself as they drove along the rutted farm track.

"It's a good job the suspension hasn't been lowered too far, or we'd never get over these potholes," he said.

She rolled her eyes and winced at the pressure of the baby on her groin as they bounced through a gate into a field. Finally they pulled up on a patch of level ground and he turned the engine off.

"Here we are." He was watching her guardedly, obviously awaiting her reaction.

"It's just a farmer's field. Not even a proper campsite. It smells of cow pats."

She could tell she had annoyed him. Good.

"Your observational powers clearly haven't deserted you," he said, tight-lipped. "Obviously, if I'd realised you'd be joining me, I would have booked somewhere with a few more home comforts. But it's not all that primitive: there's a toilet and shower in the shed at the end of the barn over there."

He indicated a breeze-block outhouse and her eyes widened at the prospect of a hundred yard walk every time she needed to pee.

"It's really cheap, and it's quiet: even allowing for the Bank Holiday, I've been the only person camping here this week. Now, if you would like to make yourself comfortable, I'll go and let the farmer know that you're staying. He might charge a bit extra for two."

∞ ∞ ∞

Tom strolled over to the farmhouse, ignoring the frantic barking of the farm dog. He waved through the kitchen window, seeing the farmer and his family seated around the table at their meal, and heard the scrape of a chair on the kitchen floor as the man rose to greet him at the door.

"What can I do you for?"

The farmer was a vigorous and weather-beaten man of indeterminate age with sinewy brown forearms below his rolled-up shirt sleeves. He eyed Tom with little curiosity, still chewing a mouthful of food.

"I just wanted to let you know that my wife has arrived to join me tonight. And I'll be going home a bit earlier, probably sometime late tomorrow morning."

The farmer nodded, unsurprised. "Ah, you'll have heard, then. There's a storm coming in tomorrow."

"Hmmm. With the wife turning up, I suspect there may be a tempest brewing already."

The other man chuckled. "Oho - like that, is it?"

Tom responded with a wry hitch of an eyebrow. Having established that the farmer didn't expect any further payment for Megan to stay, given that he would be leaving earlier than expected, he returned to the van.

Megan was waiting, her back towards him, contemplating the patchwork of rolling fields and interlocking hedgerows that slipped towards the coast. The breeze made her glorious auburn curls shift and caress her shoulders. Unable to stop himself, he stooped to kiss the exposed skin, breathing in the familiar smell of her perfume. She shivered.

"It's a beautiful place," she conceded, and he put his arms around her to gaze with her across the countryside. He felt her muscles tighten in response to his embrace; but for once, she didn't shrug him off.

"You haven't seen the best of it yet," he murmured into her ear. "We're facing west: we'll get a clear view of the sunset later." His hands rested on her abdomen and the baby kicked at the unwelcome weight. They both laughed, unexpectedly unified by their shared amusement.

She rested the back of her head against his chest. "She seems to feel quite indignant about you leaning on her."

He tucked a loose strand of hair behind her ear before leaning down to kiss the tender lobe, very gently. But he had gone too far, it seemed. Abruptly, she pulled away and stomped back to the van. She obviously wasn't ready to forgive him yet, had decided to punish him a bit longer.

"I thought you were hungry?" she said, opening the bag of supplies he had bought at the shop.

"I am."

Her brusque rejection had made his voice gruff. He *was* hungry - in more ways than one. The sight of her here, so altogether lovely despite the obvious strain and tiredness in her features, and their brief moment of accord when they laughed together about their baby, had encouraged him to let his guard down. He squared his shoulders and set about preparing dinner, grabbing the portable gas barbecue from its locker in the van and setting it up at a safe distance.

With the barbecue warm under its lid, he threw on a few chicken portions and drizzled over a marinade mix, generating mouth-watering aromas that drifted across the grass. Soon a few liberal handfuls of pasta were boiling on the two-burner camping stove, ready to be mixed with some pesto, and a bag of salad was torn open to complete their meal. Megan watched. He knew she was impressed, and also knew she would never admit it.

"Thank you," she murmured as he set up a folding canvas chair for her and handed her a plate.

"You're welcome." A teasing note entered his voice. "You can wash up." He chuckled at the horror on her face at the idea of washing dishes in the confined facilities of the van.

"You're so predictable, Meg." He sat down in the open doorway of the van, using the edge of the floor as a seat. "Don't worry: I'll do it."

Relief swam over her face.

"It really isn't that bad," he said, attacking his food with the hearty enthusiasm of a man who has been engaged in vigorous physical activity all day. "And as you see, it's possible to eat well without too much hassle."

"Trying to convert me?"

She watched as he sucked chicken juices off his fingers.

His only response was a shrug. So she had seen through his ruse to prove to her that camping food didn't have to be a constant round of instant mashed potato, tinned sausages and baked beans. It was a shame they couldn't share a bottle of wine, but given her condition he didn't like to suggest it. And as much as he would love to crack open a beer, it would be ill-mannered to do so when she had to abstain. Still, he thought - hopefully there would be other occasions in the not-too-distant future when they would make up for it.

She picked at her food, apparently unable to summon up much enthusiasm for eating despite the trouble he had taken to make a tasty meal for her.

"Don't you like it?" he asked after a few minutes.

"Oh, I do. It's delicious. I just don't have much appetite: it's been a bit of an emotional rollercoaster of a day." She laid down her fork and gazed mournfully at the plate in her lap.

He chewed a mouthful of pasta meditatively, unsure how to proceed. An inept move might lead to another argument, and he didn't know if he could stand it.

"I'll finish yours if you don't want it. It'd be a shame to waste it, after all." He hoped that a practical approach would be suitably inoffensive. Besides, he hadn't yet satisfied his stomach after the day's surfing. The hours in the sea, grappling with the board and the waves, had given him a prodigious appetite.

"Carry on." She attempted to stand up to pass him the plate, but getting up out of the sagging canvas chair was easier said than done. She gasped out an indignant laugh.

"I can't get up! I'm like a beetle stuck on its back – oh, I'll be so glad to get this baby out."

He smirked knowingly, rising to take the plate from her. "You'll take those words back in a few weeks, when you're stuck on the sofa feeding it."

"What's up?" he asked softly, after a few moments had passed without any explanation for her pensive frown.

"There's something that I find confusing. When you first saw me in the car park, you seemed genuinely pleased to see me."

It was his turn to be puzzled. He dropped a chicken bone onto his plate and rubbed his fingers vigorously with a wet wipe, handing a clean one to her.

"I don't understand why that's confusing. Why wouldn't I be pleased to see my wife?" he asked cautiously, getting up to pour each of them a beaker of water.

"Well, you evidently didn't want to let me know where you were." He stiffened in response to the accusation. "You didn't say in your note where you'd be staying, and you didn't bother to phone or even text home to tell us where you were or what you were doing. I was beside myself with worry. I only found out you might be in Saunton because I checked the browsing history on the computer."

He handed her the drink and sank back down, sipping the cold water broodingly. So that's how she had tracked him down. He had been wondering about that.

"So when I came to find you, I imagined I'd be about as welcome as a police officer in a crack den," she went on. "Especially when I saw you with that girl. I mean, it's like your mother arriving home unexpectedly and catching you smoking pot in your bedroom or something... But then you ran over and threw your arms around me as if you were glad I'd come."

"I *was* glad. I'd missed you."

"Huh! If that really was the case, you should have let me know where you'd gone."

He rose to his feet, picked up the barbecue tongs and empty food packaging, then just as abruptly put them down again, facing her.

"Okay. Do you really want to know why I didn't say anything?"

She waited, arms folded.

"Quite honestly, Megan, I would rather face a scrum full of snarling six foot seven inch rugby players than get into an argument with you. You were never going to agree to me going off for a week on my own, and certainly not in Greta, when you didn't approve of me buying her in the first place. I admitted to you earlier that I took the cowardly option: quite frankly, it's because I just can't cope with you when you're in a temper. When you get that furious expression on your face and put on your teacher voice, I have to fight the urge to put myself in the corner with my face to the wall. With that Margaret Thatcher glare of yours, you'd make Medusa look like a pussycat!"

She looked daggers at him, inadvertently confirming the truth of his description.

"I'm sorry." He held up his palms in a gesture of surrender, but his tone was more sharp than contrite. "I shouldn't have done it. I shouldn't have planned it. I shouldn't have booked it; and I shouldn't have left without telling you."

"Consulting me," she corrected him, equally sharply.

He rolled his eyes. "Fine: *consulting* you. I apologise unreservedly. It was weak; it was cowardly; it was inconsiderate. And, as you rightly pointed out earlier, it was juvenile."

His expression soured as any vestige of high spirits disappeared, and he rubbed his face in exasperation. So much for his hopes for a civilised evening. They were as prickly around each other as ever.

But she was only slightly placated.

"Well, you may not have given me an adequate explanation, but at least you've finally apologised," she replied tartly.

He took refuge in activity, unable to make her understand. "I'm going to tidy up," he declared. "Then I'm going to have a shower and wash all the salt and sand off from today. You do what you like, Megan. But I hope we aren't going to spend the whole evening at each other's throats. There's only so much arguing any couple can do before they lose sight of why they were ever together in the first place."

Chapter Sixteen

Diamond Jubilee Bank Holiday:
Tuesday 5th June 2012
Saunton, North Devon

Megan sat as if frozen in the canvas chair, making no offer to help as Tom set about clearing away the detritus of their meal. She looked dazed, as if she had been stunned by a blow.

Grimly silent, Tom tidied up with his customary economy of movement. If she wanted to just sit and chew her fingernails instead of offering to help, so be it: he had made his apology and ventured a truthful explanation for his actions. He was damned if he was going to grovel. With the van set to rights, he grabbed his wash bag and towel and stalked off towards the lean-to shower room. It was a relief to wash the day off, even if he did have to push twenty pence into a coin slot to pay for two minutes of hot water.

Afterwards, he stood before the tiny basin and shaved for the first time in days. His reflection in the cracked and mottled mirror was more like his usual self: the scruffy, laid back surfer was scraped away and replaced by the careworn family man who had always been buried just below the surface. He patted his cheeks dry pensively and dabbed at a scarlet nick on his chin with the damp towel.

Where were he and Megan going from here? As much as he loved her, and as much as he wanted to work things out, her simmering anger was so wearing. He hated confrontation. He didn't know how much more of it either of them could take; if they carried on as they were, there was a good chance that the atmosphere between them could be soured beyond any chance of recovery.

The air was cooler when he walked back slowly towards the van. Its sunny orange paint, such a happy colour, seemed discordant with his mood. For once, the sight of Greta failed to cheer him up, and only served as a visual reminder of the conflicts with his wife. A cowardly thought flitted through his mind: perhaps he should just sell Greta, abandon all hopes of a freer lifestyle with the family, and pay for the damned kitchen. Resolutely, he fought back the temptation to acquiesce. He had come too far to back down now.

He couldn't see Megan at first, and a sharp spasm of anxiety knotted his stomach. Where had she gone? He broke into a jog, then spotted her huddled in one of the seats in a corner of the van. Thank goodness. The air was cooling, the evening wearing on, and goose pimples studded her arms as she sat alone, her face as bleak as winter.

He paused, unsure how to broach the impasse between them. Finally, he reached into a locker under one of the other seats and pulled out a pink blanket of polar fleece. It was bright with cartoon characters: Alys had chosen it, with great excitement, when he took the children to the camping shop. Megan had refused to come with them. Carefully, Tom draped the blanket around her, tucking it in gently. She seemed so woebegone with that enormous baby bump on her tiny frame, skin stretched so tightly across it that her navel protruded under the light floral fabric of her sundress. He felt a surge of protective love, so strong it hurt.

Her face crumpled suddenly, as the retaining wall of pride that she had constructed to guard herself from emotion over the past days weakened in the face of his solicitude.

"When I saw that note, I thought it was the end. I thought you'd never come home," she cried, her voice cracking with pent-up emotion. "We'd been so at odds with one another for months. I haven't slept for four nights, imagining all kinds of things. I couldn't bear the thought that you'd left me. It tore me apart to think you didn't want me any more."

He crouched before her and framed her face in his hands, oblivious to anything but the pain written there. With one thumb, he stroked away a teardrop that had trickled onto her cheek. As he leaned in to kiss her forehead softly, trying to soothe her fears away, she gulped back a sob.

"Shhhh," he whispered. Unwilling to break the physical contact, he rested his forehead against hers, trying to communicate comfort through his touch. Nose to nose, he willed her to let go, to allow herself to be vulnerable.

"I only ever planned to be away for a week," he murmured. "My home is with you and the girls: how could I be at home anywhere else? Come on, Meggie. We're like a dovetail joint, you and I. The glue may have weakened lately, but we were made to fit together and stay together, whatever happens."

She mumbled an incoherent response, and with a sob, buried her face against his neck and threw her arms around him.

"I was so scared. I thought you'd never come back. I really didn't think you loved me any more."

He rocked her gently, stroking her hair and crooning inarticulate reassurances, crushed to realise the misery he had caused her. The extent of her distress tormented him.

"Hey, hush now…. Shhhh…… Sweetheart… I expected you to be cross, but I never imagined you'd be frightened. I'm so sorry," he told her quietly, against her ear, planting kisses in her hair like blessings. "I never meant to hurt you like this…. Megan – darling, please don't cry. I really am so, so very sorry."

Face buried against him, she nodded acceptance of his apology between fits of weeping.

Her hands tunnelled under the thin cotton jersey of his t-shirt and she spread her fingers, cool against the warmth of his flesh. His flesh responded instinctively to her touch, an ache springing in his gut. He fought it down: now wasn't the time. But in a movement born of an almost-forgotten habit, one of her hands hand shifted to his side and her thumb brushed over his nipple. It hardened immediately, making him gasp and pull away a little. Had she meant to touch him in that way? It had been so long since she had made any advances. If it had been accidental, he needed space to regain control of his responses.

But no, her eyes had darkened with her craving for closeness. Her lips parted as she leaned in to close the distance between them, and he returned the embrace eagerly. Their lips clung; the hot, moist meeting of their tongues arousing a fierce longing in each of them. Her tears were forgotten in the heat of their sudden leap of desire. As if desperate for his taste as much as his affection, she pressed herself against him so ardently, he lost his balance and toppled backwards onto the narrow floor space of the van. Megan clutched at him, landing awkwardly on top of him with a gasp of surprise that was almost a laugh.

"Are you alright?" he gulped, fearful that she might have hurt herself or the baby in their fall. She gave no answer, but knelt over him and bent her head to cleave her mouth to his again, grinding her groin against his and groaning with frustration at the barrier of their clothes and the fleecy blanket between them.

"I need you," she whispered, and he offered no resistance when she tossed the blanket to one side, gripped his t-shirt in both hands and tugged it over his head.

He was overwhelmed by the intensity of the sensations tripping to his head as she nipped and licked a trail across his chest, raking through the soft hairs with her fingertips. Straddling him, she looked almost wild, empowered by his helplessness in the face of her passionate assault. Teasingly she flicked her tongue in a circle around his nipples, clearly relishing making him gasp and push against her before she finally relented and sucked the peachy areola. His fingers dug into her thighs as he lost himself: it had been so long since he had been touched like this, he felt he could explode. Her tongue was slick; her teeth pinched at his skin and set it on fire. Apparently oblivious to the discomfort of their cramped position on the floor of the van, she began moving her head lower, the heat and soft moistness of her mouth following the trail of darkening hair towards his waist.

"Meg," he finally managed to pant, as if winded by the force of their mutual desire. "Meg – the door is open."

She looked up, eyes glazed, as if she hardly knew what he was saying. It was only when he gasped her name again that she realised they were fully exposed to the view of anyone who happened to glance over from the farm towards Greta.

"Ah… Whoops." Her mouth curved in a breathless smile. She sat upright, deliberately sliding her hips against his and thrilling to the sound of the deep groan that her wanton movements elicited.

He was bewitched. She was so erotically uninhibited, astride him with the straps of her dress slipping from her shoulders and her titian curls tumbling voluptuously over her shoulders. There was something shamelessly pagan about her, with her rounded fertile belly and her irresistible power to render him helpless with longing.

"God, I've missed you." He wasn't referring to the last few days so much as the past months of more or less enforced celibacy. His eyes burned with unabashed adoration.

She stroked a slow path with one finger from the hollow of his throat down his breastbone.

"I think it's my turn to be confused," he continued. He hesitated, wary of spoiling the intimacy between them, but a new warmth in her expression invited him to explain.

"You haven't wanted me for such a long time. You saw me as some kind of pest. And yet here you are… here *we* are: as hot for each other as we ever were."

She coloured. "Well… I suppose I've realised that I've missed you, too." She happened to glance up, out of the side door of the van, and froze.

"Tom," she hissed, eyes wide as she stared out of the door.

"What's wrong?"

"We're being watched."

He jerked upright, as far he could manage given that she was still sitting on his hips, and rested his weight on his elbows to try to give himself a view over his shoulder out of the door. He hadn't noticed the laughter in her eyes.

She chuckled as he finally glimpsed their audience and gasped out a relieved laugh. A few metres away from the van, a lone sheepdog stared towards them, as if puzzled by what they might be doing on the floor.

"You had me going for a minute there."

He grinned, lying back down to relax with his arms pillowed behind his head.

Her eyes widened again and lit with a mischievous gleam as she glanced back out of the doorway.

"Hello!" she called cheerily, and waved.

"Behave," he scoffed, then sat bolt upright again as he heard a gruff voice.

"Alright?"

The farmer was strolling past, only a minute or so behind his dog. Gazing at Megan astride Tom in the gap between the seats in their camper van, the man kept his expression politely blank.

"Yes, thank you. We're fine."

She smiled shamelessly at him, as if she wasn't really pinning her half-undressed husband to the floor, and as soon as he had passed out of earshot they both collapsed in a fit of giggles like a pair of naughty teenagers.

"We should really close the door." He stroked her thighs with his palms.

"Mmmm. My knees have gone to sleep. I need to get up, but I might need a bit of help."

There were more giggles as he wriggled out from under her – no mean feat in the narrow channel between the seats - and dragged her stiffly up to her feet. The moment of passion was gone, but they both felt closer as they stepped outside into the fresh evening air.

∞ ∞ ∞

The evening had grown chilly; Megan shivered. Tom reached to replace his t-shirt, then delved in a locker to pull out a couple of hooded fleecy jumpers. He tossed one of them over. It swamped her, of course, but at least it was warm; and it smelled comfortingly of him.

She sank back into the camping chair and watched as he perched on the edge of the camper floor, in the open doorway.

"You should have brought two chairs," she said.

"If I'd known I was going to have such delightful company, I would have."

She fluttered her lashes at the compliment. Now that her heart rate had settled again, she was thirsty.

"I could fancy a cup of tea."

"Mmmm. Good idea. There's water in the kettle if you want to make one."

She gave a little huff, but he didn't take the hint, so after a moment she heaved herself out of the chair and began rummaging in the van for mugs and teabags. Straight-faced, he handed her a box of matches to light the gas for the kettle.

"Has it done you good, getting away?" she asked, while waiting for the kettle to boil. She had no doubt that she looked bloody awful, herself, after her sleepless nights. Lucky swine, getting all that time to restore himself at his family's expense. He'd been having fun, getting a tan that exaggerated the colour of his eyes and toning up his muscles, flirting with young blondes... The thought of the girl needled her again. She tried and failed to keep the ice from her voice.

"You look pretty good on it, I must say. No wonder that surfer girl fancied you."

"Did she? I can't say I noticed."

She snorted, tapping the back of her hand impatiently with a teaspoon.

"Don't be disingenuous. She was all over you like piss in a wetsuit, and you know it."

"I only have eyes for you," he replied, his tone light but his expression serious.

"Hmmm… I think she was a bit disconcerted when you spotted me and nearly dropped your surfboard on her toe."

Her eyes gleamed. Their renewed intimacy had provided a measure of reassurance that she was secure in his affections, but a part of her still couldn't forgive him. She attended to the kettle's shrill whistle and poured hot water over the teabags.

"Yes, it has done me good. Things were getting on top of me. It had reached the point where I couldn't think straight."

She handed him his mug of tea, then clambered back out of the van to nurse her own drink, grateful for the warmth against her hands.

"I had a lot on my mind," he went on.

She bit her lip. "You didn't talk to me about it."

"I wouldn't have known what to say."

"You could have told me how you were feeling?" She knew she sounded accusing, but couldn't stop herself.

"Perhaps if we'd been getting along better, but we seemed to be at each other's throats most of the time. I felt as if I couldn't do anything right. You didn't seem to want to be close to me. Whenever I touched you, you shook me off as if I was some kind of sex pest. In the end I felt that there was no room for any kind of intimacy between us."

"I was tired," she said irritably, sitting down again. He wasn't going to get away with suggesting it was all her fault. "And after your birthday party, when we rowed about so many things, you seemed to despise me, almost. Seeing that animosity in your eyes – I was really hurt. I didn't want to make love with you because I didn't feel close to you. How could I want to be intimate with someone who didn't even like me?"

"But if you think back, it never used to be like that. You used to touch me all the time. Little things, like pinching my arse as you walked past, or touching my leg while I drove. You used to light up when I walked in through the door. These days, you just bark out criticisms or orders. I walk into the house and all I get is 'that tap's dripping again'. I feel like I need a hard hat and a flak jacket to protect myself from the sniping when I get home and open the front door.

"I can't understand how we went from being so close to having so little common ground, apart from the girls. It happened so suddenly: all at once we were angry with each other about the party and the money from Dad. We couldn't agree about Greta or the kitchen. And I couldn't shake off my resentment about the way you told me about the baby, and Bethan knowing about it before I did."

Not that again. "I tried to explain how that happened. I did say sorry…."

"I know, but I struggled to get past it. And then there's the house: it's been getting to me. While I've been here, I've realised that I need more time to relax when I'm off work, rather than constantly decorating or fixing things in between trips to Dad's. Life is so ridiculously busy these days. There's been so much to sort out, especially with the baby due soon. And work is – well, it's hellish at times. Really, really full-on. I think I just reached breaking point."

Megan twirled her wedding ring as she listened, doing her best to curb her impatience. It was on a chain around her neck, as her fingers were too swollen from pregnancy to wear it comfortably on her hand. She flicked the last dregs of tea onto the grass, then stood up and dropped the empty melamine mug onto the ground next to her canvas chair. Like the steam in the camping kettle a few minutes earlier, her indignation had brewed inside her and now it erupted.

"Tom, I'm sorry to say it, but I'm finding it hard to have much sympathy for you. I mean, there are people out there who are really suffering: people going through hell. People with terrible debts, losing their homes; people with painful illnesses; people whose kids are disabled or dying. People living in fear of violence outside their front doors. People who are scared of losing their jobs. People who've lost limbs or been bereaved. Compared with them, your life is a walk in the park. Everyone finds everyday life a bit of a grind. That's the way it is: it's called reality. And let's face it, unless we win the lottery and can pay staff to run the household and look after your dad and Auntie Jean, it's never going to change."

She paused, irritated by his blank, frozen expression as he heard her out.

"What do you think my life is like, eh? Do you imagine it's so much better than yours? I can assure you it's a continuous slog of work, cooking, cleaning, grocery shopping and laundry. I tidy up the same toys fifteen times a day. Sometimes I feel like I do nothing but load and unload the dishwasher and washing machine. But unlike you, I don't run off whinging about it. I can accept that a certain amount of responsibility comes with the territory of being an adult. So what makes you so special that you think you have the right to desert your wife and children to go off and find yourself? For God's sake, I've never heard such self-indulgent crap. I don't even get to go to the toilet by myself, and yet you think it's okay to go off on your own for a whole week."

His face was hidden from her, his shoulders hunched as if to defend himself from a blow. The hand threaded into his hair seemed knotted with tension. Every pore radiated misery.

Her words had been born of frustration and a childishly spiteful desire to see him hurting as she had been hurting over the previous few days. But, observing their effect upon him now, she wished she could call them back, stifle them and snuff them out. She felt ashamed, as if she had slapped a toddler in a fit of temper. The initial release of giving in to the temptation to lash out, to shock and to cause pain, was followed at once by a stab of guilt at her loss of control.

She reached out to try to touch him, make contact again, and offer a silent apology; but he flinched from her fingers as if they burned his arm, and she cringed.

"I'm sorry," she said, all too aware of the inadequacy of the word. Now they had both said it, within the space of a few minutes, and yet it was clear that neither of them felt any better. The rift between them yawned more than ever.

He got up and took several steps away. She shifted uncomfortably from foot to foot, her back aching from tension and the hours spent on the road earlier. The mournful lowing of cattle in the barn nearby seemed to give voice to her sadness at the sight of the familiar broad shoulders of her husband slumped with hopelessness. There was no pride in his bearing. The shame in his eyes when he finally faced her mirrored her own.

He scuffed heavily past her to sink back onto his perch in the doorway, gnawing at his lip. The sun was low in the sky. A flock of rooks swooped to their roost in a tree, moving as one entity, and she envied their ability to communicate so effortlessly. If only she and Tom were more like them.

For several minutes she watched his long fingers fussing at a loose thread on his shorts, winding it around and around as he brooded in silence. It was curiously irritating, an activity every bit as fruitless as their lack of communication, heightening her own sense of going round in circles. She hated being made to feel guilty. *Just talk, will you? You should have talked to me before, and here we are sitting in silence again.*

"I couldn't help noticing that you brought your guitar with you," she said eventually. "I haven't heard you play it for years." Grunting at the twinge in her back, she sank back into the too-low canvas chair.

When he spoke, his voice was subdued. "I was horribly out of practice, but I've been having a go again in the evenings since I got here. I've found it quite therapeutic. Sometimes music says things that it's hard to find words for."

Maybe if you made more effort to find some words on occasion, we wouldn't be in this mess... No – don't say it. For once, don't say what you're thinking. She sighed, suddenly weary of it all. Too weary to keep the sarcasm from her voice. What melodramatic nonsense had he been playing on these solitary evenings? *Everybody hurts? Suicide is painless?*

"Why don't you play me something now, then? Something to explain the existential quest for meaning that you've been engaged in since Friday."

He fetched his guitar, still with that hangdog expression, and settled with it on the edge of the van floor. Lifting the strap over his head, he rested the instrument on his thigh and checked the tuning, plucking the strings and deftly adjusting the pegs just enough to make it sound sweet again.

"Honestly, I'm really interested to hear what kind of music has had such a restorative effect on you. I've been asking myself: which tune could be so wonderfully therapeutic?"

He strummed a few chords, his face serious, then looked her in the eye, increased the tempo and sang.

"*Ging gang goolie goolie goolie goolie watcha, ging gang goo, ging gang goo…*"

She didn't know what she had expected, but it certainly wasn't the Boy Scout campfire song. Silly sod. In spite of herself, she burst out laughing and kept on laughing as he sang it through, including the chorus, right up to *Shally wally, Shally wally.*

"Idiot!" she exclaimed when he stopped. Sheer ridiculousness, the idea that he had consoled himself by vigorously singing Ging Gang Goolie every night. But she had felt a lightening in her chest, a lessening of the tension that had built up between them like a barrier. If he could still make her laugh, even when she clung to anger, maybe there was still hope.

"You always manage to do the unexpected, don't you?" she said.

He had permitted himself a brief, roguish grin at the end of the song, but it died with her words.

"No, actually," he said, his expression grave. "I always do exactly what's expected. And, quite frankly, Megan - therein lies the problem."

Chapter Seventeen

Diamond Jubilee Bank Holiday:
Tuesday 5th June 2012
Saunton, North Devon

om didn't explain further, but fixed his attention on the
strings of his guitar and began a plaintive song that she
hadn't heard before. It was ages since Megan had heard the
warm, rich timbre of Tom's singing voice, and her
expression softened as she listened. The song was undeniably
melancholy: slow and wistful, it revealed much of his feelings.

"Our recent disconnection
Cost our love its energy
My heart and soul rejected
Intimacy neglected
Only anger now reflected
We're crushed by misery.

If I could learn to live with me

Each day a fresh new start
Maybe you could tolerate
Overlook my past mistakes
Help me to elucidate
The anguish in my heart."

Not quite what she had been expecting. Not mere self-indulgent crap, after all, but a lament for his state of mind and the state of their marriage. Her irritation had begun to fade by the second verse and evaporated entirely by the end.

"It seems to sum up what I have to do. I have to learn to live with myself. To stop being my own worst problem." His mouth twisted, as if tasting something sour.

"Have you been feeling like that? As if you're struggling to get through each day?" She paused. "What about us? Have we really disconnected? Do you feel that I've rejected you?"

He blinked rapidly, apparently unable to answer, so she persisted, studying his expression. This was like digging out a splinter or lancing a boil: a short-term pain for long-term gain. Even if the answer hurt, she had to know how he felt about her. About them.

"Is that what Greta was really about? Did you spend the money from your dad on a camper van to get away from me?"

To her surprise, his eyes glittered as he slipped the guitar strap off his shoulder. Was he actually going to cry? She hadn't seen him weep since they watched *Up.* She remembered how they had both pretended to have a sudden attack of hay fever, hiding their tears from the girls, and then laughed at themselves for getting so caught up in a cartoon.

"It wasn't to get away from you," he mumbled, looking at his feet. "It was to get away from life in general. To escape from reality, I suppose."

"Right."

"I feel sometimes as if I'm wading through treacle… or pushing an elephant uphill. It's exhausting; and somehow it feels so pointless. I'm forty now, Meg. My life is slipping by, and what have I really achieved?"

"You've got a good job, a comfortable home, two beautiful daughters who adore you and are growing into lovely little people; you're married…"

"Oh, I've got a respectable job and yes, I'm thankful for the girls, of course I am. But you can't deny that for the last six months or so we couldn't have described ourselves as happily married – in fact I don't know how long you'll be able to put up with a miserable old sod like me." He rubbed his face with his hands. "I don't expect you to understand. I know how crazy it is. I mean, I'm surrounded by people all the time, and yet - I've never felt lonelier. I didn't know it was possible to feel lonely in a marriage, but I have been. They don't tell you that when you start out, do they? They say two become one, but they don't warn you that afterwards, when the oneness starts breaking down, you become so much less than even a half.

"My whole life, Meg, I've done what other people have wanted me to do. I didn't want to go to university: I went because my parents expected me to. It seemed wrong to go against them when they'd done everything they could to support me; and my mum was ill at the time so I didn't want to upset her… Then, when I left university, the last thing I wanted was to buy a flat and saddle myself with a mortgage; but Dad and Rob said it was a great investment and I shouldn't pass up the opportunity. Dad gave me the deposit to start me off, it would have been churlish to refuse - and of course I had the job at St Dyfrig's High… So I just gave up on my plans to go travelling and told myself it wasn't meant to be. And then, more recently… If I'm honest, I didn't want the head of department job, but you were so keen for me to do it, I didn't want to let you down."

That hurt. She remembered pressing him. It had made such perfect sense at the time, or so she'd thought.

He hadn't finished: it seemed he wasn't going to stop until he'd emptied all his thoughts and fears out onto the grass in front of her, like Nia tipping the entire contents of her toy box out onto the floor and stepping back to gape at the resulting mess.

"I barely sleep – I just lie awake every night, worrying. And then when I do manage to doze off, Nia comes in and starts tickling my ear or kicking me in the kidneys, and my brain starts whirring round and round again... I worry about how on earth we'll cope with three children when the house is already in chaos. I worry about how we'll manage for money while you're on maternity leave. My savings haven't been so meagre since I was a student."

Her eyebrows flew up. "You had savings when you were a student? Lucky you: all I had was an overdraft and a loan."

"I worry about Jean, especially after those falls she's had recently. I worry about Dad and having to help him downsize. I wonder how I'll split myself between Ludlow and home when he needs help … Then there's work. I keep up a pretence of coping, but some days I yearn to play truant, probably more than the students do. And home has been more like a combat zone than a sanctuary. Coming in through the front door each evening is like trying to cross No Man's Land with a target pinned to my chest. I know I'm a dreary old fart. I wish I could just snap out of it somehow, but I can't. I've never felt like this before. It's as if a scratchy, grey blanket has draped itself over everything that used to give me joy, and just dimmed it. I'm like a television with the colour and brightness turned down. My life has turned grey, along with my hair."

He shook his head, as if he couldn't quite understand it himself.

"I wish you'd told me," she said, but he carried on as if he hadn't heard.

"It would have been so easy to let you have that kitchen. You'll never know how tempted I was to give in because I knew how much you wanted it, and it might have smoothed things over between us. But… I felt so strongly that for once I had to do something for me. When Dad gave me the money it was as if he was giving me permission to do that. Greta was a way for me to get away from everything, all the demands that just keep pressing in on me. It was never my intention to go off on my own. I hope you know that. The plan was for us all to go together. But then, you hated her, and I got so tired of it all. In the end I thought, if I could just get away, I'd be able to recharge and come back a bit stronger, ready to support you when the baby is born. I took the surfing lessons because I thought if I could challenge myself physically, maybe – oh, I don't know… Maybe it would mean I'm not really past it after all."

He buried his face in his hands.

"You must think I'm so fucking stupid. I'm just a ridiculous, useless old fool, having an absurd mid-life crisis and running away from reality like a stereotype. Just a pointless, self-pitying excuse for a man. I really think, sometimes – no, often - that you and the girls would be better off without me."

"Hey! You mustn't say that."

Enough was enough. Megan forced herself out of the low chair with an effort and knelt beside him. Gently, she tried to pull his hands away from his face, but he resisted, as if embarrassed at being seen in such a moment of weakness. Rising to her feet, she pulled him close; he hid his face in her swollen abdomen while she stroked his hair and waited for him to stop shaking.

"I don't think you're stupid at all," she declared when he had a measure of control over himself again. "Nor are you ridiculous. Or useless. You're not a fool. And I am most definitely *not* better off without you."

She took his face in her hands and made him look her in the eye. He had to hear this, had to know that she was sincere.

"I would be infinitely *worse* off without you, and so would Alys and Nia."

He sat back a little, wiping his hands on his shorts, calmer now, but still radiating despair.

"Tom, for goodness' sake - you're forty, not eighty! The best years are not behind you: they're yet to come. In twenty years' time the kids will be independent and we'll be free to do our own thing. You don't have to give up on the idea of travelling; you'll just have to put up with me tagging along with you instead of going on your own, and accept that I'll give you hell if there are spiders, or the accommodation isn't up to scratch, or if the food is disgusting… It's never too late to live your dreams, cariad. We can live ours together.

"I don't know how you can think so little of your achievements. The kids at school think you're an inspirational teacher. God knows how you manage it, because P.E. lessons when I was at school were enough to put me off exercise for life. But somehow you've done it, and all of your colleagues respect you for it. Everyone in your department looks up to you… And what about the triathlons and the marathons you've done? You've raised thousands for cancer research over the years…"

Shaking his head, he cut her off abruptly. "That was no hardship. I enjoy pushing myself – it's only admirable if there's some sort of sacrifice involved."

She shrugged. "Well, you can belittle it if you like, but to me you're a hero. You're *my* hero. No, don't look at me like that – I mean it. You always have been, from the moment you whirled me around on the dance floor on the night we first met."

His grip on her hand hurt, but there was no way she was going to let go now.

"You've never said that to me before," he said.

"Haven't I?" She could have sworn she had, but maybe he hadn't been listening, or maybe she had neglected to say it recently, or often enough. "If that's the case, I'm sorry. I suppose I just assumed you realised. It goes without saying, doesn't it? Like one of those truths that should be self-evident. All men are created equal; the Pope is a Catholic; Bill Gates has got a few quid put by… Thomas Field is my hero. It doesn't stop you being a prize idiot at times, but you're most definitely a hero to me."

He had rested his cheek against her. Had her words sunk in now? Did he get it?

"I wish you'd told me about these negative feelings before," she said. "I might have been able to help." A deep intake of breath. "I could certainly have behaved in a more understanding way, instead of going on and on about the bloody kitchen. I'm truly sorry… and I'm glad you've told me now."

To her relief, he nodded.

"There's one other thing… and to tell you the truth, it kills me to admit this…" He looked up at last, met her gaze. *Just say it, for God's sake.* "I can see now why you bought the van. I can see that your motives weren't as selfish as I thought at the time."

The way his jaw dropped, as if he'd just witnessed a miracle, made her feel even guiltier for the resentment she had shown when he brought Greta home.

"So there you go," she went on. "Thank you for sharing your feelings with me. I'm glad you trusted me, in the end. Glad it isn't completely all my fault. And I hope you know that I'll do my best to help, in whatever way I can. I'll be there to help you get out from under that nasty grey blanket."

He straightened, paused.

"I hope you realise that you're everything to me, Megan Field."

"Thank you," she said, surprised and moved all at once.

"You to me are everything," he quoted. As she raised her eyebrows, he went on: "You're the first, the last, my everything… Everything I do, I do it for you…"

With a self-conscious grin that she couldn't help returning, he continued: "God only knows what I'd be without you… I just can't stop loving you… You're the best thing that ever happened to me."

By the time he finished, they were both laughing softly. Thank God: a spark of the man she fell in love with. He was still there, hadn't been entirely smothered by that grey blanket he'd talked about.

"That's the power of love," she replied.

He caught her hand and kissed it.

"I don't claim to be clever with words, like you are, Meg. There's nothing I could say that wouldn't sound like a cliché. You're the sun, moon and stars to me – how do I tell you that without it sounding trite? But it's true. I love you. Passionately. Profoundly. Powerfully. And because I love you like that, when you don't want me it tortures me, body and soul. It makes me feel unlovable. It makes everything bleak and meaningless. That's how much I need you. And I know that whatever happens I will never want anyone else the way I've always wanted you."

She swallowed hard. For a man who claimed not to be clever with words, he was doing pretty well.

"Tom, I feel the same about you. When things aren't right between us, it makes me edgy. We skirt around each other, nervous of putting a foot wrong. I constantly ask myself: What have I done wrong? Did I say something wrong? Because when you're so unhappy, and you're holding back from me, I have to assume that I'm the problem. It's as if we disconnected…

"I haven't known how to *be* around you over the past few months. I've had to think about my words and choose them carefully because if I didn't I'd offend you somehow. But then, you'd get annoyed anyway, so after a while I just started to think, sod it - I can't pretend to be what I'm not - and the words come out sounding angry or unfair or grumpy. One way or another, we have to find a way to stop making each other unhappy. I need to be side by side with you, not contending against you. That's the way we'll get through. We *can* get through this… Think of your mum: what would she say now if she could see you in this state?"

The lines like brackets around his mouth deepened at her mention of his mother. "She would say to me: 'Don't just stand there – pray something!' That was always her answer in a crisis."

"And have you? Prayed, I mean, while you've been here?" She felt strangely awkward asking the question: religion wasn't something they talked much about.

"Not exactly, no… My mum used to pray every day. I'm sure it's what kept her going for all those years, when she was ill. All those setbacks, all that bad news, and yet her faith was rock solid. I envy that, you know? She used to say: 'I prayed to see my boys grow up, and I did.' She was thankful. If I had gone through all that, only to still face death so young, I'd feel cheated."

His voice drifted off and it was obvious that he was lost in thought, remembering. But she took it as a good sign that he saw life as precious, worth holding on to.

"My mam's the opposite," she said, wryly.

"Not exactly the model of a Christian woman, is she?"

"Hardly. Can you imagine my mam praying? She'd never say 'Thy Will be done'. She'd be more likely to tear God off a strip for making such a mess of the world. And then she'd tell him all the ways he could have done it so much better."

The baby in her belly heaved, pushing against the pressure of Tom's cheek. Megan's own sense of wonder was reflected in his face. He kissed her abdomen with tender awe.

"It's ironic, isn't it?" he murmured. "There you are, expecting a baby in a couple of weeks: I'm the one who's supposed to be strong for you at the moment. I'm the broad-shouldered ex-rugby player. But, of the two of us, you're the strong one... You remind me of my mum in that respect. She was stubborn and determined, too; but even she wasn't as fiery or resolute or as resilient as you. You may be tiny, but you're one of the toughest people I've ever met."

"It comes with being a woman. Nature designed us tough so we could withstand childbirth. Growing up without a dad to fight my battles for me, I had to fight them myself. Coming to think of it, I probably get a lot of my toughness from *my* mother."

His horrified expression at the suggestion of any similarity between herself and Olwen made her chuckle and ruffle his hair.

"I can think of one thing you do struggle with," he said.

"Oh?"

"Changing wheels. Even on a Mini…"

Her quizzical frown cleared as she remembered.

"That was the day I really fell for you. I'd never met a woman who was so determinedly, pigheadedly independent before. I was in awe of you."

"I was so cross with myself for not being able to get those stupid wheel nuts undone. And then I was cross with you for arriving after most of the hard work was done, like the Yanks arriving late to the War or something. I'd struggled and struggled, and you got them off with one little stamp of your foot. I sat in your car and watched as you did it. The sight of your muscly thighs has turned me on ever since."

She sank down next to him on the step, thinking.

The feelings he had expressed sounded so bleak. Could he be depressed? Not just a bit low, but – she almost didn't want to think it – well, ill? But no, he couldn't be, could he? After all, he hadn't done himself any harm. He hadn't confessed to any plans to drive Greta off a cliff or into a wall, thank heaven, for all he said he believed she'd be better off without him. He was still managing to function: he didn't lie in bed in the mornings, unable to face the day. Maybe it wasn't that bad. She'd make damned sure it never got that bad.

"Right: here's the plan. You're going to book an appointment with the GP when we get home tomorrow. No, you can protest all you like - it's non-negotiable. From what you've told me tonight, you should have gone to see her months ago."

"What can she do? She can't change anything. She can't make my dad get younger or give me the body of a twenty year-old so I can play rugby again. She can't make the kids at school any easier to deal with. Or the staff, for that matter. Let her deal with sick people. As you pointed out earlier, there are plenty of people worse off."

"Maybe there won't be anything she can do. But on the other hand, there might be options worth exploring."

"What? Happy pills?" He glared at her.

"Possibly, but not necessarily. I don't know. But maybe there's a medical reason for the way you've been feeling? Why not speak to your dad, if that would be easier?"

"Quite frankly, I'd rather have my prostate examined by Captain Hook than whinge to my dad about feeling a bit sorry for myself."

"I'm sure you couldn't tell him anything he hasn't heard from a thousand other people before." But she knew him well enough to recognise the intransigence in the set of his jaw. He could be as stubborn as she, when he wanted to be. "Anyway, pills might not be the only way to start feeling better. You've already identified one coping strategy… Getting away to ride some waves."

Teasingly, she mimicked the shaka hand gesture he had shown her earlier. "It would be a lot less worrying for me if you could stay local and go to Porthcawl in future rather than a hundred and thirty miles away, of course; and next time, do me a favour and let me know where you're going."

He tutted at this reminder of his recent misdemeanours.

"So, tell me. Why did it have to be Devon, not Porthcawl?"

He squinted towards the setting sun as it gilded the hedgerows.

"I wanted to really get away. I didn't want the embarrassment of falling off my board into the water and hearing some kid say 'Ooh, hello sir, what are you doing? Not very good at surfing, are you, sir?' If I'd gone anywhere local, it would have been bound to happen."

She couldn't help but smile. They frequently encountered current and former pupils wherever they went, so it was undeniable that this could easily happen. She watched him scuff at a dusty patch in the grass with his toe. He had the most handsome profile, she thought, his jaw still firm despite all his worries about ageing. If anything, his face had grown more attractive with a few wrinkles to give it added character. And she didn't mind his grey hairs in the slightest.

She nudged him with her elbow. "You know, you're not bad looking, for an old man."

"Hmph. Thanks – I think."

But she knew she had him. He had read the invitation in her eyes and couldn't look away. She tilted her chin flirtatiously.

"Promise me you won't get any tattoos or piercings to go with the camper van and the Surfer Dude necklace. And don't grow a beard like some old hippy. It just makes you look scruffy."

"You're such a spoilsport. I was thinking of getting a big VW logo tattooed over my left nipple, and a CND badge over the right. Wouldn't you like that?"

She giggled and tugged at his hooded top. "Perhaps I should have another look at those nipples, just to check whether that might actually be a good idea?"

In a swift movement that took her by surprise, he lifted her onto his lap.

"That sounds like an excellent plan," he murmured, warm hands clasping her hips. "If I set the bed up, you could subject me to a very close examination."

"Purely in the interests of checking out potential sites for tattoos?"

"I've got a lot of potential sites that would bear closer inspection."

She leaned in, her lips almost touching his. "Only if you promise to close the door this time," she said, watching his pupils darken involuntarily. She was rewarded with a deep and passionate kiss that made desire leap inside her as strongly as a kick from the baby she carried. The taste and smell of him, clean shaven and freshly showered, and the strength and warmth of his body, made her long to be even closer to him. How had she gone so many months without feeling this thrill at his touch? Being in his arms now made her want to make up for lost time. Moreover, she sensed that he needed the reassurance of knowing he was wanted.

"Why don't you set the bed up while I go over to that revolting hut and brush my teeth?" she suggested, sliding off his lap. "It's been a bit of an emotional roller-coaster of a day... I need to cwtch up in your arms."

∞ ∞ ∞

He kissed her softly on the forehead and jumped up to fetch his toilet bag and towel for her to use, as she didn't have one with her. They'd been together too long to be precious about intimacies like sharing a toothbrush.

Re-arranging the seats and table, he set up the double bed. When she returned from the wash-room, he explained:

"I only brought one sleeping bag, so I've opened it out like a duvet to go over us. I've put the girls' blankets down for us to sleep on, and I'll manage with cushions while you take the pillow."

She looked doubtful about the improvised arrangements, but shrugged her acceptance. Good: it was the best he could do, in the circumstances, and he wanted her to enjoy her first night in the van. It was important that she should sleep well, if he had any chance of getting her to go camping with him again in the future.

"I'm tired enough to sleep on a tightrope," she admitted. "And it does look cosy with all the curtains closed. I'm sure we'll manage."

He let out his breath, hardly aware that he'd been holding it, and left her to undress in the van while he took his own turn in the wash-room.

By the time he climbed back into the van, sliding the door closed behind him, she was already in bed. Her abdomen made a surprisingly large mound under the sleeping bag. She had dark circles under her eyes and was clearly worn out by the day's events, but watched him unblinkingly as he quickly stripped off his clothes and tossed them under the bed.

"It's not like you to be so untidy," she remarked. "I'm usually the one who leaves clothes lying around, not you."

"Ah, well. The laid-back surfing lifestyle has obviously mellowed me."

He lifted the sleeping bag on his side and slid into bed to snuggle against her.

"Your feet are cold," she grumbled, putting her warm ones against him to transfer some of her own body heat.

"Now who's acting out of character? I usually get thumped if I put cold feet on you. It's very considerate of you to help me warm up."

She nestled a little closer and gazed enticingly at his mouth.

"I am feeling....unusually accommodating tonight."

The invitation made his mouth go dry. The last thing he wanted was to spoil their tentative reconciliation by misunderstanding her signals. It had been so long since she had wanted him: perhaps he was allowing his own desire to cloud his judgment. He licked his lips nervously and reached out to sweep a stray auburn lock back from her cheek.

"I thought you were tired?"

"I am."

"We can just go to sleep if you like. You know, if you'd rather…"

"You're tired too, but when have you ever let that stop you?"

"Well, I know, but I don't want you to feel under any pressure to…"

"Tom – for goodness' sake, will you just shut up and kiss me?"

He didn't give her time to change her mind, but complied eagerly with her request, pulling her close to maximise their skin contact, relishing the sensation of naked flesh on flesh under the cosiness of the sleeping bag.

The snug shelter of the van seemed to lend itself to intimacy: with the curtains closed, the world outside seemed miles away. Her kisses were a healing balm, restoring the wrecked foundations of his confidence. He had needed to feel desired, to know he was needed as more than just a provider. The longing in her dark eyes told him he was wanted as he leaned in to cover her mouth with his own and drink in the taste of her. Exploring the soft heat of her mouth with his tongue, hands in the cool silkiness of her hair, he was gentle.

"Have I just imagined you?" he murmured, stroking her hair. "I can't quite believe you're here with me: it's like a fantasy. I'm not sure if I'm just dreaming it, after conjuring you up by the strength of wishing."

"I'm definitely real. A phantom couldn't do this." She scratched a provocative path down his back with her nails.

"I love you," he breathed against her ear as he paused to take in the scent of her. Desire was changing their body chemistry and their skin seemed to ooze the musky smell of sex. It had been a long time since he had smelled it, and it thrilled him.

"Show me…" she said.

He felt swept along by the intensity of love that had been rekindled within the past few hours. He couldn't hide how much he wanted her: even if his expression had not betrayed him, his body would have done so.

His kisses, light and soft as a breath across her skin, left her gasping. Her response as his fingers stroked a teasing trail across her breasts and belly left him in no doubt of the power he could still exert over her. Eyes closed, lips parted, she was lost in the moment, too overcome to do anything for him in return. It didn't matter: he was aching for her, and the sight of her rendered helpless by his lovemaking was more than enough to turn him on. She moaned softly, eyes blurred with passion as he moved lower to probe and taste. His body throbbed; she was already wet and swollen with longing, tugging at his hair.

"Tom, I need you."

"Are you sure you're ready? There's no hurry."

She clutched at his shoulders to reinforce the message. "We've waited for months. I don't want to wait any longer. I want you now."

Without pausing to gauge his reaction, she manoeuvred herself onto her side and pressed herself against him.

He groaned. "I want to immerse myself in you. You have no idea how much I've been longing for you."

Nestled together like spoons, his upper hand cupping her breast and his mouth against the back of her neck, Tom slowly pressed a little deeper. He was cautious, nervous of hurting her after so long, and also aware that his own excitement was in danger of running out of control. She moved against him, building her own rhythm, holding her breath with the intensity of the sensation, and arched against him with a gasp as she climaxed.

Slowing his pace, striving to maintain his self-control, he revelled in her satisfaction.

"I love watching you come," he told her, stroking the softness of her skin, damp now with a light film of sweat from the strength of her orgasm.

"Do it again, then."

She turned her head to try to kiss him, but closed her eyes and broke off with a moan of pleasure as he thrust more firmly. This time, he couldn't hold back. As she reached a shuddering climax he let go, and together they slowed to lie in each other's arms, desire sated at last.

∞ ∞ ∞

Rolling over with a not inconsiderable effort, Megan snuggled against Tom's chest and buried her face there, reassured by the strength of his arms around her as the pounding of his heartbeat and his ragged breathing slowed. The hairs on his chest tickled her nose and made her smile.

Dreamily, she traced the smoothness of his skin; the line of his collarbone towards the joint of his shoulder, then skimming along the curve of his bicep. In contact with the firm heat of his body, she felt more secure than she had in months; but there was a part of her that felt if she let go of him, he might disappear.

"Are you alright? I didn't hurt you?" His voice was a low rumble in his chest, under her ear.

"I'm fine."

"Was it okay?" He sounded uncertain.

"No, it wasn't okay."

He raised himself on his elbow, anxiously searching her face.

"Silly." She shook her head and pushed him back down with her hand. "It was much better than just okay. It was wonderful."

His sharp exhalation of relief made her laugh inwardly. "Was it okay for you?" she asked in turn, knowing the answer in advance.

"Much better than okay," he echoed sleepily, and there was a smile in his voice.

She snuggled against him again, and he relaxed, closing his eyes to welcome the temporary oblivion of sleep.

"I do love your chest, you know," she murmured, stroking her palm across it.

"Mmmm? I'm rather partial to yours, too."

She saw one eye open blearily to cast an admiring glance at her bosom before closing it again with a smug smirk that made her hug him all the more.

Several minutes passed. Tom was drifting into sleep when she spoke again, startling him back to wakefulness.

"I need to pee."

He groaned. "Can't it wait till morning?"

"No. Sorry. I've been lying here trying to persuade myself that I don't need to go; but I'll never get to sleep if I don't."

"There's a camping potty thing under one of the seats: I'll get it out for you," he offered.

"I'm not going on that disgusting old thing, thanks all the same. I'll go over to the toilet if you pass me a torch and my dress."

He fumbled about and passed them to her, then jack-knifed involuntarily as she clambered over him, all knees and elbows. She slipped her dress over her head, briefly wrestled with the straps and bent with a grunt to find her flip-flops. Cool night air rushed in as she slid open the side door of the van.

"It's dark out there," she hissed, suddenly reluctant to venture out alone.

"Well, yes – it's late, and there aren't any street lights out here. You're not in Cardiff now, Meg. You'll be fine with the torch."

"I can't go over there on my own! What if there's somebody out there?"

He tutted and huffed, but she made it clear that he was going to have to accompany her.

"I'm not going in there with you, so if there are any moths or spiders you'll have to deal with them yourself," he warned her, slipping his shorts on with obvious reluctance. "I'll wait outside. Hurry up, won't you?"

When she emerged from the lean-to toilet hut, he was gazing towards the heavens. She nudged herself under his arm and they stood there together, wondering at the silence and the remarkable array of stars pricking the sky.

"Look at all those millions and millions of stars. You can see them so much more clearly here than at home, without the light pollution," he said.

She nodded, and he drew her to face him, locked within the circle of his arms.

"I'm glad you followed me. I'll remember tonight until the day I die. I'd been wondering if we'd ever be right again, but I feel now as if I've reconnected with you. I don't want us to be like we were, ever again."

They kissed deeply, pouring their love and relief into their embrace, before strolling back to bed hand in hand.

Chapter Eighteen

The next morning: Wednesday 6th June
2012
Saunton, North Devon

Morning brought sunshine streaming into the van, its brightness barely dimmed by the thin curtains. Megan woke at half past eight, stifled by the temperature and humidity in the van. She lifted her hair off her neck and kicked out to unravel the sleeping bag from around her legs, struggling to expose some skin to the air to cool off. The muggy air was suffocating, but as she gradually roused from sleep to full consciousness, it became apparent to her that it wasn't only perspiration making her feel so damp.

She shifted her hips. Yes, that was definitely a wet patch underneath her. Surely last night couldn't account for the extent of it, though? But then, she couldn't have wet herself... She felt the damp patch with her hand. Could she have wet herself, in fact? She'd be mortified if so, and how the hell would she explain it to Tom? The thought was enough to make her cheeks feel even hotter. Then it occurred to her: she needed the toilet, so her bladder was definitely full.

Which left an even more worrying possibility.

As she lay, wide-eyed now at the thoughts racing through her mind, Tom stirred in his sleep.

One azure eye opened dreamily. Seeing Megan lying awake next to him, he closed it again and snuggled closer.

"Hello," he murmured. "You're a sight for sore eyes."

She said nothing for a moment. When she did reply, she did her best to keep her tone calm and conversational.

"Tom?"

"Mmm-hmm?"

"I need to tell you something."

He opened both eyes sleepily at that and gazed across the pillow towards her.

"What is it? I've been having the most fantastic dream... We went skinny dipping in the sea and then made love on the beach, under the stars."

She snorted. "That doesn't strike me as a good idea at all. I'm told the sand gets into any number of uncomfortable places."

He stretched out, emerging from under his side of the sleeping bag like a merman exposed by the receding tide. She gazed at him for a moment, able to appreciate even in her current state that he was a magnificent specimen. The hours of surfing in the previous few days had hardened his muscles. First thing in the morning, it wasn't only his muscles that were hard.

"The thing is," she continued hastily, lest he should start making any early-morning advances, "I've either wet the bed or my waters have broken."

He jerked bolt upright, as startled as if she had poked him with a cattle prod.

"You're kidding?"

"I'm pretty sure I haven't wet myself because I still need the loo. Which only leaves the alternative, really…."

Her voice trailed off. She wasn't sure what horrified him more: the idea of her going into labour prematurely, or the prospect of amniotic fluid seeping into the upholstery of his precious camper van.

"But the baby isn't due for nearly four weeks!"

There was panic now in his sleep-gritty eyes. He rubbed them with his fists and blinked, adjusting to the sudden shift of events.

Megan was surprised how calm she sounded, considering the circumstances.

"I know, it is a bit early; but they say thirty-seven weeks is full-term and we're only two days away from that, so hopefully everything should be fine."

"Are you having contractions?"

"No, not yet."

Decisively, he stood up and hurried to pull on his underwear.

"We need to get you to the hospital," he said, staggering in the limited space available. He forced his feet into the legs of his shorts, still scrunched up from the night before. "I'll go and ask the farmer where the nearest one is." He reached for a clean t-shirt out of a locker and pulled it over his head, his voice muffled. "I expect Barnstaple will be the closest. It's about ten miles away, I think."

"I'm not having my baby in Barnstaple."

He barely glanced at her, so great was his haste to gather up their belongings. "They might be able to do something, make it stop. You hear about it all the time, women go in to hospital with contractions and they give them something to stop it."

She stared at him. Had he heard her at all?

"Tom, once your waters break that's it – there's no going back. They can't do anything to stop it. This baby will have to be born within twenty-four hours, one way or another."

She sat up, swinging her legs out of the bed with as much dignity as her swollen belly would allow. As she stood upright, fluid dripped down her legs onto the floor of the van. They both stared down at it: Tom in horror, Megan with some relief.

"Oh! That's good," she said, trying to sound positive. "It's not green. Clear is good: it means the baby's not in distress."

He gaped, speechless.

"Pass me my bra and my dress, would you?" she prompted, taking charge. "I'll head over to the loo while you pack up ready to drive home. I'd better sit on a towel, in case I leak all over the passenger seat as well as the bed."

"Megan! It's a bit late to talk about driving all the way home. It'll take us three hours or more –"

She, snatched her dress out of his hand.

"Exactly. We've got plenty of time. I'm not even having any contractions yet: just a tiny bit of backache, and that's probably due to sleeping on a bed made of nothing more sophisticated than an arrangement of cushions. I was in labour for twelve hours with Alys and seven hours with Nia. Seven hours gives us more than enough time to get home, have a cup of tea and fetch my hospital bag before we even think about phoning the midwife."

Having tugged her dress over her head, she pulled the sliding door open and eased herself out of the van, holding on to the door for balance. She was still stiff from lying down all night, and it took her a few steps to get moving. The fluid dribbling down between her thighs was uncomfortable and embarrassing, as she had no control over it. By the time it reached her ankles it was cold, and it made her thighs chafe together. It was a relief to reach the privacy of the toilet: as she bolted the door, she realised her hands had begun to shake.

"Take deep breaths," she told herself. Her bossy confidence with Tom had been a front, to make him co-operate and get her home before the baby came.

"Your timing is bloody awful, little one," she whispered to the baby, stroking her stomach. "Why the hurry to be born, eh? Just listen to your mummy now, and stay where you are until we get back to Cardiff."

Quickly, she dashed cold water over her hands and face. They couldn't afford for anything to delay their departure. If only she had thought to bring a change of clothes when she travelled to Devon with Matt yesterday morning. It was a bit embarrassing to be still wearing yesterday's sundress, crumpled like an old rag from its night on the floor and smelling powerfully of the previous evening's barbecue. She rubbed at a smudge of pesto, but it wasn't going anywhere.

Stuffing some folded toilet paper between her legs, she tried to hold it in place as she made her way back to the camper, acutely conscious that doing so made her waddle. A good job no one would see her. Except perhaps the farmer, and he had seen her in an even more compromising situation last night.

Tom was like a man possessed, hurling cushions about in his haste to get ready. Hair sticking up, face was still creased from the pillow, he was clearly oblivious to everything but getting his wife to a place of safety. Fair enough - as long as he didn't think that meant Barnstaple. She was shocked at how speedily he dropped the elevating canvas roof and clipped it into place. Usually he treated it as if it was made of glass, fussing and adjusting it to ensure that none of the elderly canvas was trapped where it might get damaged, but anxiety had obviously made him reckless.

With a grunt of effort she attempted to clamber up into the passenger seat, cursing softly as her wad of toilet paper fell onto the dew-soaked ground. Tom was already belted in with the engine running. His lips were pressed tightly together and a muscle twitched in his cheek as she abandoned the attempt to embark.

"Hang on, I'll be there now in a minute," she said, and went round to open the side door.

He muttered under his breath, something about how it would either be now or in a minute, it couldn't be both; but she ignored him. He was just asserting his Englishness again. He'd lived in Wales long enough to know that "now in a minute" made perfect sense to anyone born there.

The knickers she had discarded the night before were still on the floor of the van. Glancing around to make sure she wouldn't be seen, she pulled them on and stuffed a fresh pad of tissues into the gusset to minimise the mess she was making.

"Home, James," she joked a little nervously as she finally returned to the passenger door, "and don't spare the horses."

Fortunately, he had left a folded towel on the seat. He must have been horrified to see the wet patch she had left on Greta's rear cushions. She perched on it and held on to the door handle as he set off, the van bumping uncomfortably along the uneven farm track.

"Did you tell the farmer we're leaving?"

"No, I didn't want to waste any time. The sooner I can get you to a hospital, the happier I'll be. He knew we were going today, anyway. There's supposed to be a storm coming in later."

Out of the farm gate they went, and Tom accelerated quickly to the speed limit, crunching the gears in his anxiety to be going. Usually she knew he nursed Greta along, careful to preserve her ageing engine as long as he could.

"There's no need to panic. I'm fine, honestly."

Better not tell him that she was beginning to feel the first low-down twinges of contractions; he would flatly refuse to take her back to Wales if he knew.

"Isn't the river pretty this morning?" she said as they passed, trying to keep the conversation light. His response was a glare that made her press her lips together and look away out of the window. Clearly he was not in the mood to chat about trivialities.

As they reached Barnstaple they encountered more traffic, but they had missed the height of the morning rush hour so weren't delayed too much through the town. He kept looking over at her, trying to gauge how she was getting on. Defiant, she kept up a bright smile to disarm him.

"Right: this is your last chance," he said as they crossed the river and negotiated a roundabout. "Do we need to go to the hospital here or do you honestly think we've got time to get home? Tell me the truth, Meg - we can't take any risks with your health or the baby's."

"Honestly, I'm as sure as I can be that we've got time." Of course they had time. They'd have more if they had a decent vehicle to travel in, but better not to dwell on that. It would be hours yet, she knew it would. The contractions had barely begun. "If you make me have this baby in Devon, when there's absolutely no need, I'll never forgive you."

"Alright. But if you have this baby on the hard shoulder of the M5, I'll never forgive *you*." He drew in a ragged, anxious breath, but drove past the hospital without another word of protest.

She allowed her shoulders to sag a little with relief. Soon they would be properly on their way. At least he had trusted her, hadn't tried to force her to go to the nearest maternity unit, as he had obviously wanted to do. She couldn't bear the thought of giving birth in an unfamiliar place, surrounded by strangers and miles away from her family. Alys and Nia might not be able to visit her. And, although she knew Tom would regard it as unimportant or even irrational, she desperately wanted her child to be born in Wales.

They didn't talk much as they drove across the busy town and finally emerged onto the A-road that would take them towards Tiverton and the motorway.

"Any contractions yet?"

"I've had a few mild ones," she admitted now. Seeing his frown of concern she hastily added: "Like I said, they're only mild. And they're a long way apart. Don't forget, the early stage of labour is like a game of cricket – long, boring periods with nothing much happening, broken up by brief busts of activity. Plenty of time for tea and cucumber sandwiches. It's only towards the end that it gets exciting and physical, like a rugby match. You'll know when I get to that stage: I'll be mooing like a cow if it's anything like last time."

He chewed at the corner of his lip, driving as fast as he dared.

"Do you think it's my fault?" he blurted out at last.

She stared at him, bewildered.

"How could it be your fault?"

The tips of his ears went pink, as they always did when he was embarrassed.

"Well, after last night. You know – maybe I damaged something, made things start off. It's been so long since we... You know."

"Look, even if having sex had started things off, it wouldn't just be your fault. It takes two to tango, remember."

She felt a wave of sympathy at the guilty look on his face. Reaching over to pat his leg, she grimaced as a stronger contraction gripped her stomach.

"Are you sure you're okay?"

"Are you going to keep asking me that all the way home?"

"Probably," came his equally sharp response. "Seeing as you're in labour. You'd think I was a bit of a heartless shit if I didn't ask how you're doing."

She bit her lip and he slowed down for a roundabout at the edge of Tiverton. Every mile they covered made her feel a little better, but there was still such a long way to go before they would be home. They weren't even out of Devon yet. Her heart fluttered at the thought of it.

"How far are we from the motorway now?" she asked.

"About ten miles, I expect. I'm not sure, exactly. Why do you ask?"

He rolled his eyes when she explained.

"I need the loo again. I seem to remember there were services at the junction where Matt and I left the motorway yesterday."

Knowing how much he would want to avoid any delay to their journey, she wasn't surprised when he didn't answer straight away. "Okay," he conceded at last. "But don't take long in there, will you? We don't need any hold-ups."

By the time they arrived at the services, she was uncomfortable.

"Why don't you get us some coffee and something for breakfast while you're waiting?" she suggested, lowering herself out of the van. She had eaten very little since she found his note on Friday, and was ravenous now as her body craved energy for the task ahead.

He locked the doors and stuffed his wallet into his pocket as he followed her towards the building with an uneasy frown that had deepened still further by the time she emerged from the ladies' toilets.

"I was just on the point of sending a search party in to look for you," he rebuked her, automatically thanking an elderly gentleman who held the door open for them to pass. Tom's hands were full, with two Styrofoam cups of coffee and a couple of chocolate muffins.

"Sorry." She followed him meekly across the car park, glad he was ahead of her, as it meant he didn't see her face when the next contraction made her wince.

"You should phone Bethan and tell her what's happening," he said as they reached the van.

She held onto his coffee cup obligingly while he drove out of the service area and joined the M5, passing it to him from time to time once they were on the motorway. Apart from the slow pace and the unreliable brakes, this was another failing of his silly old van: no cup holders.

She sipped her coffee. It tasted good, and the milkiness and caffeine helped her feel a little more energised. He had stirred in some sugar, even though she didn't usually take any, and she was glad of it this morning. She drained it quickly, searched around for somewhere to put it, then dropped it onto the floor for want of any other option.

"Hey," he said, seeing her throw it down. "Don't get coffee on the carpet."

"Well, what do you suggest I do with it? I can't exactly go climbing into the back to find a bin bag, can I? And I'm not holding two empty cups all the way back to Wales. I need to get my phone out of my bag."

Rummaging in her handbag, she took a deep breath as a wave of discomfort gripped her abdomen. She counted in her head to distract herself. It wasn't agony yet, but it wasn't pleasant. Above all, she had to pretend it wasn't too bad, to prevent Tom fussing.

As she took her phone out, her eyes widened in dismay.

"Damn! I forgot to turn it off last night. The battery level is only showing one bar."

"Shit. That's not good. My phone has been dead for days – we need yours just in case of any problem."

"I won't phone Beth after all, then," she decided. "I'll just send her a text to tell her we're on our way home. If I tell her what's really happening she'll be bound to ring me back, and then I'll end up with no battery at all."

∞ ∞ ∞

Tom fixed his eyes on the road ahead, struggling to maintain his concentration while Megan composed her text message. He wasn't stupid: he knew she was pretending to be in better shape than she actually was. He'd seen her in labour twice before, and he knew exactly when she was having contractions from the way the rhythm of her breathing changed. He tried to keep half an eye on his wristwatch to gauge how far apart the contractions were, and was not reassured to find that they must be about six minutes apart.

The trouble was, he couldn't remember whether that was a good thing or not. He tried to think rationally. When she had been in labour before, she had been unable to speak coherently when the pains had been really bad, and they had still arrived at the hospital in plenty of time. Right now, she was still able to hold a conversation. So he could only hope that there was no immediate prospect of the baby coming. Last time, they hadn't had to face such a long journey to the maternity ward; part of him wished he had had the courage to defy her wishes and take her straight to the hospital in Barnstaple, where at least they would have been safe. But their reconciliation was so new, and such a relief after months of discord, he didn't dare do anything to risk spoiling it.

He was startled out of his thoughts when she suddenly pointed out of the window at a flock of sheep in a field.

"Ooh, look! Sheep!" She made as if to turn towards the back of the van, then drooped, crestfallen.

"Baaaaa," he said.

"I forgot Alys and Nia aren't with us. It's like a reflex action these days to point out sheep or cows as we're driving along. They get so excited about it."

"You're not the only one. I very nearly pointed to a tractor earlier, but caught myself just in time."

"I miss them." Her lower lip wobbled. "I'll be glad to get home and give them both a big cwtch. As much as it was lovely being on my own with you, I don't like being so far away from our girls."

"I've missed them too."

"It was strange last night, getting into a bed that didn't have anything hidden in it. On Saturday night I sat on a plastic dinosaur when I got into our bed at home. It didn't half hurt. And I've had to tell them that our bed isn't the place to have picnics with their dolls. I'm getting sick of all the crumbs."

Another contraction bit into her. This time, she couldn't suppress a little groan.

"How are you doing?" he asked a minute or so later, when it had passed.

"They're getting a bit stronger," she admitted.

She unwrapped the chocolate muffins, passing one over for him to balance in his lap. The rich, chocolatey smell filled his nostrils and made him realise how hungry he was. He broke off a piece, one-handed: the chocolate chips melted on his tongue and he could almost feel the sugar rush hitting his bloodstream.

"Can't we go any faster?" she asked plaintively, nibbling around the edges of her muffin.

He shook his head, swallowing another chunk of muffin in a lump. "Garin warned me not to go over sixty. If I blow the engine up, you could end up having the baby on the hard shoulder."

Her eyes widened in horror at the prospect. "Better carry on as you are, then."

Another VW camper van passed by on the opposite carriageway, and Tom exchanged a wave and nod of acknowledgement with the other driver. It was still a source of amazement to him that driving a classic camper had automatically enrolled him into a community of enthusiasts. Hailing complete strangers on the road with admiring glances at one another's vehicles was considered perfectly normal behaviour.

The next contraction hit, making Megan rock gently to and fro in her seat. She groaned a little louder, and Tom's knuckles whitened on the steering wheel as he fought against his instinctive urge to drive faster.

"I'm glad I'm not a woman," he said as she emerged from the wave of the contraction and regained her composure.

"I suppose it isn't as bad as some types of pain. It's not like the pain from cutting yourself, or from having your appendix burst, or a kidney stone or something. It's not frightening, because you can understand what's causing it: it doesn't mean there's something horribly wrong with you. It comes and goes, and you have time to get used to it. It isn't like you see on the telly sometimes, when they seem to go from perfectly normal to screaming agony in a couple of minutes. And I know it will be worth it in the end when I hold our baby in my arms."

He digested what she had said. The worst pain he had ever experienced was from appendicitis, though broken bones would come a close second. He'd had a few of those in his time, mostly from sport but also from his childhood days of reckless tree-climbing and seeing how fast he could skid along patches of ice. His wrists still ached from time to time, especially in cold weather, and his nose would never be perfectly straight after all those years of playing rugby.

"What do the contractions feel like?" he asked, curious.

"Like strong period pains."

"That doesn't really help. I've never had those, either." He waited while she cast about for words.

"They feel like a really nasty cramp, low down. A bit like the yucky, griping feeling you get if you've got a tummy upset and you need the loo - but more in the front, if you see what I mean. It's hard to describe... It makes your whole tummy go hard, too, as if it's being stretched like a drum skin. I don't know if I can explain it any better than that, really."

Her voice tailed off and it wasn't long before another pain made her gasp and close her eyes. He gritted his teeth, wishing he could do something to make her feel better. He guessed she was counting in her head to divert her attention away from the strength of the sensations.

They passed a road sign indicating that they were approaching Bridgwater. Still a frighteningly long way from home. And to make matters worse, he had begun to notice occasional dips in engine power. He hoped fervently that Megan wouldn't detect the problem: she hated Greta enough, without worrying that the van's elderly engine might let them down. If they broke down now, she would have no choice but to have their baby in England, and he couldn't let himself contemplate the problems that would unleash. Not only would she loathe Greta even more, but she would inevitably blame Tom for causing their predicament by going to Devon. His only hope of redeeming himself was to keep the van going and get her back to Cardiff before the baby was born.

"I've been thinking about what you told me last night," she remarked after a time, in a lull between contractions. "You obviously need a bit more personal space. Perhaps we should think about getting you a shed?"

"Seriously? If I needed somewhere to go and read porn or build Airfix models, I'd sit in the camper on the driveway. I don't need a shed. At least in Greta I can make myself a cup of tea."

"You're showing your age," she scoffed. "People don't *read* porn these days. They download it."

"People never did read porn, Meg. They just looked at the pictures."

The engine power dipped again, but she seemed too bent upon teasing him to notice. He did his best to appear unconcerned, mulling over the possible causes of the problem in the back of his mind.

"Stop trying to change the subject. I'm serious. Things can't continue as they were. We need to take steps to make things easier for you."

Back to that again. "I'll be fine," he told her firmly. "I've had a bit of a break now, and at least things are out in the open between us. If we keep the lines of communication open from now on, I'm sure things will improve."

She nodded. "Tomorrow, I'll book that appointment for you to see the GP."

He looked askance at her as another contraction began its fierce grip. "I think you might find you've got your hands full tomorrow."

"I'll make time," she gasped peevishly before turning her attention to riding the wave of pain. It was obviously much stronger than the previous one.

"What would I say to the doctor?" he asked when the contraction ended and she could focus on him again. He was as irritable as she, worried about the possibility of the van breaking down but unable to share his concerns. "I suppose I could say 'I got so fed up, I jumped in my van and went surfing.' But I can't see her taking me very seriously, can you? I mean, it's hardly a life-threatening condition, is it?"

She glared at him. Her voice was sharp. "No, but it's a marriage-threatening one."

He pursed his lips and kept his eyes on the road. He didn't want to get into another argument with her – not today, not in the circumstances. Hopefully she'd have her mind on other things soon enough, and would forget about this idea of sending him to the doctor. He had no intention of going along and wasting a busy GP's time with minor complaints about things getting on top of him. He may have been feeling as if he was wading through quicksand in a fog for a few months, but wasn't he coming out of it now? Physically, he felt stronger; and if he wasn't exactly full of the joys of spring yet, he was at least hopeful of improvement in the future.

More pressingly, what had Garin had told him about common problems with these old air-cooled engines? He cast his mind back to the days when he had owned Bessie, his wreck of a Beetle. She had been as irrational as Megan at times. Scanning the dashboard, he suddenly found himself missing the array of warning lights a modern car would have to indicate the source of any problem. *What's wrong with you, old girl? Don't you get awkward with me now; I'm getting enough grief from the wife.*

Breaking off another piece of chocolate muffin, he had a flash of inspiration. Greta's fuel gauge was showing only a quarter of a tank of petrol. Knowing how unreliable the ancient gauge was likely to be, he considered the possibility that there might actually be less petrol left in the tank. Perhaps Greta was running on the dregs of dirty fuel, and needed a top-up with fresh petrol. As much as he resented the delay necessitated by a visit to a petrol station, the thought of running out of fuel or the engine getting blocked on the way home was simply too terrifying to contemplate.

∞ ∞ ∞

As Greta continued to forge her occasionally jerky progress northwards, there was soon no way Megan could hide the effect of her contractions. Each one absorbed her full attention. She did her best to ride each one out calmly, telling herself as she had done in her previous labours that each pain was a good thing, bringing her closer to having her baby. However, on this occasion, when they were still miles from the safety of home, it didn't seem such a reassuring thought. In fact it was frightening to feel how inexorably her body was opening up, little by little, to allow the baby to be born.

If only she was more like a cat. Didn't they always wait to have their kittens until they had managed to find a nice, safe, warm place? She was sure she had read somewhere that cats were able to delay their deliveries until the circumstances were right. It would be such a relief to be able to do that: to have a pause button, to make her body wait a little longer, until they were securely back in Cardiff at the hospital. Why had her cervix chosen today of all days to get busy?

Tom's face was tight with obvious anxiety. "We're not far from Sedgemoor Services," he said. "We can stop for a couple of minutes for some petrol, and you can pop into the loo again if you need to. Hang on in there. You're doing really well."

Her expression softened. Tom wasn't one of those who dispensed lavish words of praise willy-nilly, so when he said something was going well, she felt reassured that it must be. She could imagine him at school, working with kids who needed encouragement. Even if she hadn't been aware of his reputation among his colleagues, she would have known instinctively that he would be a brilliant coach. If he approved of a child's performance, she knew how good that would make them feel, and how it would spur them on to do better.

They went in separate directions at the motorway services, and when they started up again she was glad of the sandwiches and water he had bought.

After setting off again, it was clear to them both that the pain from Megan's contractions was rapidly getting worse. She groaned aloud now every time the pain came, rocking herself and gripping at the dashboard as if her life depended on it, oblivious to everything but the tightening clench of the spasms in her womb.

It was so frustrating, just sitting there, waiting passively for things to happen. Her back ached and her nerves were beginning to jangle. If only she could walk up and down, as she had been able to do at the motorway service station. It would help with the pain and give her something to do. Their car would have eaten up the miles, but Greta only nibbled at them.

Suddenly, she remembered something that might help her feel better. She fumbled in her handbag and retrieved her phone.

It was okay: there was still a bit of battery power left. Swishing her finger across the screen, she found the icon she wanted and relaxed marginally as the app gave her something new to focus on.

∞ ∞ ∞

Tom raised an eyebrow and fidgeted in his seat as he realised Megan wasn't going to give any explanation for her sudden interest in her phone. He debated inwardly whether to tell her to save the battery for an emergency call later, then decided it would be safer to say nothing. She had been increasingly tense, but at least now she seemed happier.

As another contraction gripped her, she appeared to be trying to press something on the screen. Her expression changed to something akin to frustration along with the pain; she dropped the phone into her lap and clutched at the dashboard of the van, knuckles whitening until the rush of pain had passed.

"Are you alright?" he asked again, feeling useless in the face of her discomfort.

"This *stupid* app is about as much use as a sticker that's fallen on the carpet and got hairy."

"What app?" He was mystified.

"I downloaded a contraction timing app a few weeks ago. The idea is for your birthing partner to press the button when the contractions start and when they end. It tells you how far apart they are, and how long they're lasting. But I can't concentrate enough to get the timings right, doing it myself. It should be *you* doing it, for it to have any chance of working."

She scowled accusingly at him, and he blinked in disbelief. It was impossible to keep the impatience out of his voice.

"I'll tell you what then, Meg: we'll swap places, shall we? You drive; I'll press the buttons on the app and monitor the contractions. Would that satisfy you?"

She glared at him and gripped the dashboard again, gritting her teeth against the pain. "Don't be ridiculous! The battery's nearly dead, anyway," she muttered furiously before closing her eyes.

It seemed she had forgotten everything but the sensations overtaking her body.

Tom wiped his forehead, conscious of his rising anxiety levels. Greta was behaving a little better with the fresh petrol, thankfully, but Megan's contractions were growing increasingly powerful. They were passing Bristol now: there would surely be a good hospital in the city. Their most sensible course of action now would be to find the nearest maternity unit as quickly as possible.

"I'm sorry," he said to her as her breathing slowed back to normal. "I'm just worried about you, that's all. I know I shouldn't have snapped at you, but you must realise this whole app thing is completely barmy. Women have been giving birth for thousands of years without apps, Meg. You've done it twice before, yourself. For

God's sake, we don't need an app to tell us that we haven't got much longer to get you to a hospital... Why don't we head into Bristol and get you to a maternity unit there?" he suggested in his most placatory voice, ignoring her black look.

She cut him off furiously before he could make any further attempt to reason with her. "Tom, listen and take note: I am *not* having my baby in Bristol, or in any other part of England. It will be born in Wales, even if I have to give birth at the Severn Bridge tollbooths."

He struggled to control his annoyance and focus on the road ahead.

"You're being ridiculous. What in God's name is so bad about having a baby in England? People do it all the time!"

"*English* people do it," she snapped. "My baby is Welsh."

His answering glare was as fierce as hers. "*Your* baby is it, now? Well, *your* baby is half English, so its place of birth will hardly matter!"

"Don't fucking remind me!" she spat back at him, rage and pain making her tremble. "I should have found myself a decent Welshman who wouldn't have gone *pissing* off to *fucking* Devon when the going got tough! Ngggghhhhhooooooo!!!" She roared aloud in anger and pain as another contraction took hold.

There it was. The attack he had been half expecting since yesterday, like a knife between the ribs to punish him for his many failings. Once, he had let her down. Once, in seven years. Was she going to remind him of it every time something went wrong? And yet, he knew her well enough to realise that colourful swearing was a powerful indication of her current stress level. He had heard her tell a pupil at school once that "overuse of the F word demonstrates a woeful paucity of vocabulary and a lamentable poverty of imagination". He had had to turn away to conceal his mirth at the time, he remembered. Especially when he overheard the boy tell his friends, waiting around the corner, "I wish she'd speak English. I don't know what the fuck she was on about."

Gritting his teeth now, he fought to suppress his indignation. He should probably just shut up and drive, spare himself another verbal assault, but he couldn't stop himself speaking out against this recklessness.

"This obsession with getting back to Wales is sheer lunacy. I have to say, I have never, ever known people as jingoistic and parochial as the Welsh."

"Jingoistic and parochial? My, those are big words for a P.E. teacher."

God, he hated it when she asserted her intellectual superiority. He kept his eyes on the road, to avoid seeing the sneer he had heard in her voice mirrored on her face.

"Well, at least we know the money my parents spent on my education wasn't entirely wasted," he muttered.

She was silent for several minutes, arms folded defensively over her belly, ignoring him and frowning at the view as they crossed the Avonmouth Bridge. The atmosphere in the van was thick with resentment from both sides. However, by the time the next couple of contractions had passed, Tom was feeling guilty for giving way to his angry feelings. She was nervous and in a great deal of pain, he reminded himself. Under the circumstances it was only to be expected that she wouldn't be behaving entirely rationally.

"I just don't want you to put yourself or the baby at risk," he pleaded, reaching out to touch her arm. She shook his hand off with another mulish glare.

"We aren't at risk. But our marriage will be if you don't keep going and get us back home."

The last exit for Bristol passed by, and he closed his eyes briefly, his heart heavy. Staying on the motorway went against every instinct. He found himself praying silently that he wouldn't have cause to regret his acquiescence. His gut screamed at him to drag her into the nearest hospital, however much she might hate him for it.

"It's all your fault, anyway," he heard her grumble spitefully from the passenger seat.

Now that was too much.

"Yes, yes, yes," he snapped back. "Guilty as charged. Everything's my fault, Megan. You getting pregnant was my fault. Me spending my birthday money on something we can all enjoy, instead of your precious kitchen: that was my fault, too. You going into labour early: I'll admit, that may have been my fault. Us being in Devon when you went into labour – obviously, that was entirely my fault. I daresay global fucking warming is my fault too. Third World debt... The Banking Crisis... The plight of the fucking polar bear. Go on, lay it all at my door. I'll take the blame. Why the fucking hell not?"

His voice had risen, and he smacked the steering wheel with the heel of his hand.

She stared, so taken aback by his sudden outburst that she started to laugh.

"Oh, Tom. You're so funny. You really crack me up sometimes!"

Hysteria. There was no other explanation for her bizarre behaviour. "I'm glad you find it amusing," he muttered, keeping left to join the M49 motorway and head westwards at last, towards the Severn river crossing into Wales.

"Oh, please don't make me laugh," she panted. "My pelvic floor muscles can't take it."

He grunted. "Your pelvic floor muscles were perfectly fine last night."

"No, stop it now or I'll wet myself!"

Although relieved that the tension between them had eased, he was white-faced with worry as another remorseless contraction caused her to moan loudly with pain. In a moment of perfect clarity he knew, with as much certainty as he had ever felt about anything in his life, that there was no way they would make it home in time.

Chapter Nineteen

Wednesday 6th June 2012
Westbound: The M4 Motorway

Tom continued driving towards the bridge spanning the river into Wales. If this was a movie, he thought, now would be the moment when a male voice choir would break into a rousing rendition of Hen Wlad Fy Nhadau, the Welsh national anthem, to serenade them over the border. To be fair, he had to acknowledge that it was a good national anthem. At international rugby matches he had been to, the crowd always sang it with gusto. It wasn't unusual to see brawny Welshmen with passionate, patriotic tears rolling down their cheeks as they sang.

Chugging along in Greta, it seemed to take forever to cross the bridge. He had never noticed before how long it was, curving gradually over the threatening brown waters of the Severn. Megan was almost crying with relief to see the low-lying coastal plain and distant hills of south-east Wales appearing up ahead. Neither of them had ever been so pleased to see the green, green grass of home.

"Oh, thank God! Thank you, Tom!" she gasped out huskily, her voice choked with emotion. "I knew you'd get me back home."

He was too tense to feel any great sense of relief.

"Don't let go yet," he told her hastily. "We're still twenty-five miles from Cardiff. And we've got to get through the Brynglas Tunnels." His heart thumped as he contemplated the possibility of getting stuck at the notorious traffic black-spot that still lay ahead.

Slowing down for the tolls, he fumbled in his back pocket for cash to pay the fee. As they pulled up at the booth, Megan was groaning fiercely in the grip of another strong pain. The man in the tollbooth stared, startled by the noise she was making as Tom wound down his window to hand over a ten pound note.

"My wife is in labour," Tom said needlessly, his face lined with worry. "We don't have any battery power left on our mobile phones, so we can't phone ahead to the hospital to tell them we're coming. Is there any possibility that you could...?"

The toll collector handed over his change and shook his head apologetically.

"I'm really sorry, sir. I haven't got any way to contact a hospital. I'll speak to the Chief Collector on duty and see what he says, but I can't promise anything."

"Right." Tom bit his lip in dismay.

Megan's face was etched with pain.

"I don't think we're going to make it to Cardiff," he confided.

The toll collector nodded. "The nearest hospital is in Newport," the man advised. "Your best bet is to get off the motorway at junction twenty-four, then head for the city centre. There'll be signposts for the hospital when you get into town. It should only take you about twenty minutes to get there, if the traffic is alright."

Tom nodded his thanks and set off, pocketing his change. Twenty minutes didn't sound too bad, and at least by leaving the motorway before the tunnels they would no longer risk being delayed in a queue.

Keeping to the slow lane, with cars, motorbikes and even lorries overtaking him while Greta took her time to pick up speed, he prayed that he wasn't making the engine work too hard. The fresh petrol had helped for a while, but she was still coughing from time to time. It was almost as if she was attention seeking, jealous of Megan.

"A horrible thought has just struck me," Meg gulped in between contractions as they made their steady progress westwards.

"What's that?" he asked, dealing with enough horrible thoughts of his own.

"I haven't had a shower," she said, wide-eyed with worry.

"So?"

"What if the midwives can tell?"

"Can tell what? I bet they deal with much smellier people than you every day of the week."

She shook her head impatiently. "No, that's not what I mean. What if they can tell – you know – what we did last night?"

He blinked, temporarily dumbstruck. Did she really think this was the worst of her problems?

"Meg, you must have leaked a couple of pints of amniotic fluid since then. I hardly think there'll be any evidence left... And in any case, they'll have seen it all before."

His heart flooded with sympathy as she swayed and leaned into the flow of another contraction. Her plaintive groans sounded like mooing now, just as she had predicted earlier.

"Hang in there, darling – it's not far now," he urged.

"I don't think I can!"

A sob burst from her. She was trying hard to be brave, clinging to the dashboard, but it was clear that she was nearing the limits of her courage.

"Yes, you can. We're nearly there," he insisted, hoping he sounded more positive than he felt.

The traffic grew heavier as they approached the city and Tom had to queue at traffic lights on the roundabout as he left the motorway. The Celtic Manor Hotel squatted on the side of the hill a short distance away. It spoke of ease and luxury, a world away from their situation now as Greta spluttered mutinously and Megan crumpled against the window.

"Oh, I'm so tired… I just need to go to sleep," she complained, overwhelmed by the next contraction. Her head hung limply, her hair bedraggled by sweat although she appeared to be trembling as if chilled to the bone. No, no, no – he didn't like this. She really didn't look good.

Past semi-detached red-brick houses, modern flats and shops they chugged, Tom hyper-vigilant for any signs directing them to the City Centre and the hospital. Everyday life went on as normal around them, all the other drivers, shoppers and pedestrians completely unaware of the drama unfolding in the little orange camper van. His world suddenly felt very small, very separate from everyone else, and very much under threat.

Pulling up at another red light, he cursed. It took an age to turn green. Megan was groaning, beside herself with pain, the powerful contractions coming with only the briefest of breaks in between to allow her to catch her breath.

"Aaaagh! It bloody hurts!" she yelled angrily, teeth chattering.

He dragged a shaky hand through his hair, willing himself to keep his nerve. The volume of traffic had increased and was hampering their progress. Would this road go on for ever?

Finally they approached a larger set of lights at a busy junction. Which way now, damn it? He chose the right hand lane, signposted towards the City Centre. But as he pulled forward to cross the junction, trying to close his ears to the animal sound of Megan's groans and keep his attention on the road, he spotted a small road sign pointing left, almost obscured by trees: "Royal Gwent Hospital".

She lurched towards the dashboard as he stood on the brakes and began indicating left. Horns beeped harshly, but he ignored them and crossed to the inside lane to make the turn.

"Sorry! Sorry!" He waved in acknowledgement of the irate drivers, avoiding eye contact and pushing the elderly engine to go faster. Sweat prickled on the back of his neck.

"Are you alright?" he asked her, uselessly.

Her only response was a groan. Eyes closed, she seemed blind to everything but the overwhelming pain she was in.

In his head, he ran a commentary to focus his attention. *Okay, under this railway bridge… Damn the speed camera to hell… Shit! More traffic lights!* Although the light was changing to amber, he ignored it and chugged through.

Out of the blue, blinking a little as if surprised, Megan spoke in a voice that was quite calm although thick with weariness. "Oh. I'm alright now. I think it's stopped."

"Really? That's good," he said, not believing for a second that her labour had stopped.

As they continued up onto a steep concrete bridge, Greta's engine gave a little cough and his senses cranked even higher. Above the thick tidal mud of the river they drove. There was an excellent view of the city from this bridge, but Tom was in no mood to spot local landmarks. All he wanted was to keep Greta going and find another road sign to follow.

Megan's respite was brief.

"Ohhhhhhhhhhhhh," she moaned, sitting forward on the edge of her seat. Her voice had changed, was now a low, guttural howl. She sounded like an animal, the noise coming from deep inside. He had heard her make that sound on two previous occasions, and he knew what it meant. Heat suffused his face as he saw more traffic lights ahead.

"Don't push yet, Meg! Try not to push!"

He had no idea how close they might be to the safety of the hospital, or whether the spluttering van would be able to get them there.

She barely seemed to hear him, her head swaying with the force of the sensations sweeping over her. However hard she might try not to push, her body seemed to have its own ideas. Powerful and inexorable, the force of the contractions would not be stopped.

And there - an ambulance on the road ahead, travelling in the same direction. Perhaps he could flash his lights and flag it down? Then a better idea struck him. He would follow it.

Yet more traffic lights now. He kept going as they changed to red, then blanched, realising he was passing a police station. Hopefully none of the police officers had spotted him running the red light. He couldn't stop if they tried to pull him in: any delay now could be disastrous.

"You need to take my knickers off," Megan growled, clutching fiercely at his leg.

"Meg! This is hardly the time…"

"They'll be in the way!"

Oh God – not now, not yet.

The ambulance moved across in its lane and indicated right. Praying that it hadn't been called away on an emergency that would take it away from the hospital, Tom stayed on its tail. And he had done it, he realised suddenly: they had arrived at the hospital grounds.

Where now? There was a queue of cars waiting to enter a very full car park on the left. By the time he found a space, it could be too late. Decisively, he followed the ambulance and pulled up as sharply as Greta's soft brakes would allow outside the entrance to the Accident and Emergency department.

He was out of the van in an instant, running round to the passenger side and hollering "Someone help us, please!" to whoever might hear.

Wrenching the door open, he saw that Meg had released her seatbelt and perched on the edge of her seat making a fearsome, deep noise. She had lifted up the hem of her dress and was making a clumsy attempt to pull her knickers down her shaking thighs. Too panicked to be embarrassed, he grabbed the flimsy cotton fabric and tore it away. Stunned, he saw her arch her back and hiss in pain. Had he hurt her?

But no. There was another reason, and it nearly floored him.

"Jesus, Mary and Joseph!" Tom gaped. The top of the baby's head was visible. This couldn't be happening here.

As Meg gave out a yelp from the sharpness of the pain, the baby's head emerged, facing downwards towards the passenger foot well.

"Well done, Mum. Another couple of pushes and you'll be there," came a cheery voice at Tom's side. Glancing up, he saw a paramedic clad in green overalls calmly assessing the situation. Megan panted in her seat.

The paramedic pulled on some gloves as she pushed again, her face red with the effort. "Ready, Dad? Just have a quick peek now and check the cord hasn't slipped out. And then get ready to catch. Hope you're a good fielder."

Eyes wide, Tom patted Megan's knee in a helpless attempt to reassure her. Thankfully, there was no sign of the cord around the baby's newly exposed neck.

With another great heave and a raw groan from Megan that made Tom wince with pity, the baby turned and slipped with a rush of hot fluid into his waiting hands. Its warm, purple-grey flesh was wet with mucous and greasy under his fingers.

"Well done." The paramedic nodded approval. "Now, pop him onto Mum's chest... That's right, tuck him in under your dress, my love, to keep him warm. Good girl. We'll have you both inside in a jiffy."

Tom grabbed the paramedic by the arm. "Is it alright? It's blue."

The man gave him a reassuring pat. "We'll get him checked out straight away; but he's going nice and pink now, see?"

Dazed and overwhelmed by the emotional power of the moment, Tom's brain couldn't take it all in. It had happened so quickly. His hands had started to shake, and his knees had turned to liquid, and he wanted nothing more than to sink to the ground, but he knew he couldn't fail Megan now, not when she had been so brave. He kept a protective arm around her, supporting her as she sagged in the passenger seat, cradling the baby protectively to her chest. They were still joined by the thick, rubbery umbilical cord.

Another member of the ambulance team had arrived with a cosy blanket and a wheelchair.

"Let's get you both wrapped up nice and warm, my lovely," the paramedic said to Megan, pushing past Tom to tuck the blanket around her. "And then we'll get you inside and make sure everything's as it should be. I bet you could murder a cup of tea after all that."

Gently, Tom reached in and scooped her into his arms.

"I'm so proud of you," he whispered into her ear as he lifted her down into the wheelchair. Her face was white with shock and her long hair was plastered to her cheeks with perspiration. She had never looked more beautiful to him.

"In we go," the paramedic said, moving calmly but swiftly to whisk Megan and the baby away into the hospital building.

"I'm coming!" Tom called behind them and moved to lock the passenger door.

"You can't leave that by there, mun," said a gruff Welsh voice.

Tom stared blankly at the stranger who had spoken. "What?"

The man exhaled a long plume of cigarette smoke. "I'll tell you for why. The traffic warden'll be along now in a minute. If you leave it by there, they'll tow it away and you'll have no end of bother getting it back."

Tom fought with his instincts. He was desperate to follow Megan and their baby into the hospital, but the man was quite right: he couldn't leave Greta blocking the ambulance bay.

Quickly getting directions towards a car park nearby, Tom climbed back into the driver's seat and drove off. The trawl for a parking space did nothing to reduce his stress levels, but finally he found one about a quarter of a mile from the hospital. At last he was able to turn off the engine. He laid his palms on the dashboard, slumped for a moment against the steering wheel, and addressed Greta in a voice that croaked with emotion.

"Well done, old girl. I know it was a struggle for you, but you did us proud."

There was an awful, slimy mess in the foot well on the passenger side. Megan's blood, he realised with a shudder. His mind started to race.

What if the baby wasn't alright after all? It wasn't due for another few weeks: what if it couldn't breathe properly? What if Megan had taken a turn for the worse since he left her with the paramedic? They hadn't had time to give her an injection: what if she had started to bleed while he was finding a parking space? Panic made his head swim.

Think, now. What would she need? They didn't have her maternity bag but her handbag was on the floor, a bit messy now, but he knew she'd be lost without it. He grabbed it, gave it a quick wipe with a tissue, locked the doors and then sprinted back towards the hospital.

What had the paramedic said? *Pop him onto Mum's chest... That's right, tuck him in under your dress... We'll get him checked out straight away... He's going nice and pink now...*

It hadn't even occurred to Tom to ascertain whether the baby was a boy or a girl: his only concern had been for Megan and the baby to be safe. But the paramedic's words made it sound as if he had a son.

He reached the hospital and ran to follow the signs through its labyrinthine corridors towards the maternity ward, side-stepping people who had apparently made it their life's mission to walk as slowly as they possibly could in front of him. Automatically opting to take the stairs rather than a lift, he dashed up two steps at a time, so high on adrenalin that he was barely out of breath when he arrived at the correct floor.

Once allowed onto the ward, he forced himself to slow his steps before entering the bay where his wife was tucked up in bed wearing a hospital gown.

Tearing her gaze away from the baby in her arms, Megan's face was a picture of joyous delight.

"I know you two have already met, but you haven't been properly introduced." She beamed. "Tom, say hello to our son."

His heart swelled, full to bursting. He gulped down the lump in his throat, blinked back the stinging in his eyes and perched gingerly on the bed next to them.

"Hello there, little man... Is he alright?" he whispered. "He's so tiny!"

"He's perfect. His breathing is good. He's had a little go at feeding, but was too tired to do it for long, so they want to monitor us for a day or so before we can come home... He's not that tiny either, not really: he's already six pounds two! He'd have been a bomper if he'd gone full term." She gazed proudly at the baby again.

"And you?"

"I'm fine too, thanks to you. You got us back to Wales, and to a hospital. I couldn't have asked for more. Didn't I tell you you're a hero?"

He choked out a little laugh. He didn't feel much like a hero, but still - their son's tiny fist curled around his finger. They were safe.

He looked at her, gnawing at the inside of his lip. There was something he knew he had to say, and he knew it would hurt; but there was nothing he wouldn't do for her at this moment, nothing he wouldn't give up to make her happy. Even so, the words tasted bitter on his tongue as he forced them out.

"Listen - about Greta. You're going to hate her even more now, after this. I'll get rid of her. As soon as you're home, I'll arrange it. You needn't worry."

"What are you talking about?"

"Well – you know, I won't blame you if the memories are too traumatic for you...You never wanted me to buy her in the first place: she caused such a wedge between us. And then, it took so long to get home today. I can imagine how much it upset you. So I'll sell her on. I should get a good price for her once I've cleaned her up. Some new mats. Maybe a new seat cover, no one need ever know... We can spend the money on the kitchen, if you like."

"Greta stays," she said firmly. "I don't know how you could even think of getting rid of her. Our baby was born in that van, Tom. When you first bought her I thought she'd come between us, but when you think about it, she actually brought us back together. And at the end of the day, she got us back to Wales, even though she was coughing like a chain smoker most of the way... yes, I know you thought I hadn't noticed, but I'm not completely dense. No, there's no way she's going anywhere but home with us. I wouldn't get rid of Greta for a million pounds."

He nodded, the lump in his throat robbing him of words.

A midwife bustled in with a plate of toast. "Lunch won't be long, but I expect you're ravenous."

Megan accepted the toast with a grateful smile, nudging the baby towards Tom. "Do you want to hold him while I eat?"

He didn't need a second invitation, but scooped up the child with exquisite tenderness and stood beside the bed, rocking him gently in his arms. He gazed at the little boy's face, taking in his screwed up, puffy little eyes, snuffly button nose, tiny earlobes and pink rosebud mouth. A faint, downy fuzz of fine hair on his temples made him a look like a little peach, but the white stockinette hat provided by the hospital made it impossible to tell what colour his hair was.

The midwife cast an appraising glance over the sleeping baby and nodded, apparently satisfied.

"Have you given him a name yet?" she asked.

"I thought we'd name him after my favourite poet," Megan said.

"Over my dead body," Tom declared, tearing his gaze away from the baby's face.

Both women stared at him. Megan swallowed her mouthful of toast and pushed out her lower lip in an indignant pout.

He kept his face carefully straight. "Megan, as much as I love you, there's no way I'll allow you to call our son Sylvia. The other kids would kick the crap out of him at school."

"I didn't mean Sylvia Plath, you idiot. He'll be Dylan Thomas Field. After the poet, and after his father..." She paused, suddenly unsure. "If that's alright with you, of course?" she added.

He raised an eyebrow, considering the notion. For once she was actually stopping to consult him about something instead of just forging stubbornly ahead with her own plans.

Dylan. He tested the name in his mind. It made him think of Bob Dylan. Well, that was no bad thing... On the other hand, it also brought to mind the rabbit on *The Magic Roundabout*. That particular

Dylan had been stoned most of the time. Tom hadn't realised this when he'd watched it as a child, of course. Still…

"Whatever you want." He bent his head to kiss Dylan's forehead.

The midwife seemed relieved that a potential crisis had been averted. "It will be nice for you to have a little boy at last, Dad," she said. "I expect you'll have him playing football or rugby in no time."

"I don't care if he wants to prance around in a tutu and never picks up a rugby ball in his life. He'll be his own man. He doesn't have to live anybody's dreams but his own." As Dylan stirred, Tom began a slow, swaying walk around the bed, soothing him.

The midwife nodded, handing Megan a couple of paracetamol tablets and a plastic cup.

"Oh, of course. Quite so. Now Megan, you'll need these for the afterpains. They're generally worse after the third baby, I'm afraid." She watched Megan swallow the tablets, then asked brightly: "So, will you be planning to have a fourth baby at some point?"

Tom spun around.

"Ooh, look at his face," Megan said. "Last time I saw him look as scared as that, he was in a lift."

Confounded, the midwife left them to continue her rounds.

Megan finished her toast and set the plate down on her locker, brushing a few stray crumbs off the waffle blanket that covered the bed.

"Have you spoken to Bethan yet?" she asked. "I can't wait to see Alys and Nia, and for them to meet their little brother."

"Not yet. I wanted to check that you were both okay first. I might as well tell them in person – Dylan is waking up anyway. Judging by the way he's rooting about, he's decided he wants a feed after all." Their son's name felt strangely new on his tongue. Dylan had stretched his lips sideways in an attempt to latch onto Tom's hand where it cradled his head. Smiling at the baby's creaky whimpers, Tom passed him over as if he was made of the most precious crystal.

Megan adjusted her hospital gown and offered her breast to the gaping, searching mouth.

"Good man. Keep your mum out of trouble while I go and fetch your sisters." He leaned down and kissed her forehead, then brushed his fingers tenderly across the baby's cheek. Taking a few hesitant steps towards the door, he lingered at the threshold, gazing back longingly at them.

Megan looked up, apparently satisfied that the baby had latched on.

"Don't forget my hospital bag. And my mobile phone charger. Oh, and charge your phone – I want to be able to contact you the minute they say we can come home. Mind, there'll be a hundred messages on it from me, I expect… You'll need to dig out the baby's car seat, it's in his room. They won't let us travel home without it, so pop it in the car ready…. And can you get some wine, and some pâté and Brie ready for when I come home, please? Oh -and some nuts. I could kill for a glass of wine and a bag of cashews. Eight months without was beginning to feel like a life sentence."

"I'll bring Alys and Nia later. Just relax now and leave me to take care of things. You need to rest."

He paused in the doorway. She looked up at him, looking all at once unsure and vulnerable propped up against the plump white pillows.

"We will be alright, won't we?"

He nodded, his throat too tight to speak. Yes, surely by now, after everything, they would be.

Greta's engine sputtered fitfully as he drove home to Cardiff.

"I'll speak to Garin tomorrow, and get you sorted A.S.A.P.," he promised her. As if dealing with Megan and the girls wasn't enough, by buying Greta he seemed to have brought another temperamental female into his life. It was a good job the baby had turned out to be a boy. Having another male around the house would help to even things up a bit.

Opening his front door, he was struck by how quiet the house was without the rest of the family at home. Usually the girls' voices would be raised in welcome above the sound of the radio or television. On autopilot, he picked up some toys that had been left lying on the floor and tossed them back into their box. He would deal with the kitchen later: it was clear that Meg had left in a hurry, as yesterday's breakfast dishes were still in the kitchen sink. Dregs of milk had curdled in the cereal bowls; the flaky remains of Nia's Weetabix had set like concrete. Grimacing, he ran hot water into them to allow them to soak.

Then he saw his note. It was on the table, next to a mug containing the skinned-over dregs of cold coffee.

It seemed a lifetime since he had written it. Picking it up, he remembered how desperate he had been to get away. In his haste to avoid a confrontation with Megan that day, he hadn't stopped to think about the effect his actions would have on her or their children.

He couldn't bear to look at it any more. He crushed it brutally in one hand and threw it in the bin. But on his way out of the kitchen to fetch Megan's hospital bag, he spun on his heel and marched back. Reaching into the bin, he fished out the screwed-up paper and stepped outside to the recycling bag on the driveway. The note, and the feelings that had been attached to it, were better disposed of outside. It felt more final that way, as if its power to cause harm had been neutralised.

Having gathered up everything he thought Megan might need, Tom showered and changed into more respectable clothes, then dialled Bethan's number.

Her initial greeting suggested she had their number on her caller display. "Did you sort things out with Dickhead?" she asked, not bothering to say hello. "I hope you gave him hell for going off like that."

"Hello, Bethan."

"Oh! Tom. Er...Sorry. I thought it would be Megan on the line."

"Obviously."

"How are things?"

He sighed and rubbed the back of his neck. "Megan is in hospital," he began, but she cut him off at once.

"What the hell? What's the matter with her? Is it the baby? What have you done?"

He bristled. "All I've done is bring her back to Wales, against my better judgment I might add, and get her safely to a hospital. She went into labour this morning and had a baby boy. They're in Newport, we couldn't get to Cardiff in time – and they're both fine. I'd like to take Alys and Nia in to visit them later this afternoon. I presume that will be alright with you?"

Although he worded his request politely, his tone brooked no room for refusal. If Bethan had made plans, she would have to unmake them.

"Oh, wow! A boy, you say? That's wonderful. Really wonderful. She was so convinced it would be another girl. Congratulations – I'm so pleased for you both. And yes, of course you can come and get the girls. We were going to head to the park because we hadn't heard from either of you…"

"Megan sent you a text this morning."

"Did she? We didn't get it. Come over whenever you're ready."

Her manner was still a little frosty when Tom arrived on her doorstep, but there was nothing cool about Nia: she bolted at him like a greyhound after a rabbit and he swung her into his arms.

"Daddy, Daddy!" she cried, throwing her arms tightly around his neck and planting a wet kiss on his face. "We've made Welsh cakes with Auntie Bethan!"

"Wow! I hope you saved one for me?" He beamed at her, settling her on his hip and reaching out with his free hand for Alys. She had hung back, but ran now and clung to his leg.

"Where have you been, Dad? Uncle Matt said you went to the seaside with Greta. Why didn't you take us?"

His throat constricted at her hurt expression. What could he say? He could hardly tell his children the whole truth, but neither did he want to tell a lie. He dropped to one knee to look them both in the eye, aware of Bethan watching from along the hallway.

Carefully, he said: "I needed to go away for a few days. Next time I go, I promise I'll take you with me."

"Cross your heart and hope to die?"

He yielded readily to her insistence, crossing his heart and then adding a pinkie promise, hooking his little finger around hers, to seal his vow. She smiled, happier, and took his hand.

"Did you tell them?" he asked Bethan.

"No, I thought their father should be the one to do it."

The girls' eyes, green and amber-flecked like their mother's, opened wide as he explained that their baby brother had been in a hurry to meet them. He was only too glad to obey their demands to be taken to see him at once.

It felt strangely dispiriting to be driving a modern MPV again. Its expanse of plastic trim, with its host of buttons and functions, its illuminated digital display, USB port, cup-holders and lockers, seemed somehow impersonal after the simple, nostalgic honesty of Greta's dashboard.

Yes, it was comfortable, he thought; yes, it could easily do ninety on the motorway if he fancied risking a brush with the speed cameras. Yes, the brakes were sharp and it had air-conditioning and he could flip down the DVD player for the girls to watch cartoons when they grew bored with the view. At the flick of a switch he could check his mileage per gallon and know to the last drop how much fuel was left in the tank. It would tell him how hot or cold it was outside, and warn him if there was a risk of ice or if someone hadn't fastened their seatbelt. But it didn't satisfy him. It wasn't fun. It might have the horsepower and torque to get him out of trouble at busy junctions, but it had no soul.

Give him Greta any day, with her kitsch garland of silk flowers along the bottom of the windscreen; her inefficient heater; her asthmatic, rattly engine and weak brakes; her petrol gauge that could only be relied upon to tell untruths; her lack of luxuries, and her basic, utilitarian finish. She made him feel as if he was on holiday as soon as he climbed into her driving seat.

At the hospital, Alys and Nia gazed in wonder at their sleepy brother and delighted their mother with hugs and a bunch of flowers hurriedly obtained from a petrol station en route.

This is it, Tom thought. *This is what it's about: all of us being together. A family. It goes without saying, really. Even when the baby's screaming that horrible, raucous cry that sets my teeth on edge; even when Alys is in a sulk or Nia is crayoning on the walls; when Megan is a crosspatch from the stress of trying to sort everyone out and there are school reports to be written and guttering to unblock and Dad is on the phone grumbling about Auntie Jean and his bowels and the state of the NHS. I don't really want to be anywhere but with them.*

For the first time since he had turned forty, he had hope in his heart and a spring in his step. He wasn't going to wait until he had retired and the kids had left home to start living. He was going to follow his dreams. And he would take his family with him.

Acknowledgements

To Martin, my soul mate: thank you for always believing in me, for inspiring and encouraging me, for your advice and expertise regarding all things to do with VW campers, and for never buggering off camping without me. I couldn't have created this book without your unwavering love and support.

To the rest of my family, thank you for everything. I'm not sure how you put up with me, but I'm glad you do. I love you loads.

To Jonathan, for the fantastic cover design for the first edition. I owe you many, many beers, Bro.

To Lisa, for the beautiful cover design for this edition. Your attention to detail is second to none.

Thanks to Mum, Julia, Sara, Liane and Seran for reading an early draft and telling me it had promise, even though it still needed so much work.

Thank you Siobhan for your words of wisdom.

To Ciara, thank you for helping me believe it was possible, and for your immensely supportive feedback.

Thanks to Terry for casting a midwife's eye over chapters 18 and 19. Any inaccuracies are of course my own.

To Fiona and Nigel, who share the camper love, thanks are due for checking Garin's advice and the specifications of Tom's camper van.

Also for not laughing me out of town when I said I was writing a novel.

Finally, thank you Carl for buying a camper without consulting your wife, thus proving that my plot idea wasn't so far-fetched after all.

About the author

After narrowly avoiding being born in the back seat of a Ford Cortina, Luisa A. Jones was perhaps destined to have a keen interest in popular vehicles of the 1960s and 70s. She and her husband are the proud owners of Gwynnie, a classic VW camper van. They enjoy nothing more than touring and camping with Gwynnie and like-minded friends.

Luisa and her husband live in Wales. Besides their camper van and two VW Beetles (apparently one old VW is never enough), they also have three children, who are arguably cheaper to keep and less troublesome than classic vehicles.

Luisa studied at Royal Holloway and Bedford New College, University of London, and the University of South Wales, Newport. Becoming an author has fulfilled a lifelong ambition.

Luisa hopes that you have enjoyed this book. If you have, please recommend it to your friends and, consider posting a review. Follow Luisa A Jones on Facebook to hear about future releases and to send her your feedback. She would love to hear from you.

By Luisa A. Jones

Printed in Great Britain
by Amazon